Hidden Man of the Heart

by Ruth Sauder

HIDDEN MAN OF THE HEART

by
Ruth Sauder

Copyright © 2000

Library of Congress Number: 99-75901
International Standard Book Number: 1-930353-02-2

Printed 2000 by
Masthof Press
220 Mill Road
Morgantown, PA 19543-9701

"Whose adorning let it not be that outward adorning of plaiting hair, and of wearing of gold, or of putting on of apparel; but let it be the hidden man of the heart, in that which is not corruptible, even the ornament of a meek and quiet spirit, which is in the sight of God of great price." 1 Peter 3:3

Preface

This book was written to release some of my imagination. It is fictitious with no names describing a real person or settlement written in the setting of the Old Order Mennonite Church. My imagination may have stretched certain things somewhat to make the story more interesting. Forgive me if I offended anyone.

I have enjoyed writing as a hobby ever since I was in school. At different times, I tried to publish my stories, but never succeeded. After more people encouraged me to publish my writings, someone suggested that I contact Masthof Press who worked very hard to improve the manuscript.

Enjoy reading this story, and don't give up too soon. A sequel to this book, *Not Worthy To Be Compared*, has been written and will be published if this first book is accepted.

It is my goal that this book will inspire others to live a godly life as they read about the afflictions and disappointments that can depress one throughout life, and know that God in his almighty power and love leads the broken and contrite spirit out of the gloom. Yes, I have experienced many of these hard times as well but can also testify that God continues to lead today just as he led the Israelities out of the wilderness.

- Ruth Sauder
January 2000

Chapter One

Streaks of blue in the east made the sky appear as if it had been washed and was drying off at places. The earth had been washed, and the silent morning with its calm skies seemed peaceful after the previous evening's thunderstorm. A very sudden, insisting wind had rustled through the valley, whipping at the corner of buildings, swaying the trees, and rattling every loose object. Then the flashing of lightning and crashing of thunder had arrived, each seeming to try to outdo the other. The lightning had flashed and faded. The thunder had crashed; the lightning again had cut an instant zigzag rip in the lower sky. then the rain had splashed and beat upon the roofs. Hours later the thunder could be heard rolling in the distance while the rain gently continued.

Now, the morning sky was quiet and peaceful. Every blade of grass and leaf was washed and dripping wet as Clayton made his way down the field lane with the wheelbarrow loaded with the saw and ax. Chief, the Wenger family dog, trotted ahead as if he had been ordered to assign Clayton to his work. Suddenly, Chief sniffed the ground, turned around, and wagging his tail ran off through the hay field in a zigzag trail toward the pasture following the scent of a rabbit that had already raced to safety. At the far end of the hay field, Clayton came to the newly fallen apple tree. It was an old tree but had still been bearing fruit. The Wengers had picked the apples only a few weeks earlier.

Chief came back sniffing down Clayton's trail. Clayton picked up the ax to strip off the twigs but noticed a bird's nest which had fallen from the tree. He picked up the very carefully built nest, maybe a robin's. He studied the perfect work of a string woven with tangled

1

straw. *Some bird must build a new nest next year*, Clayton thought as he dropped it on the ground.

Clayton gazed at the fallen apple tree. He thought of a few months earlier when Doddy Wenger had died, although his death wasn't as unexpected as the demise of this tree. Clayton remembered that Bishop Paul had compared Doddy's body to a tree that bore fruit for many years.

He had said, "As the tree falls, so shall it lay. Once death strikes there is no changing."

But the tree, like Doddy, seemed to have a good landing. Doddy had been looking forward to leaving his old failing body. Bishop Paul had said more things about comparing bodies and trees that Clayton hadn't remembered or understood. Clayton picked up the ax and began trimming the twigs.

The sun had come through and as it climbed higher, Clayton soon removed his jacket. He put the twigs on a pile to burn sometime and started cutting off larger limbs.

For a moment he glanced across the fields where he saw his brother Israel and Dad with the team of horses next to the corn field. They were husking corn and filling the wagon. Once the fields dry off, a lot more corn will be husked, since most silos were already full.

The fields were beginning to look bare, changing the countryside. But the autumn had brought a change in the Wenger family that was bigger than empty corn fields, a change they would have to learn to live with. Many times Clayton wondered how things could work out, but his questions remained unanswered. Mother had said there would always be a way.

Only a month ago, the whole house had been scrubbed and the yard shined up, every corner cleaned. Some buildings had been painted. Relatives gathered at the Wenger house on that rainy day when John Irvin Horst, from way over in Elm Grove, brought his relatives and claimed Clayton's only sister Naomi for his wife. That left Mom with no help to cook, clean, and sew for all the sons that still remained at home.

Clayton saw that his parents were trying to train the boys to do more housework, even before Naomi was married, since Dad

2

had so many hired helpers. Enos had wanted to help him cut up the tree, but Mother had asked for a hand to do the family washing, and it was Enos's turn. Noah David always said it made going to school more fun, knowing that "if we were home, we'd have to do housework." Clayton found helping with the family washing not such an undesirable job; he'd do it any day rather than ironing piles of shirts or dropping cookies on a sheet and getting his fingers messy.

Over the years the boys had become immune to washing dishes. Sometimes when Clayton was with a group of his friends and they talked about their hobbies or interests, he felt sort of left out or misplaced. When he overheard girls talking about doing washing, or how it takes so much longer to peel small apples, or the drag of packing lunches and washing off ceilings, or tying up celery, it sounded more familiar to him than when the boys talked about training a dog, building a birdhouse, feeding the rabbits, or raising dogs.

Today he was enjoying himself as he swung an ax. A while ago he had heard the farm bell ring once, which meant "come to the shop," so Israel had gone and Dad was husking alone. Israel must have had a customer in the shop, as he hadn't returned since. It seemed that with Christmas only a few months away, the shop kept Israel quite busy.

The farm bell rang again. *It must be noon. Dad went in a while ago; he must have finished his rows.*

*   *   *   *

As Clayton was washing up, Enos reminded him that it was his turn to do the dishes. Clayton groaned. The scent in the kitchen revealed a tell-tale sign that the others had been cooking ketchup and there would be extra dishes.

Clayton was pulling out a chair from the table when he noticed an extra plate on the other side. Mother looked at him and smiled at his questioning look. Then she glanced over to where Dad and Israel stood discussing something in the newspaper.

3

Clayton raised his eyebrows. "Alpheus! When did you come?"

"Didn't you see my buggy?" Alpheus asked his brother as they took their places at the table.

"I really didn't look," Clayton answered. There were often cars and extra teams out front when customers were in the shop.

As the meal continued and dishes were passed, healthy men helped themselves to generous servings. The serving bowls were scraped empty till they had circled the table. Mom always said, "Just cooking for so many men is a job," but she believed in satisfying their appetites. Dad and Alpheus exchanged farm news between their bites of food.

Finally, when Mom got a word in, she asked Alpheus, "By the way, did you get sent home?" Clayton was also wondering; Alpheus hadn't been home since Naomi's wedding.

Alpheus looked up to answer and noticed the mischievous look in Clayton's eyes, and he chuckled. "No, I came by myself." Then he went on to explain. "It was too wet to fill silo, and we are still waiting on some lumber to finish the shed. I have a dentist appointment tomorrow morning first thing, and the day after is the wedding at Levi's, so Raymond said I can have off for a few days."

Dad asked about the shed they were building.

Israel scratched his head, as if he really had a problem and interrupted the conversation. "You told me you weren't invited to Lucy's wedding."

"I wasn't then," Alpheus answered as he reached for another helping of meat.

Mom asked, "Were you to town for a gift or will you get one when you go to the dentist?"

Alpheus ignored the question and took Dad's conversation up again, explaining that they had decided to put a corn crib at one side of the shed and build the lean-to on the other side.

Israel was holding his spoon in mid-air as if watching the conversation as it was pitched to and fro. Then he said, "Ach, Mom, you don't need to worry. Likely he doesn't need a gift or why would he come over the ridge to go to a wedding in Beaver Creek?"

Enos mumbled, "He probably decided he didn't want to wash dishes all his life."

4

"I'll wash the dishes for you today," Alpheus replied matter-of-factly. "I haven't washed dishes for a while."

Sometime during the course of conversation the topic changed to horses, which was a common subject in a household that had three boys with buggies. Now there were three more with buggies and three more to follow.

Alpheus said, "Oh yes, that reminds me. The other day I met William Stover at the livestock auction barn, you know, where you got that black horse for Eli Jonas? He wondered if we need a horse. He has a good one; someone moved and didn't have room for the horse. He said it's young and needs a little more training."

Now Clayton was all ears. He so much desired a horse of his own. A lot of his friends had some already, but Dad said he could use one of the other horses. Often the boys would go with each other, and not all horses were in use. Clayton had used Israel's or Dad's extra ones at times, but he still desired one of his own.

Since Eli Jonas was dating, he used his team regularly. Alpheus pulled a card from his pocket. "He said you shall call before you come, in case he wouldn't be at home. That would save a trip to Douglassville."

Clayton's heart sank. He was living for the day to go with Dad to the horse sale barn at Douglassville, but he hadn't known Dad was planning to go. Dad must be thinking about letting him have a horse. They did redo Seranus's buggy after he got a carriage for his family.

Seranus and his family lived up the road a few miles where Eli Jonas lived, and helped with the farming and his farm shop. He was the only one of the married brothers living so near to home. Ephraim and Naaman had sought land in Kentucky. Israel had the plans all made for building a house among the pines at the east side of his shop. All the paperwork was finished, but since spring when he broke up with Katie, Dad said, "No nest if you have no bird to put in, or else we'd just have another house to clean." But Israel said Katie had nothing to do with the house. They had been dating only a few months.

5

Clayton thought again of the conversation at the beginning of the meal about Alpheus and wondered what that was about. Alpheus had never dated a girl that Clayton knew of. He had been hired out to Cousin Raymond for a few years already, maybe to escape washing dishes.

To everyone's surprise, Alpheus did roll up his sleeves and fetch the teakettle from the stove. Israel had a customer and hurried out to the shop. Dad sat on the rocker to rest a few minutes and continued his visiting with Alpheus. It was most always Mom's job to clear off the table after a meal, so she knew where to find her things again. She claimed as sure as the boys cleared off the tables a few times, no kettles were in the cupboard and three different bags, each with a few pieces of bread, would accumulate in the bread box. So Clayton was assigned to put the tomatoes through the mill, and Enos was the boy who cleaned out the horse stable in the afternoon.

The front door opened; Noah David wouldn't be home from school yet. Mother looked up and said, "Well, Abe, do come in." Dad pulled out a chair for him.

Abe shook Dad's hand firmly and asked, nodding toward Alpheus, "Is this your boy, too?"

"Yes," Dad replied. "He is hired out to the next settlement west."

"I just don't get to see the young boys any more." Abe didn't waste any time to say what was on his mind. "You know my nephew is getting married. We weren't really planning to go, but now there is an ordination the same week and I have been urged to go be with the church. Three of my children live there, and Mervin's family said they would go with us if I find someone to help the boys with the chores."

Mom asked who was marrying. Clayton's heart suddenly started beating faster. He was now at the age his dad called chore-boy age. The first year his sons were out of school, Dad trained them to work at home, and at age eighteen or nineteen they usually had their regular work and jobs. But during the between years, they were not tied down. Now Clayton remembered that Enos was only a year

6

behind him. He had been home a year already as of last year; Enos only went to school once a week for the whole year.

"Well, Mom, what do you say?" Dad asked. "Since Naomi's married, the boys help her pretty much," he explained to Abe.

"Well," Mom answered, "we still have corn and tomatoes to do and sewing and—well, a whole list of things. But this may be a good time to get one of my sister Magdelena's girls to help out, as there is work piling up that boys can't do." Mom walked over to the desk and got a paper and pencil, saying, "I can spare Clayton if I have a girl to help me. I'll send Clayton over with a note, and then he can drive around by you and tell you. You say you are leaving—when?"

"We might leave Saturday and be gone a week, depends on how things turn out."

*   *   *   *

Clayton whistled as he ran to the barn for Old Blackie. She always seemed eager for a horseback errand. Clayton had rather enjoyed it the few times he had helped people with chores, but both times were at neighbors' places, where he came home evenings. He really didn't know Mervin's family well, but he thought it would be a challenge to try the job. If he remembered right, they had a dairy and some school boys to help him. And if he knew his aunt, she would provide a girl to help if possible.

7

Chapter Two

Clayton dumped the foaming milk into the step saver, put the lid back, and turned around, wondering where to go next. He asked Reuben, "Did you wash this one?"

Reuben looked up from where he was teasing a cat on the barn walk, then he threw his short piece of splinter wood down and jumped up. "No, I guess I didn't wash Bell yet."

Clayton paused a few moments while Reuben washed the cow, then continued milking. The milker on the other side started making noise and Clayton quickly went over to correct it. Reuben continued his routine of washing the next cow, whistling as he went with his one arm over the cow. Twelve-year-old Clarence was feeding the cows, and Charles and Ralph were feeding the calves. The boys seemed so good with the cows. Clayton realized that they would probably be able to milk the cows alone if they had someone to keep them at it. Whenever Clayton said something about "the cow," they would say, "Do you mean Beth?" "or Bell?" or whoever it was. They weren't just cows to the boys. They were individuals and the boys knew them all. Clayton felt a longing, the same feeling he had experienced when he had helped Alpheus do chores at another farm where they also had a dairy. He felt as if he had found work that was interesting. It seemed that quite a few of the children could help with this work.

Even Elson, the child who didn't go to school yet, seemed to know a lot about how things were being done in the barn. Clayton was convinced the children had been raised in the barn. The two youngest ones had gone with Mervin's on their trip. Clayton remembered again that this was Wednesday, the day of the ordination

Mervin's family had gone to; the wedding would be tomorrow. They had heard that Abe's daughter and husband were in the lot, and Clayton wondered what the day held.

Clayton emptied another milker and set it on the walk, folding the hose under the handle. He was now finished with that milker and went back to check another one. Clarence and Charles came around the corner and were discussing something about a near-tie baseball score at school. Clarence picked up the empty milker and headed for the milk house; he was done feeding. The boys almost always saw to it that the milker got rinsed in the evening. Reuben stood waiting for the next empty one.

With the last milker off, and the boys clanking to the milk house with them, Clayton paused at the open double barn doors. A nice autumn breeze floated in. The sky was decorated in red streaks, which bordered a purple background. He saw Kathryn was digging potatoes. She was the neighbor girl who came in the evening to make supper, get the seven children to bed, make breakfast, and pack lunches in the morning. Then she would leave for the day, except to do washing if there was any. Ralph and Elson were picking up the potatoes as fast as she was digging them.

Clayton went down to the lower barn to check if everything was taken care of. The horse snorted and blew through his nose to greet him, begging for more feed. Clayton patted him on his nose; he saw that the horse had been fed and was still cleaning up the last of the feed. Clayton went in the stable and felt his horse's long, smooth side. There was muscle there—and spirit. Doddy Abe's horse was in the next stable, a gentle slow horse, just the kind a grandfather needs. Abe's house stood near the orchard; he didn't have a barn of his own, only a shed for his carriage and a little shop to tinker in and a small chicken coop. As Clayton stood looking the horse over, he remembered again what Alpheus had said to Dad about a horse. Clayton wondered if Dad went to look at it; they never did talk about it again. Maybe Dad didn't remember either. He sure hoped he could go along if they went to look for a horse. What had Alpheus said? The horse needs a little training yet. That could mean a lot of things.

9

Clayton checked the water trough and then went out the side door and took a stroll down to Abe's well-kept little orchard. Clayton picked up a red apple that must have just fallen recently. He took a bite; it tasted good after doing all the milking. *It seems long since supper*, he thought, as he went back up towards the house.

He thought of the words to a song: "Choose my path, O blessed Saviour, just as seemeth good to thee." Every so often this week, the song would whirl around in his mind since it was one he hadn't known before.

Singing was interesting. The notes told one how to sing even if the song was unfamiliar. The words seemed to be like a story of inspiration, songs he had sung in school were just now coming alive in words. In school, students had sung the songs and never realized what the words meant. Thinking back to Sunday made Clayton's heart feel light. He wasn't allowed to go with the young folks yet. But since Dad liked singing, he didn't care if his sons went to where a group of boys gathered to practice singing.

When Seranus was still at home, the family had often sung in the evening, and they still did some when Eli Jonas was at home. But now that Eli Jonas was at Seranus's, Clayton had to go to Dad if he wanted help in singing. Dad got out of breath so soon that oftentimes they would end up discussing notes, etc. Also, Dad didn't know a lot of the songs the boys learned from the other young folks because they were using books other than what he was used to.

By the time Clayton came into the house, the older boys were lost in a storybook, and Kathryn was helping the smaller ones with a lively table game.

Clayton paused at the bookshelf and found the songbook, the old hymnal. Once they had used that book to practice some songs on Sunday. He read the words again,

Choose my path, O blessed Saviour,
Let me, trusting, lean on thee;
Order thou life's joys and duties,
Just as seemeth good to thee.
Just as seemeth good to thee,

10

Just as seemeth good to thee;
Order thou my steps, dear Saviour,
Just as seemeth good to thee.
Let thy wisdom guide me ever,
For I dare not trust my own;
Lead thou me in tender mercy,
Leave me not to walk alone

Life is full of cares perplexing,
And alone, I lose the way;
Keep me near to thee, dear Saviour,
Choose for me the path, I pray.

Clayton glanced at the last verse again, "Life is full of cares perplexing, and alone, I lose the way." Clayton thought life was a little perplexing since he was out of school but not old enough to be with the young folks. He thought it wouldn't be so perplexing if he would soon belong to a group again.

He treasured the evenings when he and Dad would walk up to Seranus's place to sing with him and Eli Jonas, which was often on a Sunday evening. Now that Eli Jonas was dating, it rarely happened. Once in a while after a good rain, they had the time to sing during the week, but the farm shop was pretty busy throughout the year.

Chapter Three

The late November skies were dull and drab. As sixteen-year-old Clayton came up the field lane with the manure spreader, the world looked even drabber since the trees had shed their leaves. Mostly the few oak trees in the north bush still clung to their brown leaves. Bud and Billy, the heavy workhorses, plodded slowly toward the barn. Clayton guided them left, down to the shed, to unhitch. "We're done for today," Clayton told them, as he patted them and stepped down from the manure spreader.

Enos had helped Clayton clean out the steer stables. There were only two loads left for this afternoon and they had had an early start, since there hadn't been much for dinner. Dad and Alpheus were at the wedding at Uncle Eli's home. *Now cousin Eldon will be the oldest of Eli's children at home—and to think he is my age*, Clayton mused.

As he put the horses away, Clayton saw that Enos was throwing down straw bales, bedding down the steers since their pen was clean. Clayton hung the harness on the hooks and left the barn. It would feel good to relax after forking all that manure.

Almost without thinking, he walked down to the lower pasture where a few of the horses were. he rested his foot on the board fence and with his head cupped in his hand and his elbow resting on his knee, he viewed the pasture—something he often did lately.

Soon after he had arrived home from working at Mervin's farm, Clayton had seen the truck arrive with the new horse. Dad had gone to look at it without him. Clayton still clearly remembered his disappointment when he had seen the horse. He wasn't really much to look at, more black than brown, and he didn't have any style when it came to holding his head or tail. Dad had said Clayton didn't have to take him for his own if he didn't like him because someone was always needing a horse around the farm. He thought he'd give a chance to anyone who needed the horse.

They had first hitched him double with one of the other horses. Later, they hitched him alone. Clayton was beginning to admire him more each time. Israel had often gone along to drive in the evenings. They had found out that the new horse had to learn to drive at night; he was rather skittish in the dark. Also, in the daytime, he was a handful to keep on the right side of the road. The main teaching he still needed was to stop at stop signs—and wait. He didn't really balk but seemed too mischievous to stand still. The same was true in hitching up.

Clayton checked his watch. It was still only mid-afternoon. They hadn't hitched the horse yet this week. As soon as Clayton opened the gate, the horses looked up expectantly and walked towards him, looking for the sweet corn stalks the Wengers had been chopping out of the garden and throwing to them. Clayton caught one of the other horses, petted him a while, and then quickly reached for the new horse and got hold of him at the second try. He was getting tamer. First, he had pulled pack when he was petted.

Clayton wasn't satisfied to just call him "Horse." Dad had forgotten to ask the man about a name; there were no papers. Clayton had finally managed to meet the Stover man and inquired about the horse's name. Stover said he might be able to find out from the former owner. Later, Stover had dropped in and said the horse's name was Clinton Worth. At that instant, Clayton had set his mind on "Clint."

Clayton let Clint into the barn. Dad's spare horse whinnied to come along as Clayton closed the gate. Minutes later, Clayton was hitching him to the buggy. The first side usually went well, but when he walked around to the other side, Clint was ready to go. Clayton tried teaching him obedience. "Whoa, Clint! Whoa!" Clint stood for a moment but then started shuffling and made a step. Enos came out of the barn, reached out and held him and stroked him. Clayton asked Enos, "Do you want to go along?"

"Where are you going?"

13

Clayton shrugged his shoulders. "Maybe I will go in a large circle. I don't know where." Enos turned up his nose and let loose of his hold since Clayton was done hitching up. Clayton called "whoa" to the horse, making him wait till he was in the buggy. Clint tried to go one way and then the other. He was neither going or standing still while Clayton got on. Then Clayton held the lines firmly, said Clint's name, and tucked the reins. Clint sprang into action, realizing he was now allowed to go.

The first half mile he tried to get to the middle of the road and go seven different gaits, if there were so many different ones. Soon he knew he was not his own boss and had to follow orders, so he dug in and went. He took short steps but moved his feet fast. At first, Clint reminded Clayton of a lively little puppy, raring to go, but hindering himself by being too playful.

Clayton was pleased at how Clint ignored the traffic. He ignored anything that came from behind, but if a truck came towards him, he expressed his disapproval by almost stopping and trying to turn into a "C." Clayton had to be prepared. Clint just wasn't a woman's horse yet. The horse seemed mischievous and was a challenge to Clayton. Dad had told Stover, "The horse and boy can grow up together."

As Clayton turned west down by Route 584, he wondered where he could go and if there wasn't an errand somewhere he could do. While driving around, he turned on Mill Stream Road since Route 584 was a rather busy road. He crossed Silver Creek Road because he didn't want to get near Uncle Eli's area with all the wedding people there. Then thinking of the wedding, he wondered if Israel or Mother would get the mystery solved. Alpheus wouldn't tell them why he was invited to the wedding when he was home, or who he was taking along. He hadn't been home since, but Israel had met him at a singing in the home area. Nobody Clayton asked knew if Alpheus had come alone. He hadn't left alone, though, but Israel couldn't see who was going with him.

Clint was getting tired, and he stopped decently at stop signs and started off obediently. As Clayton approached the Deer Creek area, he suddenly remembered where he could stop. Dad had said they need to pick up a tractor part at Elmer Groff's; someone from Indiana had sent it in with Elmer's. Clayton was a little too far north, so he took the next side road and soon saw Elmer's shop.

Clint was quite decent on the way home. He willingly stopped at the stop signs and didn't seem to notice the trucks that came towards him. Clayton still had to keep the one line firm, to keep him on the right side of the road. Clint walked up quite a few hills, so that is what he had needed—more road experience.

As Clayton turned in the lane at home, he saw Father had just finished unhitching after returning from the wedding.

Clayton entered the kitchen where Mom was preparing supper. She asked him to fetch a can of meat from the cellar, then he helped her put the rest of the things on the table. He was growing hungry, as his dinner had been scant.

The fresh potatoes with homemade butter were so good along with the green beans and sausage. Clayton was enjoying the food more than Dad and Mom's conversation, which contained mostly people's names and who was related to whom. They talked of seeing people they hadn't seen for a long time and some they just met at the wedding. Finishing his dessert, Clayton asked, "By the way, did Alpheus have a friend along?"

Mother looked at Dad with a question, and Dad's expression seemed to say, "Did you know her?"

Mother said, "I asked one of Eli's married girls who Alpheus had along. She couldn't place her, and I was going to ask her mother but forgot again."

Dad scratched his head. "After I saw the girl, I thought I had seen her in church a few times, but I had no name for her since I don't know all the young folks anymore. Then I asked Eli and he had said he wasn't sure. When I was talking with Minister Elam, a few girls were sitting at the other side of the room and I asked him who the one was. He said if he is right, she's a niece to Ammon Kilmer. She is helping at Ammon's since his wife isn't well, he guessed since mid-summer. I was trying to think, maybe he said her father is a Reiff—Mose Reiff?" Dad looked at Mom to clear matters.

Mom started gathering the plates together and nodded. "I thought I had seen her before; I guess I did see her in church. Ammon does have a sister married to Jonas Reiff's boy, but I hardly know them. They lived in the settlement on the edge of Pennsylvania, nearer to Ohio. Seems since Naomi isn't here we don't find out who is with the young folks."

Clayton said wistfully, "I'll soon tell you."

Dad looked at him and said teasingly, "So you plan to keep track of the girls?"

Clayton teased back, "And the boys!"

Dad bit his toothpick, saying, "I think this girl might be older than Alpheus."

"I know another couple where the girl is older," Mother chuckled. Dad looked at her and opened his mouth to say something but remained quiet. Mom and Dad exchanged glances, but Clayton couldn't quite read the message that Mom's eyes told Dad. Dad smiled, amused.

Clayton felt uneasy and got up from the table. He wondered again, as he had often done before. *Mom is only two years older than Dad, but from snatches they sometimes chuckled about, you would think it was ten years. There must have been some sort of story in their courting or meeting that was a little unusual.* Maybe some day he could find out, but he didn't feel brave enough to talk about it now. He was afraid they'd be embarrassed—including him.

Chapter Four

"Pass the potatoes again, Noah David," Clayton requested.

"Here's some corn, too—too little to save," Mother said.

"I'll take that," Israel said, reaching for the dish. Enos wondered if there was any meat left. Mother Lydia looked at her sons around the table and said. "I never knew it was such a joy to see you eat, till now. Last week you did not seem like my family because you were sick. Now you are hungry again." She looked at Dad who sat with an empty plate and held his chin in his hand. Touching his hand, she said, "Now if you get hungry yet, we will be a happy family."

Dad smiled weakly and sighed. He wanted to be well, but he was dragging himself around. Israel still looked rather pale. They all had had a turn with the flu. Clayton had thought he wouldn't ever feel like working again. For a few days he hadn't done much more than rest and sleep and read and drink tea that Mother carried to him. Dad sighed and passed another dish along without taking any.

Mother got up from the table and filled a cup with warm tea and put it at Dad's plate. Dad had gotten the flu soon after Clayton and Enos had it. By the time Clayton was feeling better, Israel and Noah David started, but the table was now filled again. For a week one or more had had no desire to come to the table. Somehow Mom only rested a day; the boys had decided likely it was harder on her to hear and see how they kept house than it was to not feel well.

Clayton looked at Father as he was slumped on the chair. It seemed he had aged some in the last three weeks. He had said he felt dizzy and just wasn't hungry. Clayton had had mostly fever and dizziness. Some also had had coughing while others had had diarrhea and upset stomach. Dad had had them all. The doctor had come one day because Dad's stomach was so upset that he just couldn't eat. The doctor had been alarmed and advised the family to get Dad to a hospital because he was dehydrating, but Dad had refused.

His stomach was better now, but he still was weak and dizzy and had no appetite. The other evening he had fallen while going to the bedroom, and he was dizzy and had poor balance. He had received a hard bump on the back of his head. Israel and Clayton had watched over him that night, waking him every few hours.

Dad held onto the table and got up. Mother was at his side, propping him till he got his balance. Israel got up and stood between the table and the rocking chair, in case he needed support.

Everyone knew Dad didn't need another fall. He settled on the rocker and Israel pulled his chair from the table and turned it toward Dad. Israel's face still looked pale, but he had been working in the shop again. Right after Christmas was always a dull time since most orders were filled and people didn't have money to start ordering again.

The basket of frozen wash sat in the porch entrance waiting to be hung. The boys had fetched the laundry in before supper, and the younger boys had bargained with Clayton that they would do the chores this evening if Clayton would take care of the frozen, wet wash. Mother said she could do the dishes. So Clayton was stretching the clothesline across the kitchen, living room, and hall. First he filled the small rack on the wall then started hanging up the cold wash. It wouldn't stay cold long, as the range was radiating a good heat. It seemed almost like steam waves in the kitchen.

So far, January had been frosty and rather dreary. While Clayton was hanging up the wash, he strained to catch what Israel and Dad were discussing. The other week Seranus and Eli Jonas had come over and the family had quite a discussion. It sounded as though Israel was reviewing it with Dad, saying, "Well, you see Eli Jonas will be twenty in another two months. Then he is coming home and might have a part-time job, but he plans to help in my woodworking shop. I am crowded already, so we are going to expand the shop and then we won't have to turn down so many customers."

"Did you say Clayton will help at Seranus's then?" Dad asked.

"Well, we thought so, but he wasn't interested in a repair shop. He's more interested in woodworking and he'd like to be available to help on chore boy jobs, as that way he gets a chance at dairying. Enos would much rather go to Seranus's than be a chore boy or help other people. This spring Noah David is out of school and is here to help you."

Clayton smiled to himself. When Israel talked about building his shop bigger, that meant his business was getting bigger. The delivery guys at times got him confused with other shops, so it was necessary to give his shop a name. Dad had often told them if they name a business or farm, not to use their own name, as sometimes later the business gets sold. Then the name should change. Also because in the Old Testament it counsels against it in Psalm 49. It tells of those who trust in wealth and says in verse ten, "For he seeth that wise men die, likewise the fool and the brutish person perish, and leave their wealth to others." Verse eleven is what Dad stressed so much: "Their inward thought is, that their houses shall continue forever, and their dwelling places to all generations; they call their lands after their own names."

So Israel was careful not to use his own name; he had thought of the group of tall pine trees that stood on the east side of the shop. Pine Drive and Whispering Pines were used too often, so naturally he thought of the peaceful evenings when the strong breezes sang through the pines and he would listen to their music, so he had registered the shop as "Wood Working, Singing Pine Brothers." He had painted a sign for it and put it by the lane. He also had the name printed on the mailbox.

It was Seranus who heartily chuckled over the name when he heard about the Singing Pine Brothers. "Sounds like you are advertising that we like to sing." Israel had never thought about it, as he was no great singer; he only liked to listen to singing. When Dad caught on to what Seranus thought, he was grieved. He was afraid people would think he was boasting over God's gift. He was upset for a few days, but Israel had explained that he had used "Brothers" because there would be more than only himself.

19

Somehow some of the young folks also got the same idea that Seranus had. It became a real joke when they saw the sign. Israel and Eli Jonas just laughed with the people, so it remained an interesting conversation piece. They now often called them Singing Pine Brothers instead of the Wenger brothers. Dad was severely grieved, but Israel just chuckled and said that if no one remembered him for anything worse than singing, he was quite happy. He explained to Dad that the business people don't know they have a talent for singing, so they won't even think about it. After all, the registration went through. He had written in three names and the company had picked this title.

Israel had put a telephone booth between the shop and the walk leading to the house, as delivery people and others were complaining that they had no way to contact him when there was a mix-up or a change of plans. Israel hated to bother the neighbors so often. Once when Clayton was walking past, Israel had just picked up the phone to answer it and Clayton heard him say, "Good morning, Wood Working Singing Pine Brothers. Israel speaking." Now Clayton knew the proper way to answer the phone. Israel was probably right; it would be less confusing to others because there would be a few different ones answering the phone.

Clayton could hear Dad asking, "But do you need so many blocks to add to the shop?" Israel drew a long breath, and Clayton eased over to the door to hear better. He had heard Israel and Eli Jonas discussing some of it. "Well, no, Dad. I've got enough blocks for the foundation of the house."

"The house!" Dad sounded disappointed. "I thought that idea was dropped. There is plenty of room in our house. There aren't as many people here as there used to be, and—"

Israel cut him off. "I know Dad. I listened to you last year when I was twenty-two. Now that I am twenty-three I should be able to make some decisions. I'm not sure how it will be, but I have a desire to build a house for myself. It won't make more work for Mother, and if I can't keep up with the housekeeping, I will hire someone.

"Did you realize Eli Jonas will be twenty and has been going steady for almost two years? Alpheus is going steady and will soon be twenty-one, and his girl is three years older. I'm wondering if maybe one of those might not soon ask to have the farm. It seems it's getting harder for you, and if two of us are in the shop and one at Seranus's, and one to help here on the farm and one to send out to help others with their chores, I'm not sure there would be one left to help you. I even thought that maybe till I get the house done, you and Mom would like to move in with me. If the others need the farm, I thought you might help me in the shop, too."

Dad smiled, amused, and said, "What would happen if you'd get a wife? Then where would we go? Don't you have a girl some-where that is waiting on you?"

Israel chuckled. "No, Dad. I know of no one that would have me."

Mom scolded, "Now Israel, that's not true."

"Well, I mean no one that I'm interested in, too, but if that time should come, I have it all planned out. We could easily build an end onto the south side of the new house. It would make a nice base-ment kitchen entrance and the living room and bedroom would be on the level of the other rooms. The sitting room or parlor of the new house could be handy for both parties to use."

Israel walked over to his desk, pulled out a paper, and sat next to Dad. "Here, see the blueprint." He carefully went over the details of where each room would be. First Dad was asking ques-tions, but then he was just listening. Israel was still talking. "See here, this hill on the south side. I thought we could—" Israel looked over and saw Dad was leaning back against the rocker, sleeping. "Well, at least he isn't upset or he wouldn't be sleeping."

Clayton had long finished hanging up the wash and came out to the kitchen. Israel rolled up the blueprint and said to Mom, "We want to get the foundation in yet in January, but then I want to go to Kentucky in February to visit Ephraim and Naaman and visit a few other states."

"Are you going alone?" Mom asked in surprise.

"No, Warren is going along."

"Warren?" Mom smiled to herself. People classed him as a bachelor. Maybe soon Israel, too. She asked, "Spying for girls?"

Israel chuckled, "We don't plan; we are just going. Warren didn't say anything about girls."

21

Chapter Five

Clayton eased his horse to a halt, waited on two cars, and when told to, Clint politely and willingly started off. Clint had improved a lot in the last months. He pulled willingly and waited more often to be told what to do before doing it. In the beginning, he had seemed a little like a scurrying puppy, just moving for the fun of it, rather than going anywhere. He still wouldn't be a horse for an older person. When starting, Clint would wait a little as Clayton would hurriedly get on and have his rein in order. If left go, Clint would still be in the middle of the road.

Clayton was eager to be going home, but he would also miss the cows. The last week and a half, or almost two weeks, he had been at Henry High's farm doing the milking while the Highs had gone to another state for a funeral and stayed to do some visiting. A neighbor boy came to do the feeding but went home during the day. So Clayton had spent a lot of time alone through the day, which he enjoyed because he had permission to start plowing if the ground was ready.

For supper he had gone up the road a mile to Mrs. High's parents' home and stayed for the night, but he didn't stay for breakfast. He had left too early in the morning and breakfast would have been over long before he had finished milking. Clayton hurried the horse, hoping he would find everything well at home.

It was likely that Israel wouldn't be at home; he was probably on his trip to Kentucky. Although it was March, and he was planning to be home by this time, Israel's traveling plans had suddenly stood still after Dad had gotten a weak spell. On a late January evening, the family had taken turns watching over him that night, and by early morning he seemed worse. All the children, except those from Kentucky, came because they wanted to put him in the hospital but Dad didn't want to go.

Until the doctor came, Dad seemed not to be aware, and they took him to the hospital. In a few days, it was discovered that Dad wasn't just weak from the flu, but that his heart was giving him trouble. The doctors had disagreed some, but finally agreed to let him go home on medication and with orders to try and get his body in better condition before deciding anything further.

Dad had improved. He was eating again and his blood pressure medicine helped his dizziness, but he seemed like an older man. Alpheus was planning to take over the farming later in the spring. Eli Jonas was planning to come home to help in the shop, and Enos would be taking his place at Seranus's. Noah David and Clayton would help with farming and the woodwork shop and hire out, whereever they were needed.

The foundation of the shop addition had been laid before Clayton left, and the basement had been dug out for the new house. As Clayton turned in the lane, he could see that the foundation of the house had been laid, and the shop addition was taking shape.

After Clayton had unhitched Clint, he took his bag of clothing into the kitchen. Only Dad and Mom were there; in fact, Dad was still at the table. Clayton raised his eyebrows, asking, "Am I still in time for dinner?"

"Well, yes, didn't you have any?" Mom asked.

"No, it's been a long time since I had a real dinner."

Mom bustled around getting a clean plate and taking the used one away. She warmed the meat and peas; then she scraped together the remaining mashed potatoes. "Here, put this hot gravy and vegetables on the potatoes, then they will be warm enough."

Clayton's mouth watered at the sight and smell of a good cooked meal, even if it was warmed up. The grandparents where he was getting his supper cooked more simply since they were older people. Henry's wife had shown him the freezer, canned things, and food in the cupboards to make, but it seemed too much bother for him, just for one person.

23

Enos came in the door with the mail and happily said, "Here's a letter from Israel," tossing it to Mom. She took a hairpin from her hair and slit the envelope, pulling out the single sheet and reading it so that all could hear. It said that all was well with the boys and their families in Kentucky and that Israel had dropped in to visit Naomi at the beginning of the trip. Then there were some instructions to the boys about an order for the shop, that it should be worked on to be finished next week. Israel would travel home at his own wish, as Warren had persuaded Israel to stay longer in Ohio than they had planned. Now Warren was planning to go to Ohio again after leaving Kentucky. Israel didn't know anything about his sudden interest in Ohio.

Suddenly, Mother gasped and caught her breath. Clayton looked at her and was startled. She wasn't one to get excited about something or display her feelings. "I don't know what I was thinking," she said. "Before dinner Ernie Hoover's children were here with a note wondering if their hired girl could go along to the singing, and as I am so used to it, I said that if Israel doesn't say anything, he could take passengers along. I just never thought of it that he isn't even here tonight."

"Well," Clayton began, "likely Eli Jonas could take her along if we send a message up there. Shall I run up this afternoon?"

"No," Father spoke up. "Eli Jonas was down this morning and said he is starting up country this afternoon. Amanda went to Cloverdale on Thursday for the funeral, and he is going up today to drive her home tomorrow."

Clayton looked at them questioningly.

"Haven't you heard about the boy who died in the Cloverdale settlement?" Mom asked.

Clayton shook his head, waiting.

Dad spoke up, "I think the boy was a Jonathan Leid. He lived alone and was painting in his house for a few days, and apparently he breathed too much of the vapors since there wasn't enough ventilation. He was pretty sick before he realized it and got to the hospital. Even the doctors didn't realize it was so serious; he had chemical pneumonia. His parents left the hospital for the night;

24

his lung collapsed and he died the first night when no one was there.

"How old was he?"

"I think he was twenty-three," Eli Jonas said. "He was getting his house ready for a new bride in the near future. I guess Amanda knew his girl well."

Clayton sat in deep thought, unaware of Mom and Dad's further conversation until the sound of his name aroused him. Dad repeated, "Did you hear, I guess you have to go?"

"Go where?" Clayton asked, trying to get his thoughts together. "I thought the funeral was already."

Then Mom spoke, "No, Dad decided you'll have to take Mary Emma, the hired girl, to the singing."

Clayton whistled and brushed his hand through his unruly hair, "You mean I get to go to the singing?" he asked unbelieving.

"Well, in another month you will be seventeen, so in this case you may go tonight," Dad answered.

"Where is the singing?"

"Dad and Mom looked at each other. Mom shrugged her shoulders. "The note didn't say; I guess they figured Israel would know."

Clayton rolled his eyes and said in an eerie voice, "Go to a singing before I'm seventeen, with a strange girl, and not know where I'm going."

Dad looked at Mom who pretended to frown but smiled in spite of herself. Dad was churning his spoon from the table in his hand a few times over as he said, "That's not as bad as the guy who had the wrong girl in his buggy on the way to his date and didn't know where he was going."

Mother blushed and said, "Unless you'd rather go tell her we have no driver for tonight."

Clayton gave Mom a long look. He didn't know Mom could blush. Suddenly, he got up and said, "I better go and get my buggy washed."

Sometime later, Mom saw Enos talking to Clayton as he washed his buggy. Then she saw Enos having a good laugh as Clayton

25

looked amused. She could easily guess that Clayton repeated the talk they had had in the house.

During supper there was a reunion of having the three youngest boys at home. Clayton told about his two weeks away while the others shared about the project at home. And, of course, Mom's act was told the third time.

Later, when Clayton came downstairs with his freshly-shampooed hair still disheveled, he walked over to the mirror and began combing his hair. Suddenly he turned around and looked at the clock and asked, "Mom, how am I supposed to know what time I'm to start if I don't know where I am going?"

Mom, getting weary of hearing the reminders of her absent-mindedness, gave him a motherly look and said, "Well, my young son, if you never have any worse problems than this in your young years, you will have it easy. Remember, you told us when you start going with the young folks, you'll keep us informed of everyone." Clayton smiled at her in the mirror as she passed by clearing off the table.

Later, when Mom came to empty the water glasses at the washbowl, Clayton still stood there. Mom teased, "I wonder how long it would take to comb if you were a girl."

"You can be glad you don't know," Clayton replied as he put his comb in his rear pocket. He walked over to the sewing machine to gather up his songbooks that he had deposited there and got a bag from the cellarway to put them in.

Mom paused for a moment taking in the scene. Clayton's hair were oiled down and looked somewhat dark. They would soon dry off and become lighter, with some straying. Even now after all the combing, there were a few hairs that wouldn't cooperate. Clayton wasn't the tallest of the boys, but Mom needed to make his shirt backs and shoulders broader than the rest. Tonight he had chosen to wear his silky blue shirt with small white checks and his black dress pants. His new pair of suspenders were sky blue with a narrow black "railroad" through them.

This was the seventh of her sons that Mom had watched get ready for his first singing. Some people thought the boys all resembled

26

each other. Clayton did resemble Seranus somewhat. But he was broader than Seranus, and his cowlick at the left side of his head made him comb his hair on that side while others combed them over to the right. Clayton said the cow must really have taken a big lick, but he thought his hair resembled a bird's nest. For some strange reason Clayton's left hand always came handier; he was almost three till he learned to eat right. The family kept insisting he had to use the right hand, but they finally decided it wasn't just habit. *He has Ephraim's blue eyes, like Naomi had too, one token of my mother,* Mom thought. *None of her children had blue eyes, but now it's showed up in some of the grandchildren.*

Just as he put his hat on and pulled on his jacket, Clayton noticed his mother watching him. He reached for the door and then turned back and asked, "If I behave, may I go regular then?"

"First see how this goes," Mom warned him.

Clayton drove in at the upper drive at Ernie's, turned around, and pulled up to the walk and waited. *Mary Emma must not be waiting*, he thought as he held the lines. Clint stood obediently for awhile and then started getting impatient. The porch door opened, and a little girl came running out; she saw the team and suddenly went back in. Soon Mary Emma came hurrying out. As she approached the buggy and started with apologies, Clint thought it was time to go and almost caught Mary Emma between the wheels. She asked Clayton if he had been waiting long.

"I thought I saw you coming, but then I didn't see you. I was so used to seeing you drive around to the lower drive." Then she stopped to get her breath, as she settled herself on the seat. Gathering her wraps to herself, she asked, "By the way, did you get a new horse? I almost got caught."

Clayton cleared his throat, "No, this is my regular horse. I'm not Israel."

"Oh yes, I hear," Mary Emma chuckled, understanding why he hadn't stopped at the regular drive. Israel always drove in to the upper drive and made a circle and out the lower drive to pick her up. But they had made an agreement that she'd always ask if she wanted to go along, as some weekends she went home.

27

Very teasingly she asked, "Which of the Singing Pine Brothers are you?"

Not to be outdone, Clayton answered dryly, "The cone." Mary Emma laughed heartily.

Without thinking, Clayton turned right, maybe because it was in the direction away from home, then he remembered and asked, "Oh by the way, where's the singing?" Mary Emma remained silent. She looked like she was beginning to wonder if something was the matter with him. When only silence remained, Mary Emma asked, "WHAT did you say?" Clint quickly came to a stop when she said "WHAT" loudly.

Clayton chuckled as he tugged on the lines and Clint started off just as suddenly. Clayton was still chuckling and explained his ignorance or innocence.

Mary Emma laughed and said, "It's at Edwin Reiff's."

"Come on, Clint." Clayton tugged the lines. "We have some miles to cover."

"I was sort of wondering why you didn't turn the other way, and I expected Israel would come earlier. Then I didn't even see you when you did come," Mary Emma was thinking aloud.

"I'll cut up here through Millers' lane, and get Coppertown Road. Then I don't need to turn around."

About an hour later Clayton could hear the music as he walked up to the house at the singing. It wasn't his desire to come to his first singing like this, to go in the kitchen when everyone was seated already. Then a few more arrived. When the next song was started, Clayton slipped into the kitchen a little behind the table that was filled with people singing and some standing behind it.

It sounded like the girls were leading this song. Maybe the leader didn't know it. But song after song the girls were leading and everyone sang along. Once they urged Eugene to start a song, and he had only gotten the pitch for them. It sounded to Clayton as if Eugene had a cold and, of course, Eli Jonas was up country and wasn't there to lead.

Often the girls started singers on their own pitch; once it was too high and they had to start over. At times they sang the first whole line till they hit the right pitch. Clayton could hardly contain himself, hearing how they were misusing the music.

Someone called out "page 478" from the other side of the stove. The girls looked at each other and then at Eugene. And Eugene looked at them. Clayton's heart started beating faster; he wasn't going to start a song at his first singing, much less without being told. He first wanted to get the feel of how they sang.

Someone nudged Clayton. There stood cousin Bennie. "What are you waiting on?" Clayton reached into his shirt pocket for the pitch pipe which he had brought for maybe group singing later on in the evening. Some pages started rustling, and just as he blew the pipe, another page was called. For a few minutes he forgot he was at a singing and sang the first notes as in group singing. He held his hand for alto to catch and then bass. He took a deep breath and the words came, "My God and Father, while I stray far from my home, on life's rough way, oh teach me from my heart to say, 'Thy will be done!'" They stumbled some on the chorus, when Clayton held off for others to put in the parts and no one sang the parts. Somehow none held it at the hold.

Clayton was beginning to feel like crawling under the table and thought they may as well not try another verse since it must be an unfamiliar song for them. After the last word died down, then silence, Edwin himself, over by the stove, said, "That was right; let's sing the next verses till we get used to it. I haven't heard that song for a long time."

Clayton felt his face get warm as everyone looked at him. He blew the pitch again and started, "Let but my fainting heart be blest with thy sweet Spirit for its guest, my God, to Thee I leave the rest." Without thinking he slowed his hand to lower them; then at the chorus, he held his hand for the girls to go on and he filled the parts in. As they sang the last verse the whole group had the idea of the tune and who sings what. The music blended with sweet accord—alto, soprano, and bass.

The next song was picked. The girls nodded to him, and the boy next to Eugene got up from the table and showed Clayton where to sit. This was not at all his idea of what his first singing should be.

29

But hearing their discord helped him overcome his shyness. In his subconscious mind he thought he was just singing with his small group.

Once, as Clayton glanced up while waiting until a selection was called, and while some were visiting, his eyes were drawn to the girls standing in front of the west window. He unknowingly watched the girl at the lower end who was listening to the conversation. Her rather dark hair were not really in waves but just glided back as if a soft evening breeze put them there. Her bobby pin seemed to catch them there and hold the upper part in a notch. The lower ones fell gently, neatly combed behind her ear. Her covering neatly fitted her head with the edging right where the pin had caught her hair. Her silver-toned glasses, slanted toward her face, seemed to highlight her crystal-blue eyes against her neatly-pleated lavender dress. Clayton unconsciously thought of a gentle spring breeze blowing over a mountain spring.

Suddenly, Lydia Ann looked up, her eyes meeting Clayton's for a moment. Then she smiled shyly, her cheeks glowing, and Clayton's picture was complete. The sun shown out from the red evening sky on the mountain spring. It awakened Clayton from his stupor, and he felt his own face get warm. A page number was repeated, and for the second time that evening, Clayton wanted to crawl under the table, fearing others may have noticed. His heart had fluttered when Lydia Ann had smiled. He had no idea if he had smiled back, but maybe that's what had brought him back.

Several songs later Clayton looked up just in time to see—not Lydia Ann but Barbara Ellen quickly drop her eyes. The rest of the evening whenever he happened to look up, it seemed that Barbara Ellen was just switching her glance. Clayton then turned back to his book and didn't locate Lydia Ann again.

The singing came to an end and the refreshments were brought out. Clayton had decided while singing that the best place to look was in his songbook. But now, while people stood eating and visiting, he lifted his eyes. When Barbara Ellen had her back partly turned to a half circle of girls around her and was engrossed in conversation, Clayton studied her. She had a good complexion and a friendly

30

face. Her hair were in small natural waves with plenty of loose ends that looked too excited to run with the waves. Her covering fit her well, each pleat just the right size and length to go around her hair bun.

Barbara Ellen's brown hair matched her brown eyes well. When Clayton saw the fresh green-checkered dress she wore and her brown eyes and hair, it made him think of a fine soil with green plants growing. Her brown eyes at that moment were searching the girl's beside her. The other girls laughed and Barbara Ellen said, "I knew you would, because when I came back out . . ." Clayton couldn't hear more because someone near him started talking, but her eyes were lively in conversation. She was a nice girl for someone, but Clayton hoped she was watching someone behind him.

He didn't know why Lydia Ann stirred him so, as he had often seen her since one of her brothers also was with the singing group. At times the young people gathered at her home but he had never really noticed her before. It was a big possibility that she was taken already, as she must have been with the group a few years by now. Clayton had looked around the kitchen but couldn't spot Lydia Ann. She must have left with one of her many brothers.

A half hour later Clayton came out of the parlor into the hall leading to the kitchen to tell Mary Emma they were going home. A girl who was standing at the doorway with her wrap on turned around. He couldn't see her well, but the waters still sparkled. Lydia Ann! Clayton suddenly smiled and fled; after getting Mary Emma's attention, he decided to go out out the kitchen door.

Chapter Six

Clayton shifted his position and sat up straighter. Minister Jacob was earnestly revealing the message, as if the spirit was overflowing with words. "The wages of sin is death, and the gift of God is life eternal. There is a cost of sin. Sin is a wage that must be paid, and life eternal is a gift of God. Why would we pay for something bad, when there is something so glorious to receive as a gift? It is a gift. It's not because we love God, but because God first loved us. What can we do? How can we know which way?"

Jacob paused and looked at his silent audience. "Now if we were preparing to go on a long trip, the most important thing to do is to start off; we know we won't get there if we don't make a beginning. How do we recognize God's calling? How do we know it is God calling? Now if you read some of this modern day religion, they give great visions, and the exact time they were saved, and so on and so forth. But I think of that which we read somewhere in the Bible, you readers know, the one that was in the cave and said he would come out when the Spirit of God comes. I think the first was a mighty whirlwind, but he did not come out. Then there was an earthquake and still he didn't come, but still it was not God's voice. Then a still small voice came forth, and he came out of the cave. Only a still small voice, maybe too little a thing for a lot of people to notice. We look for big things to convince us.

"And it's not just at a certain place, or a certain church. Where does God say the kingdom of God is? He says the kingdom of God is within you. Like the wind, we can't see it, but we know it is there. We see the evidence. And so we can see the Spirit of God in the people. We can't see the Spirit but the evidence that they are receiving it. That they are saying no to the world and are living for Christ.

It matters not if we have to give things up. In some cases, we may lose friends if we cease to help with something that we used to do. Are we able to endure? Jesus says, 'If they hate you, they hated me first.' It will all be things that Jesus endured, too; he went the way before. He paved the way for us, so if he suffered, we will suffer. It will be a new life, a new beginning.

"We cannot keep on in our own way, because we were born with an adamic nature, and we have to offer up that and become a new creature. We see that the trees are now budding their new leaves, the trees that showed no signs of life this winter, since the leaves fell off in fall. But if we take notice, the oak trees cling to their old leaves in the winter and they rustled as the strong stiff breezes blew through them. But now they are off. What loosened the dried leaves finally?

"My mind goes to a clipping I found in my mother's Bible. This is no scripture, only a writing to describe or explain the spirit of God like the man in the cave. There was a girl who wanted to accept Christ and be baptized, but she could not see why she had to give up so many things she wanted. She thought that it would be easy to give it up if she was born again. She stubbornly resisted every plea. The bishop tried to explain to her, and he was at his wits' end what to say to persuade her. He looked out the window and saw the oaks still clinging to the old leaves. He called her attention to the tree and told her to watch daily and see what would be able to shake the leaves from the tree. All the winds and strong blasts of winter were powerless against them. But one nice spring day with no wind blowing, the girl noticed the leaves rapidly falling to the ground. Now what made the leaves fall? It was then that the bishop was able to explain the message. New buds were coming, new life was coming in the tree, and it loosened its grip on the old leaves. Grasping the lesson, the girl became a penitent and obedient member in the church. It was not the earthquake, nor the whirlwind of the winter rough winds, but the still small voice. The new life does not come until the old life starts dying off. But like the old minister used to say, we have to sit down and figure out the cost before we start building, so that we don't start building and then can't afford to finish it. Like the song that we sing time and time again:

Alle christen horen gern fon dem reich der harlich keit,
Don sie meaner schon fon ferne,
Dasz es ihnen sey bereit,
Aber vann sie horen sagen,
Dasz mon christi kreutz musz tragen,
Vann man will sein junger seyn O so stimmer venig ein.
Leiblich ist es anzwhoren,
Ihr beladne, kommt zu mir
Uber das sind horte lehren, gehet ein zu engera thei Hort man
hoseanne singen, Lautes gut, latzts aber klingen. Kreutze ifts ein
onder tone, und ein zeder louft davon.

"Talking about sitting down and counting the cost first reminds me of the big building most of you know about in town that a big warehouse company started building. They were working on it so earnestly, but at last all is quiet. Rumor has it that their funds are gone. We think it strange that they didn't realize how much it would cost. But we see such incidents among our church, people who joined church and were obedient, willing members. Suddenly, we hear they have ceased, left off. They can't continue. They hadn't considered the many temptations that would beg them. When they promised they would say no to the world, they didn't consider the cross to bear.

"Maybe too many people get the modern religion thought: once they get baptized, they are saved, always saved. Nowhere in the Bible do we read such. Jesus was an example and right after he was baptized, Satan came with temptations. First one way and then another. But Jesus was able to live up to 'seek ye first the kingdom of God.' Scripture says then all these things shall be added unto you. Maybe not all the things that we desire in life, like the rich man. He desired to have everything good in this life, but was cast into hell as it was said, 'You had your good in this life.'

"But I'm taking up too much time. I do want to make myself clear that we are not saved by works, it's faith, through grace. But faith without works is dead. We bring forth works to show our appreciation, works brings no faith, but faith through grace shows works."

As Jacob took his seat, Bishop Paul stood solemn before the congregation, after a silent prayer for God to speak further through his servants. "For God alone knows what each need is in encouragement and admonishing. He alone gives power for the Spirit to speak further. I must ask, What can a person say further? I feel empty, as I was emptied out as the brother spoke. I can say amen to what the Spirit brought forth so far. And I can feel a thirst, that many hungry and thirsty hearts were refreshed, like a gentle rain in scorched plants now refreshed.

"It's a desire I looked forward to seeing, that some young folks would soon realize the calling of the still small voice. And I don't want you to lose faith and think that you don't understand it well enough. I think back many years, when I was at that place, I now realize how little I really understood or how little the seed was. We read that the mustard seed is of the finest seed, but it can grow into a big tree where the birds can nest. And if we would wait to eat till we know we can digest food, we would never eat. There must be a beginning, however small it may be. When it was said of comparing trees to ourselves, I had to think of another part of a tree's growth. Now we take good care of a tree in our orchard or yard. We prune it, take some branches off so that others have room to grow, but in the end it yields stronger, bigger branches and more fruit because it has room to grow. In the same way, God sees it is good to chasten us. He doesn't tempt us. The Scripture says if we are tempted, it is through our own lust, but he does chasten us. It may not seem joyous at the time, but grievous. The Bible tells us that chastening yields fruits of righteousness to those exercised thereby.

"I further saw need to take up the text which you have heard read heartily by the brother, as it states here, 'Good Master, what must I do to enter the kingdom of God?'" Paul laid down the book and looked at the audience expectantly, as if he thought someone would get up and raise an objection with him. "First, Jesus rebuked him for saying Good Master. No one is good except the Father. Jesus, too, was without failures, and he didn't want to be called good. We have failures; we see the good that is in us or that we bring forth is not of ourselves. Our own righteousness is as filthy rags before God.

Second, he says what MUST I do. Doesn't that sound rather unsubmissive? We don't want people to say, 'All right, I will join the church, but what all must I do to come up to the rules and regulations?'

"If the spirit is right, they want to know 'what all CAN I do?' Furthermore, the rules don't affect the obedient Christian; he will have no need for rules. The contrite are ready to do anything to make peace. A man was once told to keep the commandments, and he named some. The fellow replied, 'All these I kept from my youth on.' Is that how we are when we get admonished? We appear too big, and think 'I told him once. Now I wonder what he has to say?'

"But Jesus replied, 'One thing thou lacketh yet; sell all that you have and give to the poor and follow Me.'" Paul laid down the book and cleared his throat saying, "Now some people get confused here. I had people coming to me wondering if they shall sell what they have and give to the poor. Now it doesn't say that all the people have to do this. He only said it to this fellow. Why? Because he knew that it was the riches that kept him from taking up his cross. He was a man with many possessions and he sorrowfully went his way. Now what does this tell us? What do we need to do?

"Like this lad, we have to get rid of whatever lies between us and God. Whatever we have that is dearer to us than salvation. If there is something we can't give up, that's the very thing we should give up."

Clayton cupped his head in his hands, with his elbows leaning on his knee. There was so much being said, but already he knew he had forgotten some of the opening message. He was spiritually thirsty, but he couldn't quench his thirst for the many things he often questioned. One by one Jacob and Paul brought up the very issues Clayton questioned and then answered them by verses in the New Testament that he had often read and failed to understand. *Oh for the wisdom of these men*, Clayton thought hopelessly.

Half an hour later, as he stepped out of the church door, Clayton was surprised to see rain. He thought—he didn't clearly remember what he thought. He did see as he approached his buggy that he had closed it up. For a moment he stood beside his buggy, collecting his thoughts. He felt as though he was stumbling through a long tunnel or a deep forest and as he stumbled along more and more light came forth. It seemed he was seeing the sun shining in the clearing, to see where he was going. Now he only needed to go toward it.

Eldon had invited Clayton to his home for dinner. They talked awhile in the afternoon. Eldon did not seem ready yet to join church, nor did he remember much of the former message when Clayton was so eager to talk about it. Clayton left early and turned Clint out in the pasture. Dad and Mom weren't at home. Clayton leisurely walked down the back field lane and over the edge of the hay field and crossed the neighbor's land. Then he reached the woods. Chief trotted along as if showing the way and looking back as if to keep Clayton going.

At the edge of the woods, Clayton looked at a tree while his mind was pondering. Suddenly, his thoughts came to life as he noticed the whole tree. It was full of stocky branches with rough bark. *Where would there be room for fruit if branches were growing out everywhere? It should be trimmed*, Clayton thought. He stared at the tree. What did one of the ministers say about such a tree? That it doesn't get pruned? It never gave up; it kept all it had; it grew wild and was never chastened. Now there would be no fruit.

So far, Clayton wistfully thought, *I have committed no great sin. Suppose I promised and couldn't hold out against the things I yearn for of pleasures and living for myself, without giving in to another one leading?* Clayton wondered if he would be willing to let God lead him. He had a good home, many friends, and, well, why not just continue on? But there was the ever-pressing battle, a restlessness. This forenoon he had been convinced it was the still small voice knocking, and he had promised to open. It had seemed easy then, but now questions were coming up again.

The birds flew from one tree top to another, and Clayton watched and yearned. *Oh to be a bird. They need not worry about right or wrong and punishment of sin or knowing the right way, giving themselves up and being baptized on their confession of faith.* . . . Clayton trembled at the thought of going through the ordeal. He had lost some sleep over it some weeks before, but now he convinced himself: *Surely if Jesus bore all the pain to die on the cross, I can do this much.* In another few weeks those desiring to take instruction to join church would be giving their names. Clayton was beginning to look forward to it if he could settle this war of doubt and indecision. Although he had finally made a decision, he knew there would be times of doubt as long as he didn't make a public confession.

That evening Clayton sat trying to read, waiting until his brothers went to bed. Well—no, he was only pretending to read; he had given up trying to. Mother, however, noticed that he was neither reading nor attempting to, because he turned the pages too often and got up for a drink a few times or stared in the lamp-lit kitchen, not seeing. Clayton heard Dad say, "Well, boys, I think it's bedtime." Enos and Noah David were soon chattering as they went up the stairs.

When Clayton glanced up, he saw Mom looking at him, wondering. There were so many things he had planned to say. He finally stammered out something about the unusual sermon, that he couldn't remember everything. Dad and Mom looked blankly at each other. Then he felt tears pushing out as he meekly asked, "You don't have anything against my joining church this summer?" Dad got an understanding look on his face, and Mom relaxed.

"We can't decide for you," Dad said, "though I thought maybe you would. You did only turn seventeen a month ago. You must be sure it's not just a sudden notion or a desire to follow the others. But I can feel your struggle in this. Keep in mind that you don't join the church thinking that when you're baptized, God will care for you and Satan will have no power. The trying begins to see if your faith is as wood and stubble that perish in the fire or like gold, that gets purer."

Clayton felt a lot better; a heavy load was lifted from his shoulders. It meant so much to know Dad had confidence in him. He had been afraid Dad would tell him to wait another year. Dad had added that the sermon probably seemed more outstanding to him because his soul and spirit were in need of it, and "you have our prayers."

Chapter Seven

From the height of the hay load, perched almost at the top, Clayton viewed the countryside as they bumped down the field lane toward the barn. Down below, Elam Newswanger was guiding the plodding workhorses toward the barn. Clayton thought the smell of the second-cutting hay was better than perfume. Most of the grain was harvested already, and a lot of the farmers' second crop hay was in the barns. Some fields had an autumn look, but the corn was still standing tall.

Clayton could see the farms from his high perch and in his mind, named the owners. He knew most of the names now, but a month ago it was new territory to him. Now he looked ahead and saw two big elm trees on the north side of the pale yellow, spacious house with its white-trimmed shutters. Both house and shutters needed paint. The long barn and two silos and various sheds formed a cluster. The dairy cows lying down by the gate were relaxing. By now, the farm looked much like home—not his home, but a good place to live.

The wagon was slowing down. They were almost to the barn. Elam unhitched and left the horses stand, as he helped Clayton guide the wagon in to its place in the barn. Then Clayton started unloading while Elam put the horses away. Elam soon was back and stacked the bales as Clayton threw them to him.

Clayton recalled the past month's events. He had been helping some in the shop and then was hired out to be a chore boy a few times. Eli Jonas had come home to help in the shop and Enos had taken his place. Alpheus was at home doing the farming. Dad still seemed an old man. The doctors had not encouraged him to have heart surgery. They thought if he was this well, they would let good enough alone, unless Dad requested it.

Then a month ago, Elam Newswanger wondered if Dad had a boy to hire out. His wife wasn't well. The doctor thought she was working too hard, so Elam decided to get a hired boy to help with the dairying. It was actually in the same settlement as Clayton's home was, but it was so far to the edge that it was almost a part of the Cottage Hill Settlement. They could choose which singing or gathering they wanted to go to, and sometimes both settlements had them together. Titus Snyder's daughter Lavina, who lived next to Elam's, often had no way to go, so Clayton usually took her along if they were going to the same place.

Clayton just discovered he was on the second last bale of the load. He threw the last bales off and jumped down for the broom and swept the wagon, and paused for a moment as he checked his watch. Yes, it was that time of the day again. He hurried down the barn stairs and cleaned out the cow troughs, giving the leftover hay to the bigger heifers. After the troughs were cleaned, he put lime on the walkway. They usually did that in the morning after leaving the cows out, but they had cut corners today, as there was hay to rake and the baler needed some repairs.

Just then Elam came in the barn with the little children following behind. Clayton went to the milk house to put the milkers together and set up the dumping station while Elam opened the slide doors to let the cows in. Three-year-old Katie came in the milk house with her two-year-old sister Nancy following her.

Clayton never ceased to be amused by Elam's little children. He couldn't remember much of little children at home since Noah David and Enos were only one and two years younger than he was.

Katie stood watching him, then she handed him the parts and the hoses of the milkers, whichever he needed next, and the same with the dumping station. The milk house door opened a little bit and a gray cat entered; they could push the door open themselves. Katie looked around and said, "That pussy we found down by the hay field, near the mailbox. That was when you weren't here yet." She was shaking her head. Clayton smiled, amused. That was her common saying, "when you weren't here yet." *The children consider me so much a part of the family that they think I don't remember that I wasn't always here.*

40

When Clayton was finished in the milk house and entered the barn, he saw six-year-old Ralph helping his daddy tie up the cows. Now everyone could go for supper.

The meal completed, Elam pushed back his chair, still biting on his toothpick. He took a quick glance at Clayton, wondering. Clayton said, "I'll help you milk for awhile; there's no singing for this area that I know about. But since class meeting is down in our church tomorrow, I thought I'd go home tonight and then head back up after class meeting. This would be a good time to visit at home. Lavina is going along to her sister's since she has to go for class meeting too."

Clayton fed the horses, the heifers, and the bigger calves; gave the smaller calves their milk; and fed the cows while Elam was milking. Elam could finish the milking while Clayton got ready to leave for the weekend.

Clayton pulled into Titus Snyder's drive. Titus was cutting the tall grass around the gas tank and near the grape arbor by the windmill. He walked up to the buggy where he and Clayton were soon discussing the weather and exchanging information on daily work, hay making, cutting wheat, and baling straw. Lavina came from the house and stepped lightly on the buggy, and they were on their way.

Lavina inquired, "By the way, did you find out that Lester Weaver's are having a singing?"

"No, I didn't," Clayton replied surprised.

Lavina apologized, "I thought maybe I should let you know; it was announced on short notice. There are some young folks around from another state, so they quickly made a singing."

Clayton looked over at her and asked, "Do you want off there? I think I will go home."

Lavina laughed and asked, "Do I look like I was going to a singing?"

Clayton shrugged his shoulders; he honestly hadn't noticed how she was dressed. "I'm sure I don't know."

"No," she answered. "I took the chance that you aren't going, as I was looking forward to visiting my sister Marian and her family." Then she added, "But you are really spoiling me by having such handy transportation. It seems so strange that I don't have to plan half a week ahead how I'm going and ask around different places and sometimes stay somewhere if there is no other way."

Shrugging his shoulders, Clayton said, "Well, as long as we are going to the same place it works out fine, because then I know where to go. I wouldn't have known where to find some of the places up here or who the people are, but my guess is one of these times you will have a better way and send me home alone."

Lavina caught her breath and wrinkled her brow as she studied him in disbelief. Clayton looked over at her and had to smile at her expression. He chuckled as he held the reins in on Clint; it seemed Clint knew he was going home.

In his mind, Clayton pictured the time he had noticed a young man's interest in Lavina Snyder. Recently when they drove up to singings or were leaving the young folks gathering together, he first thought Jonas had an impolite habit of staring. Clayton had finally come to the conclusion that Jonas was admiring his passenger, as if he had a fear of seeing them travel together. He hadn't pinpointed it until at a singing one evening, he noticed that Jonas's attention was repeatedly drawn in Lavina's direction. Clayton didn't know if Lavina didn't see it or if she didn't want to know, because she didn't seem to respond.

"Don't worry; good things take time. And there's plenty of time yet," Clayton told her.

Lavina answered as they passed a one-room schoolhouse, "But the time is coming faster than I care for nearing the beginning of school. The teachers' meetings begin in a little over two weeks and I—" She faltered for words.

Clayton asked, "Are you planning to spend your time in school this term?"

"Yes, I guess so. The school board wanted a good excuse with 'no,' but I only had poor ones."

"Are you teaching here?" he asked, pointing to the school they had passed.

42

"No, it just reminded me about it. I'll teach at South Acres."

Half an hour later, as they approached her sister's mailbox, Lavina said, "Just leave me off here."

Clayton pulled to the side of the road and asked, "When shall I pick you up?"

"Oh, after class meeting, I can go with them to church and I'll go somewhere near for dinner, then I can walk to class meeting."

Clint willingly turned in the lane at home. While Clayton was unhitching, he glanced up at the new house, and then he looked again. Quickly he put Clint away and walked down to the house.

The shop was about completed and was in use already. Clayton was amazed as he studied the new structure that had taken place in his absence. Israel was clearing away extra boards and tools lying around. The main part of the new house was nearly closed up, but on the south side at the ridge was a foundation that had recently been added. Preparations had been made to start the walk.

Israel looked up and raised his eyebrows at Clayton's astonishment. Clayton had heard Israel discussing with Dad about sometime building a basement kitchen at the south side of the house and having one room above, connected to other parts of the house. But he thought that was only one of Israel's wistful thinking or dreams.

Still staring, Clayton asked, "What has come over you?"

"Nothing that I know of," Israel answered. "I just realized that when this house is done, there likely won't be any room for me!"

"Who's the house for?"

"Oh, our brothers. If they don't claim it, they likely will chase us out of the farmhouse." Clayton didn't know which brother— Alpheus or Eli Jonas—that Israel thought might marry soon. It was sort of interesting to hear what the other people were saying about the new house. Rumor had almost everyone moving in the house. It seemed a lot of people sort of expected Israel to have a secret friendship somewhere, and at times they wondered themselves. Israel said it was worth building the house, just to hear people's imaginations.

Clayton entered the kitchen. Father had been stretched out on the sofa but stood up to greet him. Mother pulled a cake from the oven and gave a welcome home smile to Clayton. "What brings you here on a Saturday evening?"

"I was coming down since class meeting is in our area and I thought there was no singing. Then I found out about one when I was on my way already."

"Yes," Dad spoke up, "we were hoping we'd get to see you when we thought about that."

Clayton took a chair. "I see Israel is building an apartment house."

Mother shook her head, "No one knows what he'll do next. But since Alpheus is farming here," she looked at Dad who silently listened in approval, "it seems he is thinking about bringing a house-keeper here sometime in the future."

"You mean you would move in the new house then?" Clayton asked in surprise, and interest.

Dad and Mom exchanged a silent message. "There are so many plans budding; we'll have to see which will bloom," Mother said. "Oh, by the way, did Israel tell you?" she asked with a lighter feeling.

Clayton shrugged his shoulders and said, "He said something about soon there would be no room for him."

Mother shook her head and spoke triumphantly, "No, I mean about Naomi." Clayton shook his head. "They have a baby," Mother beamed. "Another grandson."

Dad said fondly, "Of course, what else?"

Clayton asked, "How many grandchildren does that make? Eleven?"

Mother answered, "Eleven."

Clayton echoed, "And only one of them is a girl."

"This one will be Emory," Mother informed him.

Chapter Eight

The house was too quiet. Clayton got up from the sofa in the living room and yawned as he stretched his arms and body. He had heated some chicken corn soup and had a helping of the good apple pie for dinner. Then he thought he would sleep awhile since his head wanted to nod in church in the forenoon, but his thoughts had churned one way then another till he decided against sleeping. The house sounded so quiet, almost as if the clock stopped ticking, but the pendulum was still swaying. Clayton thought he could almost hear Elva, Elam's wife, softly humming, something she often did while going about her work. Seeing the sewing machine, with the chair drawn up to it and the partly sewn dress thrown on the open sewing machine wing with the scissors nearby, he thought it would seem right to hear Elva sing, as she often did when sewing.

That was another thing he enjoyed at the Elam Newswanger home. Elam and Elva liked to sing. On leisure evenings or after a sudden thundershower, they would all sing together, and it was so touching to hear the children sing. Sometimes later they would sing while they were playing, often the right words, but the tunes varied. Clayton saw the little table and chairs in the corner of the living room where Katie and Nancy had been playing house. One of the dolls sat on the rocking chair, another one slumped on a chair. Little dishes were scattered around. Clayton could almost imagine the childish conversation as they would play together. Sometimes Ralph would help the girls. Then Katie would tell him he was the dad and she was the mom and Nancy was the maid. But if Ralph didn't help, then Nancy was the dad and Katie was always the mother.

Ralph often was busy with his Tinker Toy set, building something or telling his dad what to build. Clayton looked around. He couldn't see the set under the table. Then an amused smile came to his face as he saw the small school desk beside Elam's big desk. Ralph was spending more time at his desk lately. Elva was teaching him the names of the colors and how to print his name. She would show him pictures in books, drilling him in the English words. Tomorrow would be a big day for Ralph; school was starting. A few days ago he had proudly shown Clayton his new pencil box and his new straw hat. He had, also, finally learned to drive his little bicycle alone.

If no other sound could be heard in the house, usually baby Mabel could be heard crawling across the floor. She pushed herself along, wiping up all the dirt in her path, cooing as she went. She would beg everyone who came along to pick her up, except she protested when Nancy did. Nancy tumbled over too often when carrying Mabel, but she'd always try again.

Clayton looked at the clock—2:30. It would still be a few hours before it was time to go to Willis Weaver's where the young folks were invited for supper. He had no one to pick up. Often Lavina would ride with him, but of late she sometimes chose to go to the Cottage Hill gatherings, which were often not very far, as Elam's lived right where the Cottage Hill and Stoney Creek settlements divided. Clayton still cherished his home settlement, but he now found himself often heading for Stoney Creek.

Clayton walked out on the porch and across the lower yard which led to the meadow gate. He continued on to the group of trees by the water, a slow run that branched off from South Creek and flowed through the wooded part of the pasture. South Creek flowed across the corner of the orchard where the fence parted Elam's orchard from neighbor Titus's north pasture. There was a fallen tree by the creek where Clayton rested as he ruffled his hair with his hand. A root of a tree was sprouted in the run, and the water rippled over it like a miniature waterfall. The birds called to each other from the treetops.

Clayton saw a leaf drop and float down the stream. It glided easily till it came to the tree root; it wavered but then glided down on the other side of the root. It hesitated where to go, but went on down the stream. He wondered what else would block the lone leaf from sailing. He saw a fallen branch across the stream. The leaf got pushed around when it reached the branch and it was crowded to the edge and there was swept over a stone and fell to the side, away from the water in a little ditch where other twigs and leaves had bounced. Its voyage was over until a heavier flow of water would come and catch some of its articles again. Clayton took a deep breath and sighed as he leaned his back against a tree.

His thoughts turned toward the evening. Maybe the best place to stay would be here beside the creek. Thinking of the leaf, he remembered the words of a song: "Often I'm hindered on my way." The leaf had been tossed aside. If he wanted to admit it, Clayton himself felt as if he was caught in a whirlpool of water. There was no stopping and no sailing on. Then he thought of where the leaf finally lay and the words came:

> *In the rifted Rock I'm resting,*
> *Safely sheltered I abide.*
> *There no foes nor storms molest me,*
> *While within the cleft I hide.*

All during the summer, with instruction meetings, he had tried to keep his mind on the important step he was taking and to grasp all the admonishing and instructions he received. Somehow as the older ministers pleaded, warned, and admonished the class, Clayton believed struggles lay ahead for him. The ministers talked as if they were still fighting as much of a battle as it was when they had started on their voyage.

Clayton had sort of taken for granted that once he joined church and was led to a life companion, a lot of struggles and decisions would be solved. But this must not be so because church elders earnestly preached on struggles of the warfare of the pilgrim's travels. They must be right in it, fighting on.

Clayton thought of his baptism that was only three weeks away. His thoughts had been really stirred up and churned around the other week when one of the articles at class meeting was on Holy Matrimony. He had done a lot of thinking since then.

Ever since he started going with the young folks, Clayton's heart trembled at the sight of Lydia Ann. He had read in a poetry book a short verse that said, "Your name is like a golden bell hung in my heart. Every time I think of you, I tremble and the bell swings and rings." There were times when he had looked up and Lydia Ann had looked his way. Sometimes she had recognized him with a smile, but there were other times when he had looked up to locate her that he met her looking his way and she had quickly averted her eyes, as if she was trespassing. But the short, sudden smiles he had received lately she would likely give to anyone else who would happen to look her way.

Clayton knew his desire and admiration of Lydia Ann was getting stronger since he lived at Elam's; his hopes had grown fonder. The Newswangers were a happy family. Elam seemed happy to come in the house where a cheerful wife awaited him. He discussed with Elva his troubles or whatever was going on outside. Or, if there was a joy, sometimes he would run to tell her and she rejoiced with him. At times they teased each other good naturedly. Seeing Elam and Elva was the real picture of what Clayton dreamed about in Lydia Ann. But he had a growing fear.

Lydia Ann was a few years older than Clayton and he felt a fear that some other boy would recognize her, too. She seemed rather reserved. His heart had felt warm the few times when he had smiled first and she had smiled back and blushed. But those smiles were few and far between.

The other week, the inevitable had taken place. Marcus, Lydia Ann's brother, had told his singing buddies to come on Wednesday evening, as there were some boys traveling through from Virginia. They belonged to a singing group and they wanted to meet the boys and sing some with them. Marcus and his brother Orvie were quite fond of singing.

Clayton's face felt warm again just thinking about it, how he had arrived at Marcus's place. He had left his bike standing in the backyard. He had been a little late and had hurried up the walk and stepped on the porch. Out of the corner of his eye he thought he had seen a movement. Before he had time to look or think, a voice startled him, so much that he jumped.

The voice had good-naturedly said, "All dressed up and no place to go?" His eyes followed the sound of the voice. At the far side of the porch where the garden came up almost to the porch, sat Lydia Ann! Around her was a row of flower pots nearly filled with soil and she was planting flowers in the pots. Clayton had felt rather stupid and said, "I suppose I'm late."

Lydia Ann was still looking at him rather questioningly and she answered mischievously, "I have no idea if you are late. It all depends what your appointment is for!" She looked at him, still holding a flower plant in one hand and the spade in the other. Her covering strings were untied, one swaying in the front; the other one had been tossed over her shoulder. Her hair were pulled back where the hairpin caught them, but quite a few had eluded the grip of the hair clip, falling over the stems of her glasses. But the glasses till slanted in, displaying the crystal-blue eyes, as if to give the picture a better view. The pink checkered dress matched her glowing cheeks, and the lighter pink apron with fine dashes of yellow buds against the crystal blue eyes was a picture of spring time, of a mountain spring where a rustling wind had rustled through. Clayton had shifted his weight. Lydia Ann had motioned toward the porch furniture, "Please take a seat."

Still dumbfounded, Clayton had answered her question finally, "I guess the others are all in already." Lydia Ann started planting flowers again. As Clayton sat down on the porch rocker, she opened her mouth to say something, but then didn't. The blank look said she had not understood what he meant. "I mean are Marcus's friends here to sing?"

"WHAT?" she asked surprised.

Then Clayton had explained. "Marcus told us to come over this evening since there are boys here from Virginia who like to sing. He wanted us to meet and join them." Lydia Ann had stared, bewildered, at him and caught her breath. They both paused. Then Clayton asked, "Isn't Marcus here?"

49

"Well no, not that I know of. You know he works over at Lloyd Eby's."

"No, I didn't know. You mean regular?"

"Well, yes, since, oh, maybe June or July." Then she got a knowing look on her face and added, "I think Orvie did say he was going over to Eby's tonight. Either he didn't say or else I didn't pay attention if he talked about a group from Virginia being there to sing."

"So it's at Eby's," Clayton had thought out loud.

"Guess he figured you knew he is there during the week," Lydia Ann had said as she bent down in the garden to fill another flower pot. Then she had asked, "How is your father? Getting better? I see he is in church again."

Clayton had cleared his throat, "Better than he was but not what he used to be. I always wonder how I will find him when I get home."

"Oh that's right, you aren't at home either. Are there still enough helpers at home to help your mother since Naomi isn't there?"

"Well, since Alpheus is farming, Dad helps Mom more."

Then Lydia Ann got a mischievous look on her face as her glance dropped, and she appeared to be busy with the flowers as added color came to her cheeks. She sounded serious as she asked, "Are there still singing pines left?"

"The trees are still all there," Clayton answered after a few seconds. "The house is further back."

Lydia Ann chuckled, "Oh yes, I almost forgot about the new house. Is Israel soon moving into it?"

Clayton had gotten up from the rocker and replied, "No, his rooms were just recently added on."

"Whose rooms are in the other part of the house?"

"If you tell me, we'll both know," Clayton had answered. "And if not, we'll both wait and see, eh?"

Lydia Ann chuckled at the question as she laid down the spade. Her pots were all filled and planted. Then Clayton added, "It might become Pine City yet."

Laughing heartily, Lydia Ann questioned, "Without the cone?" The smile on her face when he looked at her came to his mind quite a few times when he thought about her later. Clayton had wiped his hand across his brow, tipping his hat and saying, "I should be on my way. I've kept you long enough."

"And maybe I've made you miss some singing," she had apologized. "Did you hear that Uncle Raymond Oberholtzers are coming for the weekend of the twenty-third?"

"You mean the bishop from Missouri?"

Lydia Ann nodded in answer to his question. A solemn feeling overwhelmed Clayton as he thought, *To think that a bishop from far away cares enough to come when the young people get baptized.*

At that moment Lydia Ann's younger sister had come running around the corner of the house saying, "Mother wondered if you are making the flowers first. She wants you to finish the ironing so she can start the—" She spied Clayton turning and going out the walk, and had stopped in mid-sentence.

The previous Sunday evening when the young folks had a picnic in the meadow at Mervin's, Lydia Ann had recognized Clayton a few times. While he was roasting a twig full of hot dogs, she was along waiting in line with a bun. He hadn't noticed her, as there were quite a few waiting, until she came closer and asked concerned, "Did you meet the singers yet?"

Clayton had looked around and smiled as he answered, "Oh yes, I did. I enjoyed it. Are you waiting on me?" he asked, testing his hot dogs and burning his finger.

Then Leroy, who was a born sport or joker, always making mischief with his mouth, looked at Lydia Ann and said dryly, "And I thought you were waiting on a hot dog. I'll give it to someone else if you are waiting on a pine cone instead."

Clayton had been too embarrassed to look up, but not many people had heard. He was afraid Lydia Ann was humiliated. He didn't really care if people called him the pine cone; it was his own fault. Even now his face felt a little flushed when he realized how it sounded when he actually asked Lydia Ann if she was waiting on him.

Then there was Barbara Ellen. At times he had to admit that in a way it was a good feeling when he would lift his eyes and find her looking. She was a very friendly girl and wasn't bold at all; in fact, more often when he looked up, she wasn't looking any more. One time he had looked up quickly and found her soft brown eyes still looking his way. He had made her blush a few times. Most often when he was studying her without thinking, she would at that moment look up at him. Then she'd blush.

Clayton thought about earlier this summer when they had been at William Gehman's for supper. He had hitched up and started through the barnyard when he saw a group of girls talking in the yard. As he passed, he had caught snatches of the conversation and stopped to ask if they all had a way home. (This was one time that Lavina had not gone with him.) After some convincing, Barbara Ellen had emerged from the group. Clayton had then remembered that her brother Charles had not been with the young folks that day since a group of boys had biked to a distant settlement for an adventure or challenge. He had not known where the boys were till Barbara Ellen told him on the way home.

Clayton and Barbara Ellen had discussed their class meeting and joining church since she was in the class too. Then he realized that she understood things better than he did. Barbara Ellen's smallest sister had been in a recent farm accident, and there were so many things to talk about. A new family had moved in. He didn't remember all they had talked about; he just knew it had been the shortest ride he ever had to Harleyville!

If it wouldn't be for Lydia Ann, maybe Clayton would consider Barbara Ellen more. The words of a song came to his mind, "Oh what needless pain we bear, all because we do not carry everything to God in prayer." Then he thought of the song, "Get your knees acquainted with the cold and rocky ground; talk it over with Jesus. He will make it right. Tell him all of your troubles, day or night, so he knelt upon the stony creek side, and prayed for guidance to lead him through the evening, that thy will be done.'"

Clayton hurried home and saw Elam's were there already. He pulled his buggy in the driveway and hitched up Clint and tied him, then went in the house to prepare himself to go to the supper place.

He arrived just in time to join the second setting at the table, where the boys outnumbered the girls by quite a few and hearty conversation was taking place while they ate. Across the table, Elmer was talking about his trip to Canada, from where he had returned only last week. Eli Jonas was asking him if Eli Gingerich had been there; then they discussed his shop and some of the equipment. " . . . some Burkhart, you know where that bridge is right at the end of the lane with those pillars? It was there when William Weber . . ." It was all a strange bunch of names to Clayton. He had never been to Canada and doubted he would ever get there.

Finished with his first course, Clayton leaned back in his chair and found himself looking almost right at the bulletin board where a white paper, with easy-to-read block letters, was tacked. It read, "Breaking Point—Even a perfect egg must break for a new life to be born." Clayton thought of the ducks sitting on eggs, how after some weeks the ducklings inside start pecking and eventually the egg breaks and a new life is born. The egg must be broken before new life comes.

Clayton thought of the many sermons on new life he had heard in the past month and of different ways it was described. Then he thought of his baptism three weeks away, where a seal on the new life would be made. When he read the note again, he thought of Jesus, that He was perfect, without sin, and still needed to give His life so new lives could be born. He didn't have to; He was willing. Jesus could have sent twelve legions of angels to lift Him from the cross. But Jesus was willing. Even a perfect egg must break for a new life to be born.

Next to the bulletin board a pale simple motto hung; no decorations, only a chain around the glass frame. The words read, "Life is fragile, handle with prayer." On the other side of the bulletin board was a bigger wooden motto with scalloped edges. The words, hammered in old-fashioned script, read, "Nature forms us, Sin deforms us, School informs us, But only Christ Transforms us." As he started to memorize it, the boy beside him poked him, as he was trying to hand him the dessert bowl.

Clayton took a helping of the dessert. As he looked up to pass the dish on, he saw Lydia Ann at the far end of the table looking his way. Apparently she had watched the incident since she had an amused smile on her face, which disappeared the moment their eyes met, leaving her blue eyes with a look of wondering concern. Clayton had felt his cheeks grow warm and dropped his glance. The next dessert dish was passed to him. He passed it on and reached for his glass. But when he tipped it, there was no water there. Barbara Ellen was at the other end of the table setting down a dish of dessert and noticed he had picked up the empty glass. She gave him a knowing smile and turned around, heading for the serving cart where the water pitcher stood. Her white apron with the pink-lace edging at the pockets blended well with her pink-and-white-flowered dress. Clayton noticed that she was helping to serve the tables. But he had not noticed that Lydia Ann was at the far end of the table. He was careful not to look in that direction, after the water incident. He had heard some soft chuckles which had drawn Barbara Ellen's attention.

After supper Clayton followed the boys down to the orchard. There he took part in pitching quoits. By the time they had the game started, a row of girls were sitting on the bank, watching them and rejoicing at both their hits and misses. Lydia Ann wasn't along, and Barbara Ellen was busy in the house with the table and dishes. So Clayton gave himself wholeheartedly to the game.

Chapter Nine

This is strange country, Clayton mused, watching from the rear van window as the van traveled on, covering many miles of Pennsylvania. Since it was daylight, it was interesting to watch the scenery. The Pennsylvania hills were flattening out. There were nice large fields with big farming operations. Clayton could see that a lot of farms had added more silos in the past years. But then there were also lowlands where it was too flat and with swamps to be farmed around, but no forests seemed to be near.

The van contained Eli Jonas and his friend Amanda, Clayton, Israel and his younger brothers, Enos and Noah David. Uncle Eli, Cousin Eldon, Aunt Magdelina, and her husband and their two daughters and son Bennie, were also along. They had started off a little before midnight, heading to near the Ohio line, to the Mose Reiff residence where Alpheus's friend, Ella Mae, had once lived. She had been working at her Uncle Ammon's the past year since Ammon's wife was sickly. In the beginning of November Ammon's wife had died and Ella Mae continued to keep house for Ammon. A month later she pulled stakes and Ammon moved to his son's home when Alpheus and Ella Mae got published.

Mom and Dad had left yesterday morning with Alpheus and Ammon. Dad had been undecided if he would take this trip since he had had another spell of flu in the beginning of November. It had left him so weak that his heart acted up again. The doctors had stepped up his medication but informed him that he was just wearing out and surgery was of no help.

Two weeks ago everyone had thought David Wenger would miss his son Alpheus's wedding, but he was doing better again. Doctors counseled him to go ahead with the trip. So the Wengers

55

went the day before so he could rest before going to the wedding. They had gone to one of Mom's relatives for the night.

Within five miles from the wedding, the van stopped at a restaurant for the weary travelers to get breakfast and tidy up for the wedding. When the van pulled in at Mose Reiff's, it didn't seem like strange country anymore. There were a lot of familiar faces. Clayton wasn't even out of the van till he felt a tug on his leg. It was Seranus's three-year-old Anthony informing him of his train ride. Seranus and his family had left yesterday and traveled on the train as far as they could go. Then they had to take a bus and needed to wait a few hours. The connections weren't so great, but they had decided to use this opportunity to take the boys for a train ride.

Next to Seranus stood Ephraim and Naaman, and soon there was a circle of Wenger brothers as Israel joined them. Of course Alpheus wasn't included; he was somewhere upstairs dressed in his bridegroom clothing.

Later when Clayton went upstairs, he almost had to look a second time; he couldn't believe how different Alpheus looked in his plain suit.

During the forenoon sermon, the minister admonished the young couple that was about to step into marriage and start a new home on the importance of a Christian foundation. Clayton pictured the new house back home; the foundation of the house had been in quite a while. The minister spoke about the foundation of the home. In November, Clayton had quit at Elam's since most of the fall work was done. He had come home to help with work on the house that Israel was building. Israel had been busy in the shop. Eli Jonas and Israel were in the shop regularly. Alpheus was helping Clayton and Enos on the house. Now it was nearly finished, except for the rooms that Israel had added later. Although Alpheus was doing the farming, it was decided the newly married couple would move into the new house for the time being. But there would be some moving around yet come spring.

It would seem strange to have a new member, Ella Mae, living on the farm as one of the family, but likely it would be just the beginning of changes in life. Clayton thought of the words, "I'd like to stay here longer than man's allotted days to see the fleeting changes of life's uncertain ways." But Clayton wasn't really fond of that song. There were changes, but he'd sooner cling to how it is, or was, instead of wishing to live longer.

Amanda was sitting next to Alpheus with Eli Jonas as witness, and Clayton knew she was almost a part of the family already. Clayton glanced at Dad, who looked weaker and more aged. Something tugged at his heart. One generation passes; another generation comes. Clayton refused to think about Dad wearing out and giving others his place.

During the service, Alpheus promised that because God had led them together, he would love Ella Mae and patiently stand by her in all sickness, taking on him the heaviest part. He claimed he was free of all other women concerning marriage. Ella Mae made her promises, and they became husband and wife.

Clayton wondered what Israel was waiting on. He had come to the wedding without a friend, but then a year and a half ago Alpheus hadn't had a friend either. Things had happened fast when Ella Mae came to work for Ammons. But there were always travelers coming and going so that Israel had met other girls. (Like when he and Warren had stayed in Ohio longer and went there again. By now Warren was no longer a bachelor.) Israel had been to Ohio, Missouri, Kentucky, etc., and was still single.

Clayton glanced at Dad again. He always felt that Israel would take care of Dad if it came to that. The wedding sermon was over and people were filing upstairs. The aroma of food floating through the rooms made Clayton's mouth water. He was hungry after his long trip and a restaurant breakfast.

After dinner, as Clayton was heading outside, he met Naomi and her husband John Irvin on the porch. Naomi handed baby Emory to Clayton.

"You mean your baby has grown this much?" Clayton exclaimed.

Naomi smiled. "He's growing, but not so fast. It's just that you haven't come for so long."

"Oh, do you mean you miss me? I thought you wouldn't know which of us visited and which did not."

Naomi smiled and said, "I have a lot of brothers, but I know them all apart. But I had to look a few times at Alpheus this morning."

Clayton nodded knowingly, "The new suit does change his looks somewhat. I think he combed himself a little different, too." He returned baby Emory to Naomi and John Irvin looked at Clayton, his eyes sparkling with mischief. "Naomi said the girls here must be interesting since you can't come up our way one weekend."

Clayton didn't deny it; maybe that **was** the reason he didn't want to miss a weekend.

"Well, you're seventeen now; does that help?" Naomi asked.

"No," Clayton said, brushing his hand through his disheveled hair. "If I listen on Dad, I have to wait another good half year."

Naomi then started asking about Dad, and Clayton said, "Well, he was lower because he still hadn't come back to where he was before his first bout of the flu when we were all sick. I could feel this trip was a strain on Mom, as Dad really wasn't in shape to come. But he wasn't going to miss it."

"Is Israel still going with the young folks?" Naomi asked.

"Yes, rather regularly. Sometimes he misses a singing, but he goes regular to dinner and supper places."

"I talked a little with Mom, and I understand that Alpheus and Ella Mae are moving into the new house down by the shop. I thought Eli Jonas is the one helping in the shop," Naomi said.

Clayton chuckled and questioned, "You say you did talk with Mom?"

"Just a little bit, but then we had to sit down and eat."

"Well," Clayton began, "for now he'll move into the new house; Israel's rooms aren't done yet. I guess we wouldn't all fit in the new house until those rooms are finished. So Alpheus will go there, but not until after Christmas. They will do some visiting here before they come. It is a good time because we only have to do the chores for Alpheus, not the farming."

"But did Mom tell you about the letters we had from Kentucky?" Clayton asked, lowering his voice as people were passing by.

"I didn't get to ask her about that yet. She wrote me a letter last week and wrote something about it. It seemed she thought I knew it already. We couldn't quite figure it out." Naomi looked at her husband, who was looking at Clayton, urging him to explain.

"It's Ephraim," Clayton said. "Since the land he was renting and farming is now sold, he hardly has enough acres. He had hoped to get first chance to buy it. Now there is a place for sale just across the dirt lane which goes in along Ephraim's farm. The buildings are almost to the road next to Ephraim's. They can see to the house. There aren't many buildings, and there is not much of a barn. There is no silo and a few sizes of sheds, and Ephraim says the house is in good shape and just perfect for a retirement house. He thinks Mom and Dad should get the house; he wants the land. It runs all along Ephraim's farmland and two fields go further back yet. He says it's his turn to have Mom and Dad near. Ephraim's children hardly get to see them, and," Clayton chuckled, "he even says that Dad seems to be growing older by watching his sons carrying on so with the growing business in their shop. He says in Kentucky people live more relaxed."

"You mean they think Dad would move to Kentucky in his older years?" Naomi asked.

"Ephraim seems to think so."

"What does Mom say?"

"Well, she says it would be all right if all the children would go, because it's not nice that two live so far away. They don't get to see them; as you know, Dad is no traveler."

Naomi seemed to be thinking. "Oh, do you mean Alpheus would move in the farmhouse, and Eli Jonas would get the new house (Israel would have his rooms), and Dad's go to Kentucky?"

"I keep hearing snatches. I think that's what it amounts to."

Naomi asked, "Well, what would you do?"

"Us?" Clayton asked astonished. "Do you mean Enos and Noah David? I would never move to Kentucky now!"

John Irvin laughed at Clayton's outburst and thought, *He must know something.*

"Well, Noah David would go along but says he would come back in a year or so when he is old enough to join the young folks.

Come spring he'll be sixteen. Enos doesn't say much, only that he'd go get them settled and catch the first bus coming back and work at Seranus's. I plan to go back to Elam's in March or so. I would have stayed there and got some part-time jobs there, but we had to get the house built since Eli Jonas and Israel were so busy in the shop."

"Oh!" Naomi exclaimed. "Wouldn't any of my many brothers come to my house to live? We have plenty of room."

"And plenty of work," her husband reminded her.

"Well, I don't know what I would do if Elam's wouldn't need me anymore."

"Oh, this is where you are," Mom said, opening the porch door. "I was looking all over for you."

The people were being seated to sing in the afternoon, a part of the wedding Clayton always enjoyed. Clayton saw that Mom and Naomi went to the next room to visit. He was sure they had a lot of catching up to do since Mom didn't often meet her only daughter after Naomi married. But would Mom want to move further away yet? To Kentucky?

Chapter Ten

January was cold. December had been mild except for the last week.

Clayton went up to his room and lit the lamp. The room felt chilly compared to the cozy kitchen. He sat on his bed and reached over to the drawer in the nightstand and pulled out the green glittering diary. He'd always think of Elam's when seeing it.

Elam had invited him to come for Christmas dinner, and he enjoyed spending time with Elam's again. When he was about ready to leave, Ralph handed him a gift, saying, "It's for you!" Ralph's eyes had sparkled, and the girls stood around him sharing the pleasure of giving him something.

Clayton exclaimed, "A gift? It's quite a few years since I received a Christmas gift." First there had been a box of the delicious oatmeal cookies he liked so much that Elva baked, and then there was a songbook; it was just like the one he had often borrowed from Elam. Clayton had been surprised, but there still was a small package left.

"Open it," Ralph had chimed, hardly able to hide his excitement.

Clayton had been speechless as he pulled a diary from the paper. He thought maybe it was a joke and looked up to see Elam watching him. Elam had inquired about his sudden change of actions. When Clayton admitted he thought only flirting girls and grandmas kept diaries, Elam almost choked on a laugh and told him he kept a diary all the time. He wrote when he was with the young folks and the first year he was married, but then later he only wrote when he planted corn, or when it snowed first, etc., or if the children were sick, or if he started plowing. . . . Then he gradually quit, and

Elva started journaling. Elam had told him that this year would probably be an interesting year for him and later he would enjoy reading about it.

Clayton opened the diary he had written in almost every day for the past two weeks. Some days there was nothing to write, just a repeat of the day before. He stared at the page as his thoughts ran on. Alpheus and Ella Mae had moved into the house over two weeks ago. Mom had truly gained a daughter. Ella Mae at times came with a pie, saying she baked too much for the two of them, as it took so little with only two at the table.

Once she came up to see if Mother had mending to do, and tonight she had come with one of Alpheus's shirts. She was going to iron it, but felt it wasn't worthwhile to set up for a few pieces, so she came to see if Mom had ironing to do. So she ironed a pile of shirts and handkerchiefs. Then Alpheus had come in after he was done in the barn, so the visiting was on, as Eli Jonas and Israel had also come in from the shop. When Dad and all the boys were there, Clayton thought he should feel shy for Ella Mae, as she probably did feel out of place with Dad, but she had calmly ironed on. She helped with the visiting and when she was done ironing, she sat down next to Alpheus and made herself one of the family. Seranus had come down to use the telephone and then dropped in and the Kentucky subject was brought up, and tossed to and fro. Seranus didn't like to see them making the move. He said they could build a house on his farm if Eli Jonas needed the house. But Ephraim had sent another letter. Dad had said, "I'll see my doctor next week and ask him what he thinks."

Clayton stared at the empty page as the scenes of the evening came to his mind. While visiting, Alpheus had looked fondly at Ella Mae as they exchanged smiles. Ella Mae had spoken to him quietly as she looked up in his eyes and Alpheus's eyes spoke volumes— a perfect understanding look.

Clayton thought of Lydia Ann, but he felt a little disturbed. On Sunday evening after supper he had looked up to see the most charming smile he had ever seen on Lydia Ann's face. But it had quickly faded when their eyes met. He had guessed it was not meant for him, but who then? He had looked around but had seen no one looking her way.

Clayton slowly wrote: "Alpheus's were up this evening and Seranus was down. So I had an enjoyable family evening. As I ponder, hopes grow fonder; I believe, but Lord, help my unbelief."

Chapter Eleven

Most of the men had gathered in the backyard to visit with each other, resting their aching muscles before they would leave. Then Alpheus came out the door with a grin on his face, asking, "Does anyone know where the blanket chest is? The one with the drawers that belongs to us? Ella Mae can't locate it."

The men looked at one another around the circle. Seranus said, "Seems to me, I saw a lot of blanket chests today, coming and going. Let's look here on the truck." He led them toward the truck loaded with his parents' furniture.

Minutes later Israel came running up from the house saying, "The chest stands down in the basement kitchen entrance at my house. Remember that was a piece we weren't sure where to take." So the men backed the spring wagon down to load up the chest. With one pulling and one pushing, they soon had the chest at the door and moved upstairs. Ella Mae was calling after them to put it in the green room.

"This room looks pretty green," Israel said. "Guess it's safe to put it in here."

Some of the rooms had changed color in the last few weeks, so it was hard to remember which room they were talking about. Coming downstairs, Clayton saw Ella Mae hurrying around, tidying up the disarranged kitchen. She picked up a silverware chest and carried it to the wall closet in the living room. As she opened the door, she chuckled. "Well, this isn't even mine; I put mine away already. I didn't even notice that it wasn't mine. Maybe it's Mom's." Enos didn't think it was Mom's. Besides, it was empty.

Then Seranus remembered, "Oh, now I remember. Mom said we could have it. She had an extra one, and she knew Marriel didn't have any."

Clayton walked through the kitchen and headed upstairs. When they moved the chest up, he had seen that his room needed to be straightened up.

"Supper should be ready in a half hour," Ella Mae called after him. It sounded good to hear that because his dinner had been digested long ago, and the drink and cookies they had had at 2:30 were worked off by now. Clayton looked around the room, wondering where to start. At least the bed was in order. The fluffed up pillows had smooth, white, clean-smelling coverings slipped over them. A green and white and pink quilt with paths and blocks was spread over the bed with its borders almost reaching the floor. A rug lay on a heap near the bed, likely kicked aside during furniture moving. The dresser stood there with all the drawers out. The bureau didn't have its mirror on yet, and heaps of Clayton's belongings were piled nearby. Some had been taken out of another dresser that had been moved elsewhere. His Sunday clothes on hangers had been thrown over the chest. He decided he may as well hang these in the closet now since he knew this was his room when he is here.

While he was hanging up the shirts, jackets, and dress pants on the rod in the closet, Clayton thought he heard a team and voices. He looked out the window and gasped, "Not more furniture!" He saw a team of horses hitched to a wagon which was loaded with a sofa and recliner and sewing machine. He saw Eli Jonas run down to the wagon in the lower lane, at the shop and new house. The wagon was fixed with lights on, which they would need when going home. For a moment Clayton was stunned. Then he recognized the driver as Amanda's brother. Guess Earl's need to make room for the wedding.

After supper Clayton lit the lamp in his room and continued putting his belongings in the bureau and dresser. It seemed that he had just figured out where to start when the call had come for supper. Now, he had to figure out again what he was doing. Closing the top drawer and looking around to see what else was to be put away, he surveyed the room and mused, *This always was Naomi's room. Then when she married, it was the room to "store" things in.* At that time it had been some sort of faded lavender, yellowing with the years. Now it was a light blue, with a navy blue design of feathers rolled on. It looked like wallpaper, but it wasn't. A lot of painting had been done lately.

As Clayton folded his summer clothing and put them in the next drawer, he thought he would soon need to exchange them for his winter clothing. *This really isn't home; it's a place to store my things. And a place where I am welcome to stay to repack them and sleep a few nights when coming and going.*

An hour later Clayton sat at the south window in his room looking out in darkness. He had lost some time when he was looking at his old school things before putting them in the drawer. The moon, only half in size, was shining and the sky was dotted with stars. He looked down toward the new house, but the pine trees and the shop hid it from view. The glow against the pine trees revealed that Israel had lit his lantern. Clayton wondered if they were each alone in their part of the house, but then he remembered that Eli Jonas's part wasn't fully furnished yet, only the bedroom. Mom and Dad had furnished one room for each of their boys, so likely he will sleep in his part. Amanda hadn't moved her things over yet, only those few pieces to make room for the wedding. Likely Alpheus and Eli Jonas were batching together for this week.

Now Alpheus and Ella Mae lived in this house where his parents had always lived. Noah David was in Kentucky helping the brothers prepare the house for Mom and Dad and then help when the furniture arrived. The truck was to start off the next day. Enos was at Seranus's.

Dad had been at Seranus's the whole week already, and Mom had been here during the day packing the household things. Today she was here helping to manage the moving. Naomi had been here today till after dinner. Then Mom and Dad went home with Naomi and her husband and would be staying there till the wedding in another week. And Noah David would come up with the brothers from Kentucky for the wedding. Then Mom and Dad, Enos, and Noah David would go home to Kentucky with Ephraim's and Naaman's after Naomi had the reception for both Alpheus and Eli Jonas on the Sunday following the wedding. The Kentucky house was supposed to be all set up for housekeeping just as if they lived there and had gone on a trip and were returning again.

At first, the doctor hadn't been too thrilled about the Kentucky plans, but he had consented. If they could get Dad away from the confusion of tearing up and moving and could go from Pennsylvania to Kentucky as though he was going on a trip, then the doctor would let them go ahead. Enos was going along to help get settled, but would return for the summer and live at Seranus's.

After his possessions were all arranged in the closet and drawers, Clayton prepared himself for bed. As he lay across the bed relaxing before blowing out the light, he surveyed the room again. It seemed like home, a place he could enjoy, but then he pictured the little room eight miles across the countryside at Elam's. The room papered with little violets with tiny green stems and leaves and a deep lavender border around the wall. The bed with the brown log cabin quilt on, the night stand, and the bureau and closet where his clothing for this season were.

He had moved back to Elam's in the beginning of March but had come home to help with the moving and would stay till the wedding was over. Clayton was thinking of the upcoming wedding and meeting the brothers and their families from Kentucky. *Naaman's boy, let's see, that made four boys and one girl, if I remember right. It made an even dozen grandchildren, Dad said. With only one being a girl. Dad said it looks as if there would be one girl to each dozen grandsons, so three weeks ago when Ephraim's sent word that they had a little girl after four boys, Dad had said, that's right, the second dozen is starting. So it's a girl.* But the first dozen hadn't started with a girl. Ephraim and Naaman each had four boys and one girl, but not in the same order. Seranus had two boys and there was also Naomi's little Emory.

Chapter Twelve

Clayton nibbled at his toothpick, spitting bits of it out as he sat with a group of boys on the hill of the root cellar in the backyard. The side door opened from the house and a group of boys spilled out, some still chewing on their toothpicks, one running his comb through his hair. A little while ago the girls had called from the door, "Last call for supper," and some boys headed for the house. Now they had returned again, their stomachs filled.

A few boys were setting up the croquet game in the flat part of the spacious yard out toward the shop. A group of girls came walking along the hedge fence. The boys said they needed some volunteers for the game and in a short time the croquet mallets were all taken and the game was on. Clayton thought he might help in the next game. Croquet was a game they often played at home as a family with Dad usually being the loser.

The trees everywhere were pushing their leaves. The grass was nice and green and every plant and tree was showing signs of spring. Clayton lifted his eyes and looked across the countryside, seeing different shades of green in trees and bushes. Fields with newly turned furrows appeared like a rich brown carpet. Down through the orchard lane a group of girls were taking a stroll breathing in spring. Another few girls were walking up the road, while shouts of excitement came from the barnyard. Clayton looked back and saw that they had stretched the volleyball net from a buggy to the barn. The boys were playing, and the girls on the stone wall along the front yard were cheering.

Martin Sensenig's had opened their home and had welcomed all the young folks from Stony Creek and Cottage Hill. That always was a treat.

As Clayton watched the croquet game, one after another was being made out. He was getting enthused in the game and looked forward to helping in the next one. Mary Emma was still trying to hit the post to become free; Ralph and Eldon were cornering her up from each side. Mary Emma was pleading with them to go and try to get Susan until she is free. Ralph had a grin on his face and was anxiously and impatiently waiting until Ellen finished her turn.

Clayton cringed and said, "Ouch." He felt pain in his foot and looked up to see Marcus and the gang with their songbooks. One of them had purposely stepped on his toes to get his attention. Clayton looked at them silently. Marcus looked at his songbook and nodded his head, looking toward the barn saying, "We're going to the silo." Eugene was behind him and nodding, urging him to come.

Clayton got up slowly, but suddenly turned around as shrieks of delight came from the yard. Ralph was moaning, "Ou-u-u!" Mary Emma, still rejoicing, hit her croquet ball way beyond the middle arch. Marcus's group walked on, not interested in the croquet game. Clayton walked toward his buggy to get his songbooks.

Somehow he didn't feel very eager to sing this evening, and for sure not to be penned up in the silo. But the boys were expecting him to come. Clayton got his songbooks from the buggy box and laid them on the buggy seat as he smoothed out the buggy robe.

He had spent a few hours this week thinking about maybe tonight would be the night. He had it all planned: who he would talk to, etc., so he could take Lydia Ann home. Now that he was here, he didn't know if he would have the courage. he hadn't seen much of Lydia Ann tonight. Earlier he had seen her drive in with her brother, Paul Wayne. When Clayton had gone for supper, he had seen her with the girls on the side porch where they passed through, but she had not given any special recognition as he walked past.

Clayton picked up his books and headed toward the silo. The boys were singing already. Clayton's heart stirred as he heard the volume echo in the silo. He could hear there were a few more voices than usual. Elmer Reiff from Cottage Hill was a gifted singer and had a rich, deep voice. The words rang, "Some day these conflicts will be over, and sin and sense molest no more. And you shall pass

from earth below, to where the tree of life doth grow." After each
song another song was soon selected. They also tried some songs
that no one was very familiar with and at times switched to other
books.

Clayton put his heart into singing and enjoyed it to the fullest. Sometime later, the words echoed in the silo in sweet accord of

> *Sometime, when misgivin's have darkened the day,*
> *And faith light I cannot see,*
> *I ask the Dear Lord to brighten the way.*
> *He whispers sweet peace to me,*
> *Yes, he whispers sweet peace to me . . . .*

While the young people continued singing the chorus, Clayton
started reading the second verse to himself. The first verse had roused
his struggles again. The song went on to say,

> *I could not go on without him,*
> *I know the world would o'erwhelm my soul*
> *For I could not see the right way to go*
> *When temptations o'er me roll.*

He continued reading the third verse,

> *I trust him thru faith, by faith hold his hand,*
> *And sometimes when my faith is weak,*
> *And then when I ask him to take command,*
> *Seems that I hear him speak,*
> *Yes, he whispers sweet peace to me.*
> *He speaks in a still small voice we are told,*
> *A voice that dispels all fear,*
> *And when I'm in doubt or troubled in soul,*
> *That still small voice I can hear.*

Clayton stepped quietly out of the silo. He met Martin
Sensenig's sitting outside the silo listening, and a group of boys stood

close by. Clayton took his books back to the buggy. Some of the words were going through his mind, "I could not go on without Him, I know the world would o'erwhelm my soul—for I could not see the right way to go . . ." and something about "and when I'm in doubt or troubled in soul, that still small voice I can hear . . . sometimes my faith is weak."

A buggy was turning around and pulled up to the walk. It was Jonas, and Lavina came out the walk and stepped on. Last year when Clayton was living at Elam's he often took Lavina along. She had acted as if she didn't know someone was interested in her, but at any rate, she and Jonas became a couple soon after that.

Another buggy came around the shop. That was Paul picking up Dorcas. Clayton started going toward the house and met a few boys who stood by the hedge watching the buggies leave. Abe, one of Enos's buddies, started talking with him, asking when Enos is coming back. "I haven't heard from him for a while."

Clayton shrugged his shoulders saying, "That's what I told Elam the other day, that the buses must be on strike, because he had said he would catch the first bus back after our parents are settled."

"Does he ever write?" Abe asked.

"Yes," Clayton tried to remember, "he did write with Mom's letter. He wrote about a Mark and a Kenneth that he went along with on a long hike exploring the Kentucky wild forests. They had stayed overnight and camped out and he talked about another area they wanted to explore."

The other boys started cheering; one gave a loud, long whistle and the others laughed. When Clayton looked up from the boys who were standing in front of him, he saw Landis Newswanger urging his horse past the cheers. The horse hesitated and stepped high and guided to one side. When Landis reached down to get hold to pull up the robe, Clayton saw it was none other than Lydia Ann who bent forward to smooth her side of the robe!

Clayton's heart stood still. He felt numb, as if the yard had shocked him. He had been on the way to the house to find someone to ask Lydia Ann for his company. He had been eighteen for the last month; he had been trying to build up courage, and was planning to

71

not go home this evening without carrying it out. He had almost written to Lydia Ann this week privately, but then doubted that he should. Maybe she'd rather answer through someone else, and it was this thought that had driven him out of the silo.

Landis Newswanger? Clayton repeated to himself. *I wonder how long this was brewing?* Landis had only come home in January. Clayton tried to think when he had seen Lydia Ann with that priceless smile that had vanished when their eyes met. Had Landis been home then already? It must have been in January, as Clayton had had his diary already. His eyes felt misty. He felt depressed, but not at all angry at Lydia Ann for accepting Landis's company. Deep down he thought Landis needed Lydia Ann.

Clayton thought of Landis. His father had died two years ago when Landis was seventeen years old, and he had worked hard to keep the farm going. The only boy at home with three sisters yet, he had dated Pauline from Wesfall for about a half year, and he just wasn't so well. Doctors said it was stress. Then Landis broke up with Pauline and things went worse. One of his married brothers moved home and took over the farming, and his mother and sisters built a new house and were raising produce.

Landis had left for Indiana and was working for his uncle, but he had come back in January. He was a working hired man and was well-liked, but he wasn't quite the Landis he had been before. He was rather inferior. This was the first time he had asked a girl since his breaking up with Pauline. Clayton understood that Lydia Ann wouldn't have turned Landis down when he asked for her company, but if only Landis had asked Nora, Laura, or Sylvia—there would have been others who would have been a good help for him.

An hour later, as Clayton was going back to Elam's, his mind was churning. He wondered for the fortieth time, *Doesn't Lydia Ann care for me at all?* He reasoned with himself, *She had no way of knowing I was still interested or if I was going to ask, as I was eighteen already and didn't ask.* Then he wondered again, *Had I asked before Landis, would she have turned me down anyway?* It brought some fresh tears. He blew his nose. It felt better to release the tears. It seemed he heard the words:

On Mount Olive's sacred brow Jesus spent the night in prayer. He is the pattern for us all, all alone if we only steal away in some portion of the day—where a heart if broken up with the bitter woeful cup, there's the time to go to Christ all alone. In our blessed Lord Divine there is peace and joy sublime. When we take our sorrows all to him alone.

Clayton was now deaf to all the sounds of the joys of spring that had cheered him that morning. At Elam's place he unhitched Clint, put him in the barn, and walked behind the barn where they had cut down a tree. He knelt by the stump and relieved his tears. He tried to pray; all he could say was, "Lord, not my will but Thine be done." He sat on the stump and looked in the darkness, the stars twinkling high above and the moon shining clear. Across the miles he pictured Lydia Ann's parlor where she was visiting with Landis. He felt glad for Landis. It was the first time he realized one could feel sad and glad at the same time.

Up in his room, Clayton tried to pray, but no words came, only sighs and tears. He thought, *Then we sigh and we cry and ask, "Father, why?"*

After he was in bed, the words of a song they had sung in the silo came to Clayton's mind:

No tears in Heaven, no sorrows given,
All will be gladness when we shall join that happy land,
No tears in Heaven will be known.
Some morning yonder, we'll cease to ponder
O'er things this life has brought to view.
All will be clearer, loved ones be dearer,
In Heaven where all will be made new.

Could we ever cease to ponder on things this life brings to view? But it says, "all will be clearer," maybe some day.

Half an hour later, as he lay staring in the darkness tossing again, Clayton thought of the picture that was often in his mind, especially when he closed his eyes. He pictured a refreshing mountain stream, crystal-blue waters with flowers growing by its side. Now that picture had gone dark. He thought of the words, "A stern and rock bound coast." Where had those words come from? Where had he heard them before? He couldn't remember that it was a song. He tossed and turned again. It must be a poem he had said in school long ago. It sure described his feelings about the refreshing mountain stream; it was suddenly "a stern river." He pictured a boat traveling through stern waters, along the rock bound coast.

Chapter Thirteen

The warm June air breezed through the twilighted country-side. Maynard Weaver's had opened their home to the young folks and had served them supper. They requested they sing awhile, so the youth had sung for over an hour. Now the singing had ceased and people were visiting, some in the house, some on the porch.

The girls had started the vocabulary game in the kitchen. Some people called it Definition. A person said a word or two to describe a word, and others had to guess what word they were referring to. Some of the boys stood at the doorway watching and helping to guess, and soon they were in the game.

Clayton got up and went out on the porch where the summer air breezed through. His mind felt in no mood to concentrate on words or guessing words. The moon shone so clearly as if it was a light brightening up the yard, and the stars far above seemed to be twinkling. They were so clear.

Clayton drew a deep breath as he looked over the universe. He thought of the words of the spring song they had sung in church a few weeks ago.

> *Die sonn vird neu und reine.*
> *Der mond und sternen all*
> *Gar fielmal heller scheinen.*
> *Dasz man sich wundern soll.*

And it did seem true. As if the moon and stars were shining brighter in the mild summer skies. And man has to wonder at the great God.

With the next breeze that floated over the porch there was a smell of flowers that were blooming somewhere. Between the porch

75

and the wash house was a nice-sized flower bed. The sweet smell reminded Clayton of the song in church that they had sung that morning:

> *Die bame steter faller laub,*
> *Das erdrich decket seiner stoub,*
> *Mit einen gruner kleidi.*
> *Narcissen und de tulipian*
> *Die Zieter sich fiel*
> *Schoner en als Solomon's seidi.*

Clayton didn't know much about flowers, if they were tulips or what he smelled, but the latest breeze seemed to carry the perfume of the sweet lilacs. Elam's had a few such bushes, and he liked that smell. It was better than any perfume he had ever smelled—so pure, not artificial.

Clayton stood on the porch and held onto the clothesline that was strung across the edge of the porch, while he viewed the summer sky. He then sat down on the wooden porch, hanging his legs over the edge. Further over on the porch a few boys sat on the glider. Some stood in the yard. Others were going in and out, taking their songbooks back to their buggies. The sounds and smells of summer had cheered Clayton some already; he had felt troubled before coming to the gathering.

The other evening at Elam's when he had come in, the children were talking as usual. A nice family life, and young Ralph had so many stories to tell of his school day. Clayton had pretended to show interest, but he had failed to hear what Ralph was really talking about. He had repeated something a few times, demanding an answer from Clayton who had answered rather unkindly. Only afterward did Clayton think of how it must have sounded. When he looked up, he saw Ralph staring at him with a stricken, hurt look. He saw Elam look at his wife Elva in a way that seemed to say, "See, I told you, he's so—." Clayton didn't know how people classed him. Maybe unfriendly, short tempered, or easily upset. He himself didn't like the way he was. He knew he hadn't talked as much with Elam the last few weeks. Meal time, usually a friendly, interesting time, was rather silent except for the chatter of the children. He often sensed that Elam looked at him expecting an answer, and Clayton hadn't even heard what he had said.

Clayton longed to understand himself. It had taken much concentration to sing tonight. The singing hadn't seemed to go on its own volume or rhythm. Once he had started singing on a wrong page, and sometimes the people had sat expectantly waiting for him to start a song while he was still paging through his book. He hadn't heard that a number had been selected.

It was now more than a month since that Sunday evening when he had seen Landis driving out to the lane with Lydia Ann at his side. He thought he could accept it since it was such a joy to know Landis was being helped. Over the past weeks Landis had shown more interest in people. He visited more, showed interest in life, more than he had for a long time. But Clayton missed Lydia Ann's smiles. He couldn't help it. He felt hurt deep inside, when he saw Lydia Ann and Landis smile at each other. She had smiled a few times when Clayton's eyes happened to meet hers, but it was just an ordinary smile. The special smiles were saved for Landis.

Last evening when he was writing in his diary, he sat on the bed for a long time trying to sort his thoughts. Why couldn't he forget his disappointment and accept things as they were since he felt joy for Landis's sake? Why couldn't he shake it off and go on in life? He tried so hard and prayed to accept it and continue on, one day at a time. Surely he could endure it for this day since we are promised new strength each day.

Then this forenoon in church one of the ministers had said a verse that helped to clear his thoughts. "The spirit is willing, but the flesh is weak." *My spirit is willing to give Lydia Ann to Landis, but my flesh is weak.*

For a fleeting moment he again remembered when he had made a few blunders in singing. He had seen people smile and chuckle; others tried to hide their confused smiles. Some looked embarrassed for him. Once he did look up in time to see Barbara Ellen looking at him in what seemed to be a look of concern. Her smile seemed to be understanding, as if to say, "Keep trying; I

77

understand." The sympathy had instantly pushed tears to the surface. It was the first time in a long while that he had noticed Barbara Ellen.

A few boys came on the porch further down from where Clayton sat, and he could hear them talking in low tones. "What did she say? She can't say she is too young now anymore."

"No," Duane answered. "I asked her if she is interested in keeping company, and when I said that you sent me—she stood quiet for a few moments, and I said, 'Emily, remember it's Junior.'

"She said, 'I'm sorry; I'm not interested at this time.'"

Alvin spoke up on the other side of the door saying, "I wonder why she asks who is asking if she's not interested in **anyone**?"

Alvin said to Nelson, "Didn't she tell you she is too young? Maybe she is waiting on you now."

"I'm afraid not," Nelson said hopelessly. "I asked her since then. I wrote to her privately and she said she does not feel 'it's the Lord's will and I pray you'll understand.'"

Leon said, "I do wonder what the matter is with her."

"Did you ask her since she is eighteen?" Junior asked. "You should ask. Don't you remember at Clarence's that evening?"

"Oh, that's right, I almost forgot that."

The boys suddenly seemed aware that someone was nearby and lowered their voices. For a moment Clayton had forgotten his own struggles. He knew without a doubt the boys had been talking about Emily Rissler. Ever since she had joined the young folks, a few boys had their eyes on her and soon asked her. She had said she was too young, and Nelson thought it was only an excuse, so he asked her and got the same answer. From what he heard others saying, Clayton gathered that Junior and Nelson asked Emily again at seventeen, and to the one she said she was too young and to the other one, "Not at this time." Now she was eighteen, apparently, and it seemed about every evening someone asked her for her company. Even boys other than the popular ones had started asking since she had turned those down. Others got hope. Now it sounded like the popular ones were still trying.

Emily was a rather small girl and did not really dress in fashion. She was naturally attractive, without trying, like the Aaron Rissler family as a whole was. Their girls were swept off their feet as soon as they started attending the singings and were allowed to date.

Ida Beth Rissler had only started going with the young folks but was spoken for by Wesley ever since she was barely out of school.

Emily's father had coarse light hair which made one think of baler twine, but it was turning white now instead of gray. Her mother had black hair, and Emily's hair were a beautiful dark red, the color of a delicious cake.

The Rissler girls all had rather long hair which, when they were young had braided and looped them three-quarters of the way up the braid and tied them with a narrow material or string. Most of the sisters were rather dark complected and had small eyes.

The whole Rissler family had an unusual way of saying some of their words. Clayton rather enjoyed hearing them talk. It sounded exciting. They pronounced their A's mostly with an O sound. Some words they added an extra syllable; if a word ended with a long "ee" sound, the would add "a," making another syllable.

With their different accents and noticeable features and dark hair, and with their braids tied up when they were young, this family was what Clayton just naturally pictured when he had read the Laura Ingalls book years ago. It was easy to picture them being out on the prairie and riding in covered wagons—doing daring things.

Clayton had asked his mother long ago why the Risslers had a different way of saying their words. She had informed him that Aaron's great-grandparents had come from a settlement in Mississippi that no longer exists and some of those people had passed their slang and unusual language on to the next generations. Aaron himself never lived in Mississippi, but he still talked like his mother and grandmother. In the "Little House" books, Clayton remembered, the girls had helped their Pa, very much like the Rissler family.

The Risslers lived on the outskirts of town in a house with only a few acres and small buildings. Three houses up the road toward the small town, they owned an older building, a fake-front structure where they operated a bakery. Years ago they had had a big business when all the girls were still at home. They had done whole-sale baking for other people, but now that Magdelena and Judith were married, the Risslers weren't much in wholesale. Emily, Ida Beth, and Matilda still helped. But one thing wasn't like the Ingalls books. The girls had a brother Arthur, who was older than Magdelena, but when he was still at home he had helped the girls in the bakery.

Clayton always sort of pictured Arthur to be Almanzo of the Ingalls books. Leanna was quite a few years older than Arthur, so Clayton didn't remember so much of her being at home. As Clayton was growing up, he knew that there was a bunch of girls who weren't dependent on other people. Judith and Emily loved horses and handled their team like any boy.

Clayton thought of Emily Rissler again. Her sisters had been snatched up before they were old enough. And most of them kept the first one they dated. But Emily wasn't allowing herself to be snatched. Her rich dark hair were maybe not quite as thick as some of her sisters, but looked heavy. It looked as if it was too heavy to be combed back. The one side had like a double wave holding the other hair to come forward. The other side had a bigger wave that out-centered her hairline a little, as if that side started growing a little further out. As the day lengthened, the waves of hair seemed to be pushed from the other hair so that there was no room for more to come forward. There was a cluster of loose ends usually tangled over the uneven waves.

Emily was the smallest of the girls still at home, but not the youngest. Her small, dark eyes seemed to speak of adventures mingled with friendliness. Ida Beth was taller, not quite as dark complected. Her dirty-blonde hair curled all over wherever loose ends were, and she had sky blue eyes like her dad. One looked about as mischievous as the other! Almost all the popular boys tried to get her company and since they weren't accepted, some of the other boys had asked her for dates, too. It seemed that Emily might be the cause of breaking down the popularity of the Rissler family that had grown in the years.

Aaron Rissler's wife had been a Kauffman. Her dad had been raised by a family who had buried all their children as infants. Then they had raised two foster boys and Daniel, Aaron's wife's father, was one of them. He grew up and joined the church and never was adopted, so he kept the Kauffman name. To Clayton it may as well have been Ingalls. Knowing both the Risslers' backgrounds, it helps to understand as to why they differ a little from the majority. They were a "wonder" and their children ranked as "outstanding" among the young folks, yet the children themselves didn't seem to have pride. In fact, it seemed they were at times humbled at the difference. Ida Beth blushed easily, and some of the boys put effort into making it take place. Of course, Wesley wasn't too fond of the other boys giving her attention.

The Rissler family "stood out" more when the girls were still younger; the mother wasn't quite as talented as a lot of people are, and thus she raised them as best she could. Then as the girls grew up, things fell into place and maybe that's what made them popular, because they were raised so humble.

Clayton realized he had spent quite a bit of time thinking about the Risslers as he sat on the porch. Then he remembered Lydia Ann and sighed. It was time to go home.

Chapter Fourteen

Clayton stretched his neck, looking over the seat in front of him. At the same time, the bus driver was looking in his mirror at Clayton and asked, "This road?" Clayton got up and shook his head. He reached up to the rack and got his overnight suitcase and walked forward on the bus, steadying himself by touching the backs of the seats as he walked.

The Greyhound bus slowly moved on. Clayton told the driver, "It's the road just on the other side of the bridge, there by the rows of trees. The bus glided to the edge of the road and came to a halt. The door opened with a swishing sound as he went down the steps.

The driver said, "As eager as you look, I suppose you are welcome somewhere. Now have a good time!"

Clayton nodded and thanked him. How fresh the air smelled when he stepped outside. He briskly started walking down the road, a good two miles it would be. He needed the walk to refresh him from the stuffy bus he had been riding on. He hadn't thought of it while he was on the bus, only when he stepped out in the fresh air.

As Clayton walked down the road and turned left, he had a good look over the countryside. October was almost gone and so were the corn fields. In a few fields he could see farmers husking corn. He thought it must not have rained as much here as it had at Elam's or they wouldn't have been husking corn. Since it had been too wet to go in the fields, he had decided to spend the weekend with his sister Naomi and her family. He had been thinking of writing her but didn't get it done. While at Naomi's home, he could go to an Elm Grove singing if there was one. He hadn't been to Elm Grove gatherings for quite a while.

Going to see Naomi was as near to going home to Mother as he could do. Naomi always seemed glad to see her brothers. She had written to Clayton at times, when they didn't get to see each other for a while. Sometimes she had news from Kentucky; Mom didn't get around to writing often.

Clayton was beginning to get hungry; likely it would be dinner time soon. He took a shortcut through a well-covered hay field and then came up on the top of the next slope. He saw the familiar place—the small barn and the stone house with the shutters and the cluster of enlarged pig barns, the nursery, and the farrowing house. John Irvin had a neat set-up for pigs. The last house was a lot of pens, two rows against each other from smaller, small, medium, to large, etc. When the pigs came to the last pen, they were ready for market. The whole farm was set up for pigs. There was no frustration in sorting or chasing pigs. When the prices were high, John Irvin said they would lay money away for the time the prices are sure to drop, which hog prices are bound to do at times.

As he approached the yard and walked up to the porch, Clayton was so absorbed in his thoughts of what he was going to say to Naomi that he was quite taken aback when they almost bumped into each other at the wash house door, near the kitchen entrance.

He jumped and caught his breath, then he chuckled a little. He expected Naomi would really exclaim when she came to her senses, but she only stared at him. The girl wasn't Naomi! He wished to somehow sink through the floor of the porch, but the girl had long since vanished by the way of the wash house.

Clayton tried to think. Did he go in the wrong farm lane? No, he saw the familiar hedge half-way around the house and the big tree by the gate and the "finishing lot" that was built on the west end of the barn. He had to be at the right place. He took courage and stepped toward the door. After he had thought twice, he realized the girl had been John Irvin's younger sister. She must be here helping Naomi.

As Clayton opened the kitchen door, his mouth almost watered from the smell of browning butter and cooked dried sweet corn and browned gravy. He walked in and saw that some of the table was set. Naomi was sitting at the desk and had a tablet or book in front of her and was writing. Little Emory was sleeping on the sofa next to her.

Without looking up, Naomi said, "If you have time, maybe you could wash the window by the hand wash sink. The other windows don't have to be done this week." Clayton smiled to himself; apparently she thought John Irvin's sister had come back.

Clayton meekly said, "I'm not so good at washing windows."

Before he was half done speaking, Naomi whirled around and her eyes were open wide. Then as she looked at him, her mouth fell open in disbelief. She smiled and said, "No, you don't have to wash the window, but do take off your wraps and find a seat. Tell me where you came from and do you have more people along?" By that time the sister had come back in the kitchen.

Clayton asked Naomi, "Were you asking John Irvin to wash the window or weren't you expecting him to come in for dinner soon?"

As he took a seat on the rocking chair between the desk and the blackboard, Naomi, no longer interested in her writing, closed up the desk and wheeled the desk chair around. "Yes, we are waiting on John Irvin for dinner, but I didn't hear a truck driving in. He hired a neighbor to take some piggies up to his uncle on the other side of the mountain. But I didn't hear a team or anything either," she said looking out the window and back at him. "Where did you come from?"

"I came on the bus. I walked up from the Creek Road."

"Did you come from Elam's?"

"Yes, since it had rained so much, we couldn't husk corn and I decided to come up here and visit you. Maybe I'll attend a singing if there is one in this district."

Naomi turned to her sister-in-law, "Julianne, is there a singing?"

She shrugged her shoulders saying, "I didn't ask Samuel."

Naomi explained, "Julianne isn't with the young folks anymore. They married but aren't moved yet. I expected you to show up

84

sometime, but I just wasn't looking for you right now." Then she asked, "Have you been to see Alpheus since he is a daddy?"

"Yes, I was there the other week when I had gone to fetch some mail that Alpheus said was there for me. Alpheus was quite proud to show me the baby which broke Dad's predictions."

Naomi chuckled, "You mean that there was a girl?"

"Yes," Clayton said as he leaned back on his rocker. "When Ephraim's Etta was born, Dad said, that's right, it took another girl because the second dozen was starting. It goes one girl to each dozen of boys in this family."

A pick-up was coming up the road and a few minutes later John Irvin walked across the yard. Julianne busied herself getting the rest of the dinner on the table.

John Irvin, coming in the door, noticed Clayton right away and gave him a hearty handshake. Then he mentioned something about Clayton coming in to see his little nephew. Clayton glanced at Emory sleeping on the sofa and said, "But he just sleeps on me."

"Guess he is having night now. Last night he thought it was day."

They had started eating when Emory whimpered and sat up on the sofa. Naomi looked at her husband and he got up and brought Emory to the table. He held him on his lap and continued eating. Emory's brown eyes opened big and round as he stared at Clayton, but then soon he offered a few words in his baby language.

John Irvin asked, "I guess Enos isn't talking about coming back to Pennsylvania?"

Clayton shook his head, "Must be the buses all stopped running to Kentucky, that he isn't here yet." Then he added, "Whenever Mother writes, which isn't very often, Enos adds a few paragraphs and his name is usually connected with a Mark Shirk and a Kenneth. Sounds as if they get along pretty good. Guess they explored about every ridge and wood lot in Kentucky by now."

Naomi added, "And it sounds like he really enjoys his work at that horse farm. He repairs fences, paints, cleans out the barn, and exercises horses."

John Irvin cleared his throat, "The way Dad wrote in his last letter, it sounds as if Mark and Kenneth and horses might not be all that interests him in Kentucky."

Naomi, seeing Clayton's blank face, explained, "Enos at times complained about the girls that ask for transportation and ask to be taken here and go there. But Dad wrote that lately he has been very considerate, since, oh let me se, I think he said since Marvin Eberly's son married. He's the one who used to take Devon Weaver's girls along. Now they need a way to go and Enos seems quite willing to do so."

"Oh yeah?" Clayton said, raising his eyebrows.

John Irvin suddenly got up and headed for the bedroom. Naomi began talking about Noah David. "It doesn't sound like he is thinking of coming back from Kentucky either." Clayton looked at her to go on. Naomi said, "Mom just can hardly see it that her youngest son is interested in girls already. I suppose when Ephraim was sixteen she thought he was about grown."

"Noah David's interested in girls?" Clayton questioned.

John Irvin came back to the table and handed a bundle to Naomi. Emory joyfully exclaimed, "Baby, baby!!" Clayton stared from John Irvin to Naomi to Emory and back to Naomi, astonished and puzzled. Naomi was smoothing out the folds and rewrapped the blanket and was saying, "You know, he was working for—." Clayton forgot to concentrate on what she was saying. Naomi looked at her husband and stopped talking, wondering why he had such a different expression on his face as he watched Clayton. She looked at Clayton and hesitated. Something was wrong. She left her sentence unfinished.

Clayton, feeling that he was being stared at, aroused from his confusion and asked, "Is it, is that yours?"

John Irvin was smiling, and Naomi looked more puzzled and asked, "Is what ours?"

Clayton felt himself blush, saying, "I mean the baby."

Naomi gasped, then her face got a crooked smile as she rubbed her hand over the baby's few hairs on its head. "Sure he's ours. Isn't that why you came? To see your little nephew?"

"No, I thought you were talking about Emory when you said

meeting my nephew," he said, looking at John Irvin. "No one told me. I just had an urge to come up this way to visit."

All eyes looked up when a buggy drove by the window. Naomi looked at Julianne who was done eating, saying, "Samuel must be here to fetch you already." She looked at the clock. It wasn't early anymore and she said, "You can just go. Clayton knows how to do dishes." Naomi winked at him, then gave Julianne instructions about coming back to work next week.

Things were starting to make sense. Naomi asked, "If you didn't know that little Joel joined us, why do you think I was sitting around letting Julianne do my work?"

I had been wondering," Clayton admitted. "How old is he?"

"He is nine days old."

"So, it's another grandson for Dad," Clayton thought aloud.

"We were hoping for a boy, since he is only a little over a year younger than Emory," Naomi said. After awhile, she said, "Let's see, what were we talking about?"

Clayton scratched his head. "Oh, you were saying something about Noah David." Clayton still wondered what she was about to say.

"Oh yes, you know he works for William Horning's and a schoolteacher was boarding there. Well, Noah David got to know her, and this year when school started someone was wise enough to voice their concern. William's really weren't aware of it themselves, but anyhow the teacher is boarding elsewhere this year. I can't remember who she is."

Clayton was in deep thought trying to grasp in his mind all he had learned that day. John Irvin teased him, saying, "Maybe you should go to Kentucky, too, eh?"

Naomi laughed and said, "No, I was going to ask him. Here awhile ago when our parents moved to Kentucky, you told us forcefully that you weren't going to move there with them. I thought I'd hear why not, by now."

Clayton felt himself color, and with eyes cast down on the floor he softly said, "That bud never bloomed." Had he been looking up he would have seen John Irvin and Naomi exchanging a knowing glance.

87

Naomi was stacking the dishes and closing bowl lids, then John Irvin carried the dishes to the sink. Clayton stood and rolled up his sleeves, saying, "I could wash the dishes once again. I haven't done it for quite a while."

The visiting continued and news was exchanged about Dad's health. Mother had written to Clayton that Dad had a cold and it was quite wearing on him. Naomi said that the last letter said he was spending a few days in bed. He just had no strength.

Later, they continued visiting at the living room end of the kitchen. Naomi was catching up with the home area news. "Let's see," she began, "I think I heard that Landis has a girlfriend. Did they say Marcus's sister Lydia Ann?" Clayton nodded.

Naomi asked how Landis was and Clayton was pressing his hands along the back of the chair in front of him, expressing his joy that Landis seemed so good. "He mingles with the rest of us and takes an interest and, well, he is about back to his usual self." Had Clayton been looking up he would have seen John Irvin quickly glance at Naomi with a look of command.

Naomi weighed her words as she slowly said, "A little while ago I heard that Lydia Ann wasn't too sure about . . . about . . . their courting or continuing to see each other. Do you know anything about that?"

Clayton took a deep breath. "Well, I sure hope for Landis's sake she can see her way through." To himself, Clayton thought he'd rather be disappointed, since the shock was over, than to have Landis depressed. He seemed not to notice that Naomi's face was a little flushed and that John Irvin was holding his breath, hoping Naomi would say the right words without raising suspicion. Therefore, he didn't notice their looks of relief after his last comments. He had no way of knowing that Lydia Ann herself had talked to Naomi when she had been burdened under the strain of noticing that since she was dating, Clayton seemed at times preoccupied. "His singing didn't want to go." Lydia Ann hadn't known what to do when Landis asked her, because she had been admiring Clayton. Since Clayton hadn't asked for a date, she thought he had no such intentions.

Once when there was a lull in the conversation, Naomi looked at Clayton and said, "I don't quite trust you. Every so often you fall silent and get such a grin on your face. I have a feeling you have something up your sleeve. I wish you'd get that grin off your face." Clayton thought she must be a lot like Mother; you may as well not try to hide anything from her.

Clayton's grin widened as he pretended to look for something up his shirt sleeve, then he cupped his hands together on the back of his head. John Irvin sat front on his chair, becoming very interested. Naomi looked at him, daring him to go on.

"It was last Sunday evening," Clayton began, still smiling. Then he sobered as he continued. "Most of the young folks were at Nelson Brubaker's for dinner and some older couples. The married couples and a few young folks had left already. Some were staying for supper and some were going to David Kilmer's for supper. The cousins and neighbors and some boys were going home, and others were trying to decide where they could go, including me. But I was about ready to start back to Elam's when some of the singers were begging me to go along to sing for the grandfather at Earl Leinbach's down the road.

"There was pretty much commotion going on outside, people were cheering, or excited, then it had quieted down. Suddenly, people were yelling and whistling! The people on the porch started talking excitedly. They said something about a horse and a buggy. It was hard to understand, as two people were talking.

"Soon the girls in the hallway exploded and all ran out. David and I went out, too. I fully expected to see a buggy going out of control since there were boys running out the lane. There was a buggy almost at the end of the lane, but everything seemed all right. The girls stood in a circle all talking at once. Alvin, Junior, Wayne, and all those that always are in the lead of things just stood perplexed. I thought maybe the buggy going out the lane was driverless, and that the boys were running out to catch up to it. But they didn't try to catch up. They were heading down the corner of the field to get to the road further down, as if waiting on the buggy.

"I thought it looked almost like Israel's team, but I knew his horse wouldn't take off without him. Just then three girls came walking in the yard past us. Cousin Reba was along. I asked her if something happened, and she laughed, 'Yes, haven't you heard? That is Israel and Emily leaving.'

"David exclaimed, 'WHHHAAT?' Then we all had a good laugh."

Naomi's mouth dropped open. "Israel?" she weakly gasped. John Irvin was laughing and got out his handkerchief to wipe his tears. "They didn't have a date did they?" Naomi asked, her voice full of disbelief. "I guess he just took her along somewhere."

"Of course they had a date. Well, quite a few people found their way over to Aaron Rissler's to prove it. No one seems to know where they went for supper. There was quite a group of people at the Rissler farm, to welcome them when they got there. Everyone, of course, knew that Israel wouldn't be just taking her along or something. For one thing, they handle their own team. For another he would have to drive pretty far out of the way to go her way just to take her along home."

Naomi asked, "Well, do you mean Emily has no steady friend yet? All the others did before they were eighteen."

"No, she was being asked as soon as she was a little over seventeen like the others, but she never accepted anyone. First, she'd say she was too young, so people figured that she had a notion to wait until she is eighteen. Then when she turned eighteen, she was asked quite often, about every weekend. I overheard some of the boys talking. They were getting disgusted. After she turned down the popular ones, some others started asking her and it was just coming to the point where I thought she'll soon spoil the popular name of the Rissler family."

"And don't you think she has now?" Naomi asked in all seriousness. Clayton and John Irvin laughed.

"No, you think wrong," Clayton answered. "Israel might make our family popular yet." Naomi rolled her eyes hopelessly.

"But seriously," John Irvin said, "is that why she turned the others down? Was she waiting on Israel?"

"Waiting on Israel," Naomi laughed, "you mean till he gets old enough?" Then they all laughed.

"I mean did Emily know Israel is interested in her?" John Irvin asked.

"I was wondering about that too," Clayton said, "wondering if Israel was waiting, why he didn't ask her sooner if that is why she turned all the others down."

"Unless Israel hadn't noticed before," Naomi put in.

"Well, last evening we had a singing in the area since there were some travelers around that weren't staying for Saturday. Then when I met Israel alone out by my buggy, I asked him if this is what he wanted, why he didn't ask sooner and save the boys' irritation and Emily's predicament or good name? He said he wanted to give Emily and everyone else a fair chance. He added that they also had a date the Sunday before and no one knew it. The young folks had no gathering that Sunday and the Risslers didn't tell anyone. I told him that according to that, my girl is about to turn eleven or so, because he'll soon be twenty-five and Emily just turned eighteen."

Naomi shook her head and John Irvin chuckled. She asked, "And what did he say about that?"

"Oh let me see. He had an answer on top; oh yes, now I remember. He said she might have just turned twenty-five and is wondering where you are."

"Oh, brothers," Naomi groaned.

John Irvin got up and said, "Well, I better go check the one batch of piggies in the nursery. Maybe I have to grind a batch of feed yet. I don't know why you are so surprised. Didn't you know I made your family popular by marrying Naomi?"

"You mean popular by making us a family with all boys?" Clayton asked.

"And that," John Irvin said as he headed for the door.

"Well, I'll go over to Dan's to see if there is a singing any-where tonight." Clayton pulled on his jacket.

Naomi asked, "Do you think the Risslers don't approve, that they kept the secret?"

"No, not at all. I do think that really the Risslers don't count themselves high. It's just that people make them popular. They aren't proud." Clayton put his hat on and went out the door and up the road to neighbor Dan's.

Chapter Fifteen

The December sun shone in the living room window. Clayton could feel its direct rays, even if the weather outside was rather cold. The afternoon sun through the window had a nice warmth.

He had been helping Elam work on a puzzle since he had come home, and Clayton almost got carried away with it. Elva had finished the border and was starting to get the pieces of the barn together; then the fence pieces were attached right to the last barn pieces. And here was the bridge already. Without knowing it, Clayton was softly humming a wordless song as he fitted the pieces together. He hardly noticed that Elam was no longer helping, as Elva was trying to get the dinner dishes away. The little girls weren't getting along with each other, so he had picked up Nancy and tried to get her interested in the toys, but baby Mabel was trying to crawl on his lay and crying, too.

Clayton roused from his puzzle when he heard Elam quite sternly say, "Close the door." Clayton looked up to see Ralph standing on the rug with his boots sprinkled with snow, some dripping off, and his face rosy from the December air.

Ralph was asking, "When are you coming?" A nice cover of snow had fallen the day before and Ralph wished to play in it, but not alone. Clayton leaned back on his chair, seeing the girls each trying to claim their father's lap. He knew Elva wanted to help with the puzzle after the dishes were done, and for a moment Clayton was a little boy again. He remembered the great time he had had at home playing in the snow.

He got up and said to Ralph, "I'll come out and help you play in the snow for a while." Ralph turned to him with a big smile. Katie came running from the other room and picked up her wraps that were on the floor and followed Ralph out the door, pulling on her coat. Clayton almost had to squint; the snow was so bright with the sun shining on it. He tried to make a snowman, but that didn't work too well, so he made a ring tag. Ralph wanted him to draw more things in the snow, so Clayton was making many shapes of things with his feet.

Katie didn't stay long; she was cold. Clayton pulled Ralph along on the sled, but there was hardly enough snow to make a smooth ride. Ralph had gotten a small shovel and was pushing it through the yard and over the lane, and on behind the barn. The dog was running along. Clayton followed them and watched as Ralph took big steps and looked back to see his tracks in the snow. A rabbit quickly darted from under the wood pile and across the open field, leaving its little tracks in the snow. The dog took off, with its nose to the ground, zigzagging after the crooked trail. Ralph stood for a moment very surprised, then started running, too.

Clayton sat on a stump by the wood pile as he watched Ralph climb over the meadow fence. The dog was up ahead at the sinkhole, where they had dumped a lot of stones. Clayton sat for a while on the stump, bathing in the sun. It didn't feel quite as warm as it did when it shone through the glass in the kitchen window.

Ralph continued playing at the stone pile and Clayton waved to him, yelling that he was going back to the house. Ralph waved back and continued playing, so Clayton walked back to the house.

As he came into the kitchen, Clayton noticed the teakettle was singing on the stove while the fire crackled. Mabel and Nancy were sleeping on the sofa, and Elam and Elva were working on the puzzle. Clayton went up to his room, kicked off his shoes, and wrapped himself in a quilt to take a nap. But when he closed his eyes, he saw things that kept him from dozing off.

Shortly after he had arrived at the singing last evening, Cousin Bennie had also arrived and tied his buggy right next to his. They had talked while they waited for their horses to cool off a bit before blanketing them. Bennie stated, "Tonight I'm going to ask a girl for you."

"Oh," Clayton had replied, "who is this?" and Bennie mentioned a few names of girls he himself never considered. Then he added, "Or anyone that you say." Bennie kept urging, but he never mentioned Barbara Ellen's name. Then he had said, "Well, then tell me who I can ask for you."

Clayton had replied, "I didn't say you could ask anyone."

Bennie urged on, "Oh, I know. I'm taking neighbor Verna along home tonight; shall I ask her if she is interested in your company?"

Clayton answered, "Even if she is interested, I'm not."

Bennie kept talking as a buggy pulled up to the walk to let its passenger off. It was Charlie's high-stepping horse. Clayton could see through the shadows as Barbara Ellen stepped nimbly from the buggy and went into the house.

Warm circles moved around Clayton's heart as he remembered when he had stumbled with the singing. Some had chuckled, some had covered a smile, others stared, while Barbara Ellen had looked at him so trusting and affectionately, with no trace of laughter or ridicule.

Clayton hadn't been listening to what Bennie was saying, but more boys were standing around them and had been drawn into the conversation.

The singing went better than it had for some time before, as there were a few boys there from a neighboring district who helped lead songs. Clayton laid aside all his other thoughts while singing. It wasn't until after the singing was over and the refreshments were brought out that Clayton had noticed Barbara Ellen again. In a deep caramel-colored dress, accenting her friendly brown eyes, she, with a few other girls, had been in a deep con-versation on the other side of the kitchen, much too deep in conversation to notice Clayton watching her.

Later, as Clayton came to get his hat, only Charles was in the room. Clayton hadn't remembered where he put his hat and was looking around. Charles was leafing through postcards lying on the sitting room table, looked up and said, "Hello, Clayton. What can I get for you?" Charles was that way, an easy talker and always used the

94

person's own name to welcome a person. Everything combined made Clayton say on the spur of the moment after looking around to see if no one was coming, "You can ask Barbara Ellen if she accepts my company tomorrow evening."

Clayton had to laugh at the look that came on Charles's face. Clayton smiled a little, but felt his face get warm. Charles stood as if frozen; for once he was at a loss for words. Coming out of his stupor he put the postcards back on the table and very politely said, "Sir, I'll do that for you."

Clayton found his hat and made his way to the door and said, "Tell me in church tomorrow."

*   *   *   *

Clayton slept surprisingly well, but awoke a few hours too early, with sleep all gone. He prayed for guidance, "Lord, just as seemeth good to Thee; not my will but Thine be done." Doubts were creeping in. He sort of purposely delayed himself in going to church, as he would rather not talk to Charles until church was over. He thought he already knew the answer.

He caught a glimpse of Barbara Ellen as the girls left after church, and Clayton was almost startled to see the glow of anticipation. She looked the way he was starting to feel, but surely she wouldn't feel so just because of him. Clayton dropped behind while they walked out to their teams after church. Charles was soon by his side, dragging too, to let the group ahead of them gain on them. Charles simply said, "Barbara Ellen is expecting you."

Clayton felt his face blush as he stammered, "Oh, ah, you didn't talk her into it did you?"

"No, no," Charles said. "I just asked her if she'd accept Clayton's company on Sunday evening and she said, 'Did he ask?' I said, 'Yes, he asked me personally,' and she rode home with me—all the way in silence. When we got home, I said, 'Well, Bevy?' She said, 'If you are serious, he is welcome.'" Charles laughed easily.

They were coming up to the buggies and the rest of the boys. Clayton had broken out in a cold sweat. Charles had no idea how much his few words had affected Clayton. Clayton had wanted to get away and think. Maybe he shouldn't have done it. He took a back road and left the horse go where and how he wanted to. They explored roads he hadn't driven on very often.

It was long enough after dinner when Clayton got back to Elam's. Elam did not seem to be aware that Clayton hadn't been somewhere for dinner. They probably thought he had dinner and came right home. Clayton pulled up a chair and helped Elam with the puzzle. It was a good remedy for his wandering thoughts.

*　　*　　*　　*

Now his mind kept seeing Barbara Ellen's home, the little room on the west side of the house. He almost trembled to think of walking across the yard, past the tall trees near the walk where it leads to the double doors. There a small, narrow walk led to the parlor door. Likely the stove had to be fueled this wintry December day. What would he say when he went inside? Would she talk first? Why didn't he ask her some Sunday evening when the young folks were away for supper? That they would arrive at home together? He squirmed. He wanted to think something else, but the moment had come.

He was just ready to press the doorbell when she said his name. He looked around and she was coming on the walk from the barn with her everyday clothes on. He was starting to feel confused. This wasn't the right place! They don't even have a doorbell! A light seemed to be shining down on them, as light as day. He was confused—it was Lydia Ann!

His mind felt so tired. Is that where he had gone? *Oh yes, I guess I did, but how could I? She has Landis.* He wanted to tell her that he had made a mistake, but she smiled kindly and let him in another room. There were more people and they sat at a table. There was a lot of food on the table. No one had plates; they just reached in and spooned out of the bowls.

He didn't remember going away from the table. But now there were rows and rows of chairs; Landis had walked by and started

96

talking with Lydia Ann. But then Clayton couldn't see Landis any-more and Lydia Ann was talking about her dress. She had just made it from some odd material.

Then they went past the chairs into a small room. There were a lot of shelves loaded with food. He was trying to get a cupcake, but he just couldn't pick it up. When he did pick it up, it wasn't a cupcake but a toy instead. He couldn't find the door out of the room anymore. Lydia Ann wasn't around either any-more.

Clayton tried calling, but his voice sounded so strange. He called again. Then he tried to open his eyes. Was he asleep? Did he fall asleep on his first date? He looked around the room. It was about dark. He looked again. This was his room at Elam's!

Clayton looked at the clock, "Five o'clock?" Was it Monday morning? He thought for a while and finally it dawned on him. It was evening and he was about to go see Barbara Ellen! Clayton's heart felt lighter to know it had only been a dream; that's why every-thing was so confusing. He changed his clothes, ran a comb through his hair, and went downstairs. The Newswanger family was just ready to eat supper.

Elam looked at his wife Elva with a grin and then looked at Clayton and said, "I thought you were away somewhere, and Elva thought you were upstairs. I see she was right."

"I didn't know where I was either. I fell asleep and didn't know what day it was or where I was."

Elam took a second look at him and then with a faint twinkle in his observant eyes he said, "Just think of it. It isn't Monday morn-ing."

Elva quickly put another cheese sandwich in the pan on the stove. How delicious the toasted cheese sandwiches, stewed crack-ers, and sliced potatoes tasted. Clayton started to feel a little more like himself once he had something to eat.

He went with Elam to the barn and told him he would feed the horses and take a spin over to Charles's place. While he was feeding the horses in the lower barn, he saw Elva and the children go to the barn to help Elam. Clayton went to the house and changed clothes a little bit more. He went out through the sun porch and wasted no time in getting hitched up and was on his way.

*　　*　　*　　*

The door opened just as Clayton pulled off his overshoes. Barbara Ellen was there, wearing a gold and sand brown checkered dress with fine green leaves in the golden checks. Her smile made Clayton feel welcome. Before he remembered to say anything, she kindly said, "Bring your overshoes along in. There's a rug in the hall for them so they don't get so cold." She held open the door, and Clayton followed her in. She opened the next door and showed him where some more overshoes were on the long rug, lined up against the wall. She hung his wraps on a clothes tree beside the built-in fireplace and asked, "Is it getting colder outside?"

"Yes," Clayton replied, "the temperature has dropped ten degrees in the last two hours and it does feel rather cold or maybe more damp."

Barbara Ellen put a little more draft on the stove and welcomed him to sit on the rocker recliner, and she seated herself on the padded chair. The kerosene light on the stand halfway across the room flickered, its flame dancing up and down. Barbara Ellen got up and gave it a little turn, one way and then the other, and its flame spread even and glowed in silence.

Barbara Ellen asked, "Did you come from Elam's or were you at David's?"

"David's?" Clayton asked.

"Yes, Charles was with Raymond for dinner and said David's had invited just a few of the boys for supper, whoever wanted to come. Charles stopped in on the way home from Raymond's to change horses since his regular horse goes lame at times. So he used Dad's extra one." Then she looked at him and asked, "Say, you aren't driving the same horse either that you used to. Is it maybe an extra?"

"The one I had since I was sixteen was just a small horse, and she really couldn't take the long distance, and some weekends I travel many miles, depending where the singing and supper crowds are. Since I have Huckaberry, I decided I don't need to keep the other one to help out."

"Huckaberry?" Barbara Ellen asked, surprised.

"Yes," Clayton chuckled. "When I went to buy him, the man's name on the mailbox reminded me a bit of the word Huckaberry, so I called him that since the owner seemed not to know what his name was."

"Do you still have the other one?" she asked.

"Yes, I do. Earlier when I was sort of thinking of getting another horse, Noah David thought he would be interested, but—" Clayton left the sentence unfinished.

"Isn't he coming back to Pennsylvania? I thought someone said your brothers are coming back as they get old enough to join the young folks."

"I know, but Enos isn't coming back, and it doesn't sound like Noah David is coming back either by spring."

"Will he be seventeen already by spring?"

"I think so," Clayton replied.

"Are you staying at Elam's for the winter?" Barbara Ellen asked.

"Yes, I think I likely will be staying there over winter as Elam has two buildings to tear down near Greensburg. Israel was counting on me to help in the shop, so I might help him some. I still have some of my belongings at Alpheus's."

"It sounds as if you have a full winter, and talking about Israel, I guess he is still seeing Emily"

"Yes, I'm convinced they will continue, as far fetched as it seemed at first."

"I'm convinced," Barbara Ellen said, "that maybe this was cooking awhile before it came out. I thought they probably could hide it pretty well as no one ever would have thought such a thing."

"I know," Clayton agreed. "We should have known that Emily was up to something when she wouldn't accept any of the boys that asked her. I still wonder when it really took place or when the idea was formed."

The subject then drifted to how Clayton's dad was doing, and Clayton said, "He is still quite weak at times. Earlier he had a cold which wore him down again. I was thinking of going to Kentucky to see the folks sometime, but now until we get the shed and barn torn down, I don't know when it will happen."

Then Clayton asked, "Let's see, did I hear you were helping at Lone Willow School a few days a week?"

"I was when school started," she replied, "but now since they are adjusted, I'm not helping anymore. A couple over on the Road 66, who always get butter and eggs from my parents and took us on some errands at times when it was too far to drive with the team, found out that I have helped with housekeeping at different places. So when her mother who lives with them had a stroke, she asked me to help. I'm there most every day, unless her husband has a day off work.

"That reminds me, I have to ask Anna if she can take my place on Thursday." Barbara Ellen stopped abruptly as if she suddenly remembered something. Clayton looked at her, waiting for her to go on and wondering what she was about to say. Barbara Ellen remained silent, weighing her words.

Clayton looked again and asked, "What were you starting to say?"

Barbara Ellen refolded her hands in her lap and continued looking at the same spot on the floor, saying, "I just remembered I haven't asked Anna for sure if she could take my place on Thursday. I'm invited to my cousin's wedding at Jonas Weaver's, down at the west end of the settlement. And now I was wondering—I guess you are invited, too." She said this without looking up.

Clayton propped his head in his hands with his elbows resting on his knees. He took a quick look at Barbara Ellen and saw the glow on her face deepen. Dropping his eyes, he asked, "Are you to bring a friend?" Clayton looked up to see her nod her head yes.

Clayton drew a deep breath and wiped his hand over the other hand and said, "I guess that's how it is then, unless you would rather go alone?"

They were interrupted by three boys who dropped in to visit them, and Barbara Ellen fetched refreshments to treat everyone. The half hour they were there passed quickly.

When they were alone again, Clayton remarked about the unusual rug on the floor, and Barbara Ellen explained that a friend of her mom had given it years ago. They had lived as neighbors, and now they lived in Holland. Clayton had many questions to ask.

Sometime later he checked his watch and asked, "Are you going to the wedding with your brothers or shall I pick you up—or what?"

Barbara Ellen had to think, "Oh, let me see. It will save you some miles if I go with Charles. I guess coming home is up to you. We can see by Thursday how it suits best."

Every half hour seemed to go faster. And in the next hour Clayton was driving back to Elam's. His heart felt lighter than it had on the way over. He found himself humming a tune. Huckaberry was eager to get home.

Chapter Sixteen

With a creaking, whirling thud, the last piece of metal roofing was pushed over the edge of the old shed. It tumbled down with a stiff shrieking sound and hit the rest of the metal on the ground. Clayton didn't have to look at his watch; he knew it was past dinner time. He had been hungry for a while already, but he was eager to get the last of the tin off before he quit for dinner so it wouldn't be such a dreadful job to start again. The roofing was such a bulky affair that he had skinned his fingers at different spots. Maybe the job wouldn't have been so difficult if two people could do it together, but Elam hadn't been feeling so well yesterday. This morning he was so chilly it seemed as though he had a fever, so he had stayed home to rest. There was some kind of flu going around; Clayton had heard that quite a few people were under the weather last week.

Clayton retrieved his lunch box from his buggy and turned over an old wooden box to sit on to eat lunch. He ate his sandwich and poured his hot soup in a little saucer. The soup smelled so good, but he suddenly realized he wasn't as hungry as he had thought he was. Was he getting the flu? Maybe he had too much stress.

While working alone all morning, a thought had tried to disturb him, and he had tried to ignore it by keeping busy. Now that he had taken a break from working, the thought seemed to be more pressing. In the past week the thought had tried to hinder him at different times and different ways, but he had refused to give it any consideration. Now it seemed to be getting stronger.

Last week he had thought he would talk with Barbara Ellen concerning his doubts about their relationship, but his doubts had vanished while being with her Sunday evening. Now since Sunday evening, the thought came haunting him with more strength.

Clayton found it interesting to visit with Barbara Ellen on Sunday evenings, and they had gone to two weddings during the two and a half months that they were seeing each other. He had gotten to know most of her family, and he did enjoy visiting with her. Some Sundays and even on a Saturday he felt uneasy, wondering what to say when Sunday evening came, but the conversation never lacked. By Tuesday the thought would start bothering him again. For a while he wasn't really able to determine the root of his troubles. It seemed to show up more as time went on.

Last Sunday evening he had been going to discuss it, but he failed to do so. He had hardly even thought of it at the time, but afterward it was bothering him again. He had finally come to the conclusion that he was guilty of not being able to return to Barbara Ellen the true friendship that she had been showing to him.

At first, Clayton had been startled at her keen memory and thought maybe something was wrong with **him**. When they would start visiting on Sunday evening, Barbara Ellen would ask him how his visit was to the dentist on Wednesday, or if Elam's brother from Ohio had their children along. Also, how was his hand that he had pinched between a cow and the barn wall? It seemed she remembered everything they talked about on Sunday evening and would think of him each day and what he was doing which day! He himself didn't remember the things she said were scheduled for her week.

Often Barbara Ellen would say, "Oh, do you remember the lady where I keep house during the day? Their son came from Utah. He was the one I was eager to meet, being, you know, I said—" and it had tuned out to be a half-hour subject! Then back to the dentist subject, saying that was the day it had been so very windy, and it wasn't so nice to be out. Clayton had almost forgotten that he had been at the dentist, and he couldn't recall that it was windy that day. This happened every Sunday evening.

Clayton was coming to the conclusion that if he loved someone, he would want to share everything. *If I loved her, I would just naturally think or remember all and share all. I often feel things are too unimportant to even mention or remember.* He also noticed that Elam related to Elva any little thing that went on outside such as if

103

someone had stopped to talk to them out in the field or whatever. They were little things that Clayton hadn't thought Elva would be interested in knowing.

As the weeks continued, Clayton also sensed that Barbara Ellen's affectionate feelings were getting stronger for him than what he felt for her. Just the way she would look up at him while driving along in the buggy or while visiting Sunday evenings. He was beginning to dread opening the subject to her. He realized he should have done it sooner.

By now he had nibbled on all his lunch he cared for. He leaned back against the wall of the shed and tried to rest before climbing up and ripping off boards. As he leaned back, he thought of Sunday being two days ahead, and he had half promised himself that he would somehow start the subject, regardless of the cost. He already knew he would hardly find the courage, but putting it off wouldn't help.

After being deep in thought another ten minutes, Clayton slowly got up and started climbing the ladder onto the roof to start ripping off the boards next to where the tin had been. The thought had come to him, and he wondered why he didn't think about it sooner. He would pray earnestly to God that he would reveal to Barbara Ellen that their friendship is not his will, that she would be aware that it's not a friendship his blessing can rest on. Clayton would pray that Barbara Ellen would feel led to discontinue. A heavy burden and load seemed to be lifted off of him.

* * * *

He tossed again; the bed was beginning to feel hard. Clayton had tried to fight off the disturbing thoughts, but they had come pressing down on him like a cow pressing on a fence and finally got through. He could now see that things weren't going to be as easy to be solved as he had hoped.

He had prayed so much to God, asking him to reveal to Barbara Ellen if it is not his will that they continue. First, he thought it might take longer, but now it was March and the battle was bigger instead of smaller. If only he would have gone through with it a month ago.

Clayton had a feeling Barbara Ellen had detected that something was amiss last Sunday evening. He had thought he would bring up the subject before he left the room, but he didn't know where to start. It would have been so much easier if she had asked if something was wrong. She never asked. Clayton knew he had heard only about half of what she had said. His mind had been so bothered and occupied that he failed to hear her.

This week had been rough. Two evenings he had written Barbara Ellen a letter when he came to his room, and both times he had destroyed them in the morning. His heart had cried out, "No!" This was no way to break up, not giving her a chance to say something. He had heard and read that too often the people quitting their partners by writing left the hurt one in the dark. They had been going steady for about four months; it had to be discussed.

Today was Saturday again. This time he was going through with it. Clayton thought firmly, *If only Barbara Ellen would give me a clue of her indecision.* He didn't want to hurt her. He wanted to pray, but he was getting tired of his same prayer. He knelt by his bed and the words came to his heart, "If it is Thy will, Father, let this cup pass over me."

Minutes later as he was going out to the barn to help milk, a song was pressing on his mind. He heard himself sing, "Must Jesus bear the cross alone and all the world go free? No, there's a cross for everyone, and there's a cross for me." *So this is a cross I must bear,* he wearily thought as he sat down to the cow where a milker was making a troubling sound. Elam was washing the next cow. When the milking was under control, Elam went to feed the cows. Clayton was responsible for all the milkers. At times, Elva would come out and do the feeding.

To Clayton it seemed that Elam came near to him a few times as if he was going to say something. But when he did say something, it was just usual things, nothing of importance. He kept going about his work. Clayton felt a little nervous. He worried that maybe he wasn't doing his work well enough. The last week he had done things without knowing it, much less knowing if it was done right.

It was not until after breakfast when Clayton had turned out the cows and was putting fresh bedding in the stanchion that Elam came with a fork and was helping fluff up the old bedding and add new bedding. Clayton knew Elam wanted to talk about something because they hadn't done this together since the week he had started working here.

As Elam scraped down the manure in the stanchion next to Clayton, he asked, "Have you been making any future plans in the line of what you want to work? Maybe you are tired of being my slave?"

Clayton leaned on his fork handle and looked at Elam, puzzled. "I have no complaints of working for you if that is what you want to know."

Elam put fresh straw in the stanchion and said, "I thought since you've been here a few years, maybe you are thinking about a change."

Clayton wasn't able to understand. "Is someone saying things? What makes you ask?"

Elam was scraping down manure in all the stanchions on either side of them, while Clayton still stood looking puzzled. "No, no. No one said anything about your not liking to work here. But I wonder what you would do if you suddenly could go work whatever you desire to do for a while." Elam rested his hands on the fork handle.

Clayton thought for a few moments, then said, "Maybe I would go see my folks in Kentucky sometime if I had no work."

"I would give you off any time to go to Kentucky; I hope you know," Elam answered.

"Well, yes, I guess you would. I really wasn't planning on going to Kentucky now, but it is a thought."

"And what about a job, if you could choose? Had you thought you'd get work in Kentucky if you were allowed to choose something?"

"Oh, well," Clayton slowly said, as he started bedding more of the cow beds, "Israel and Eli Jonas have pretty much work lined up in the wood working shop since my younger brothers are not coming back from Kentucky as they planned."

A look of relief took place on Elam's face as he seemed to weigh the next words. Slowly he spoke, as if they were heavy words. "I like having you work for me, and I was planning to keep you in a job for another summer, but Elva's brother Adam has been talking to us. Since he is dating Irene from this area, he would like being nearer. He wondered if he could get a job somewhere, and I thought that maybe it would be a good time to change work hands and give you a chance to do something else. And I wonder if it might not be a good idea to go see your parents in Kentucky."

Clayton was almost happy to have something new to weigh on his mind, and there was so much to think about. He bedded a few more stanchions and then asked, "Would Adam come soon?"

"We really didn't make more plans. I wanted to talk with you first. As far as I'm concerned, it can go another month, unless you want off sooner. I think maybe it could be worked out."

"I'll think it over," Clayton said.

"You do that. We can decide later."

Clayton finished scraping and bedding. Having something else to think about was almost like wearing new comfortable shoes. As he thought what was before him, he remembered that maybe it would help make that easier by saying that he is planning to go to Kentucky, maybe soon. Earlier he had decided not to go to the singing as he hadn't been feeling up to singing, much less leading the songs. Others led if he wasn't there, and he had a feeling he might do something like sing the same verse twice or something like that. He went to bed early on Saturday evening since there were so many thoughts chasing each other around that he felt a headache coming on. He didn't worry too much about Sunday evening since he had fully promised God that he would work it out. The heaviest part was over, and he could rest better on trust. He had no idea how he would tell Barbara Ellen. He had prayed and was now trusting that God would lead. He had a thirsty longing to hear the Word in the morning service. He had a feeling the message was going to be what he needed.

Clayton wasn't disappointed. He sat erect, drinking in the words as Bishop Paul was having the opening services. He reminded the congregation of the words they had just sung: "*Vas mich auf diser velt betrubt dasz varbret un kurtze zeit, Drum far oh velt mit ehr und gelt un iher vol lust hein."*

"Yes, we as Christians do have sorrows and trials here in this world. But here it tells us the things that grieve us in this world are only for such a short time and after our life is over, then the sorrow and trials are over, too. And what is there to do about our burdens and trials? Jesus said, 'Come unto Me all ye that labor and are heavy laden. I will give you rest. My yoke is easy and My burden is light.' And if we ask, we shall receive. If we seek, we shall find. If we knock, it shall be opened unto us.

"Maybe at times we look out in the world and think we could have it easier; we see people that seem burden free. We get a notion we could live like that, too, not to be against anything and enjoy all of the world's pleasure. But let us remember David who said in Psalm 73:2-5, 'But as for me, my feet were almost gone; my steps had well nigh slipped. For I was envious at the foolish, when I saw the prosperity of the wicked. For there are no bands in their death . . . neither are they plagued like other men.' And so it goes on, 'Their eyes stand out with fatness; they have more than heart could wish.' One verse says, 'He saw how good they seem to have it,' and another says, 'Behold, these are the ungodly, who prosper in the world; they increase in riches, Verily I have cleaned my heart in vain, and washed my hands in innocency. For all the day long I have been plagued and chastened every morning.' Do we feel that it was in vain? That we repented and are separated from the world?

"Like the song I quoted, *'Vas mich ouf diser velt betrubt, dasz vird ein kurtze zeit.'* David said, 'Until I went in the sanctuary of God; then understood I their end. Surely thou didst set them in slippery places; thou casted them down in destruction. How are they brought into desolation, as in a moment! They are utterly consumed with terrors. As a dream when one awaketh; so, O Lord, when thou awakest thou shalt despise their image. Thus my heart was grieved, and I was pricked in my reins, so foolish was I, and ignorant; I was as a beast before thee. Nevertheless, I am continually with thee; thou hast holden me by my right hand. Thou shalt guide me with they counsel, and afterward receive me to glory. Whom have I in

108

heaven but thee? And there is none upon earth that I desire beside thee.'

"So David, when he thought of the end of the foolish, then he was able to see the worth of not letting his foot slip to follow them. He said in the last verse, 'It is good for me to draw near to God; I have put my trust in the Lord God, that I may declare all Thy works.' Like the song we sang—'*Vas aber meine selle hebt, dasz blebt in Vagkeit*,' the glory, the crown, the reward—those things last forever. The burden only presses for a short time.

"David's foot almost slipped when he saw how easy the foolish have it, but that's what keeps us from despairing—**the reward**. It would not be worth it to give up the glory, the crown, to enjoy the pleasures of sins for a season. '*Den vas mich auf disen velt betrubt, dasz vind ein kutze zeit, vas aber mine seele liebt dasz bleubt in evagkeit, drum fahr oh velt mit ehr un geld ein valust hein.*'

"I do not want to take up more time since a visiting brother is here. Let us pray that God will let the Spirit speak through him. Let us kneel to pray."

When the congregation rose from prayer and the deacon read the assigned text, Clayton took another look at the visiting minister. He was a rather aged man. His hair were rather scarce, and his body seemed to be weakening with age.

Clayton took another quick look at him, when the deacon said the text was chosen from Psalm 37:1-26. It was very rare that a text was picked out of the Old Testament.

As the stooped, rather aged man who was on the small side, rose and clasped his hands and looked over the congregation, he looked down a moment as if to make a silent plea before starting to speak. Clayton was quite taken back when he heard the minister's husky, brisk voice when he said, "*Ich vill aw do frieda und sooge vinsha zu unser fersmling, und ich bin fro for daby voona, Ich bin net konva die veile us ich main dir sind unga lant aber nur ous liebe.*"

Clayton could soon tell by his accent that he must be from Canada. He went on to say (in Pennsylvania Dutch, but will write it in English for those reading) he didn't know what text to use and had let the matter rest, and then during the forenoon "hearing the beloved brother speak of the joy of a Christian and the evil of the unrighteous that was explained to the fullest, which I can say yea and amen to, my mind went to Psalm 37, which I will use as a text.

"Above the beginning of the chapter it says, *'Das Gluike der Goltlosen soll dem frommen nicht argenis geneichen.'* The English say the happy state of the godly and the short-lived prosperity of the wicked, just as the brother had explained of David, how his foot almost slipped when he saw how well it goes with the unrighteous. And here it says now, 'Fret not thyself because of evildoers, neither be thou envious against the workers of iniquity. For they shall soon be cut down like the grass, and wither as the green herb.'

"What more is there to say? It says it so plain. We shouldn't be envious of their doings. It will be cut down soon and it shall wither. It is things that will not keep.

"Now here is what we shall do: 'Trust in the Lord, and do good; so shalt thou dwell in the land, and verily thou shalt be fed. Delight thyself also in the Lord; and he shall give thee the desires of thine heart. **Commit** thy way unto the Lord.'

"Trust the Lord and commit thy way unto the Lord. Trust in Him. Now what is trust? I think back to a man in our congregation who was in a wheelchair. When he would come to church in the team, the people would lift him down as he would hold onto something like the back of the front seat or a brace in the back that was put there. The people would say, 'Now let go or we can't lift you down!' When he let go, he had to trust that the others had hold of him. As long as he wouldn't let go, he wasn't trusting. At times it took a lot of trusting; sometimes he feared to let go.

"Now we aren't on a wheelchair, and I am not here to talk about the things of the natural life, but the spiritual. I want to make it a little clearer as to 'our trusting' in natural things. Let's think now. When services are over, we will rise and file out. Will we hold onto something and step cautiously—one foot then another—to see if there is a floor under us? No, we get up and go without thinking that we are walking. We trust. We don't fear or doubt. Either we trust something or we fear and doubt it. We can't do both.

"Do we trust as well in our spiritual walk? What ground do we walk on? Do we trust in our next step or are we afraid to take a step? Did we ask God? Are we now trusting? Trust in the Lord and commit thy way unto the Lord. If we have something before us, a way we must walk, we shall commit it to the Lord. Give it over to Him and then step, trusting, just as we will get up and walk out of here, never fearing about the floor. We trust that it will hold us. If we fear and doubt and fret, we aren't trusting."

Clayton was so overwhelmed at the message; he saw the way before him and how much he was fearing and doubting. *How would it look if I'd walk out of here with one hand on the bench backs and with one foot at a time, feeling if there is a floor underneath? Or spend a whole night or a few hours worrying that maybe there were no boards there before taking the next step? How does God feel when I walk life's journey like that?*

A while later Clayton heard the minister say, "For in Thee, O Lord, do I hope, Thou wilt hear, O Lord my God, so when we have a troublesome walk, or a difficult journey, we pray to God for help and guidance. Then we trust he hears and we go on our way, trusting. A song came to my mind: "Yet faint but pursuing still onward I go, my Lord is my leader; of whom shall I fear?"

Clayton was deep in thought, picturing a way ahead of him, a very rough way—to Barbara Ellen's parlor—not knowing where he could step sure-footed to get there. He felt the need of calling on God to guide him the right way, to give him the right words, and then he needed to trust that He made a way. Never doubting, just stepping as we walk with Him in the light of His Word, never fearing. Only trust and obey.

When he next became aware that he was in church, Clayton heard the preacher say the verse, "The steps of a good man are ordered by the Lord, and He delighteth in His way." God knows what way we have to go. Here it says, 'The steps of a good man are ordered.' These things don't just fall on us by chance. Further, it says, 'Though he fall, he shall not utterly be cast down for the Lord upholdeth him with his hand." There it's even if we fall through an opening where the board disappeared. When we doubt, we are not cast down. He shall uphold us by his hands."

Till Clayton was again aware, the minister was reading the last verse of the text, Psalm 37:26. "'He is ever merciful, and lendeth; and His seed is blessed.' So comforting. So if we feel we do not have enough trust, here it says he lendeth. He lendeth his help. So whenever we don't have enough for the task that is before us, he will lend us if we ask.

"I wish you the Lord's blessings and will leave off from speaking. A woman likes to serve a meal if the people are hungry; it's also a joy to let the Spirit speak if you feel a hunger, and I want to say that you have eaten well. I will let the brothers testify to the word."

Clayton was glad that the young folks had no invitations for dinner. He had some "digesting" to do in the afternoon, until time to go to the supper place. He felt strangely at peace even though he had not yet planned what words he would say to Barbara Ellen. He had prayed that God would give him the needed words when the time came.

Hours later, Huckaberry was taking Clayton and Barbara Ellen to her home. A mild breeze floated over the valley; spring was on the way and so was Clayton's nineteenth birthday.

Barbara Ellen asked how they were coming along with tearing down the buildings. She knew which days it wasn't desirable, and Clayton went into detail how they had worked quite hard and put in longer days as they wanted to get it finished since spring work was starting.

Then they talked about the spring coming and the work. One thing led to another. They were nearing her home. Clayton had first thought he'd say it on the way home and leave, but decided he didn't want to spoil this drive, after the many enjoyable rides they had over this way.

Barbara Ellen asked, "Oh yes, I forgot to ask you, did you come to the singing late or weren't you there? Maybe catching up on sleep if you are putting in long days?" she ended in a question.

"No, I wasn't at the singing last evening. I thought I could use the rest and I wasn't feeling really the best."

"Are you feeling better now?" she added in concern as she looked at him with a look that he could almost feel. Her eyes were as kind as ever.

Clayton thoughtfully said, "I guess I fully recovered this forenoon in church."

"Didn't we all," Barbara Ellen said knowingly, as he let her off by the walk and drove over to the hitching rail.

Barbara Ellen had just lit the lamp when he came in the door. She took a quick look at him when he remained standing at the door, holding his hat. "Would you like to go out on the swing by the grape arbor in the spring air?"

"Sure, why not," she answered, pulling on her sweater and lowering the lamp.

Clayton carried his hat outside and set it on top of an evergreen bush near the swing. The visiting continued for another hour when something was mentioned about Adam. Then Clayton said, "Talking about Adam reminds me of what Elam was saying this week. Adam is getting tired of going back and forth every weekend and asked about staying at Elam's."

"You mean regular?" she asked.

"Yes, if I understood right."

"Would he work out or—oh, do you mean—?" Barbara Ellen faltered for words.

"Yes," Clayton scratched his head, "he will work for them."

"So you'll be looking for a job I suppose?" Barbara Ellen asked.

"I really don't have to look for one; there's plenty of work in Israel's shop. And I might go to see my folks in Kentucky sometime."

"Sounds interesting. I suppose you're eager to see where they live?"

"I have a good idea since I know where Ephraim and Naomi live, so I know about how it looks. But before I go anywhere, I—" his voice quivered. Clayton thought, *Not already*, but he forced himself to go on. "I have to tell you that I am not fair to you. I cannot return the friendship that you give to me."

Barbara Ellen gasped, as though something terrible had happened! She was speechless. Clayton took this opportunity to go on, saying, "I know I should have shared it with you sooner, but I had been praying that God would also reveal it to you."

"I have no idea what you are trying to tell me," she said, her voice full of shock. "It sounds as if maybe you have been thinking long on something till you are weary thinking about it. Maybe there is a misunderstanding somewhere that should be discussed."

Clayton felt tears budding. He half prayed and half sighed silently to Barbara Ellen, "Please don't make this so hard." Clayton blew his nose. "It's not fair to you. You think of me in a way I can't return. You think of me each day and can remember what I do at work and are concerned when ugly weather comes. You remember if it is at a time that it makes it difficult for me—and I do not return it."

"Maybe I express myself too much. I didn't know that it bothers you that I remember your doings."

"No, this is how it should be, but it's not fair to ask for your friendship if I have none to return. When you tell of your plans of people who will come to the place where you work or do something, I don't remember. I don't care enough. I respect you and appreciate that you were willing to get acquainted. And I almost thought maybe I did care, when I realized how hard it would be to tell you this. But I saw it wasn't enough."

"Did you talk with someone about this? Maybe you are imagining things," Barbara Ellen asked.

"No, I haven't talked with anyone. I didn't need to. I realized it at Elam's. He shares everything with his wife and she shares just as much with him. Elam says a lot of little things that I would think she wouldn't be interested in and visa versa. I'm sure it didn't just take place since their marriage."

"I am concerned for you, Clayton," Barbara Ellen said a little above a whisper. He felt tears trickling down his cheeks when she said his name. She continued, "This is all so new to me. I have never felt that you showed no interest. In fact, since you didn't say so many words, it made the words you did say all the more, oh, valuable. I have at times already thought of that verse, something about—oh, I don't know if I can say it. Something like, 'Words are like leaves. Where they are many, often not much fruit is underneath. But where words and leaves are few, there is fruit there.'"

Clayton blew his nose a few times and wiped his eyes. "Some day," he started afresh, "when you find a friend that truly cares, you will realize that I was not what I ought to be to you. But I feel good toward you and that is why I didn't just write you and tell you these things. I have enough respect for you that I wanted to discuss it with you."

Barbara Ellen was close to tears. Her grief was still fresh, almost too fresh for tears. She humbly asked, "Don't you want to go to Kentucky and be on a break awhile and see how you feel by then? Take time to think it over and maybe things will look different again."

"No, Barbara Ellen. You have no idea how long I had been thinking about it before I made this decision. If my going away for some time would make things look different, it will still be time to reconsider rather than dragging it on and making it harder."

"Maybe you are right. If anytime you want to discuss it more, feel welcome to it."

Clayton stood up and reached for his hat. "It's later than I usually start back, but I thank you for having patience with me. I want to part as a friend, and forgive me for having to make you go through this. Don't count on my returning. I—I do not know what the next step is—."

Barbara Ellen added, "We'll pray, not our will but God's will be done."

"Thank you," Clayton said as he turned and walked out to the buggy. On the way home his resolve broke loose. He cried freely; he had to get it out of his system. His handkerchief was wringing wet till he reached home. A peace that passeth all understanding swept over him, but the wound would need time to heal. A few times during the evening he almost thought he cared more than he knew. He almost weakened when Barbara Ellen mentioned leaves and words. He now realized how much she valued his friendship.

Chapter Seventeen

On Tuesday evening Clayton was in the milk house rinsing milkers. It seemed with each day the painful memories of Sunday evening pressed harder. He shed many a tear. He didn't know if he could make himself go to the singing on Saturday or how it would affect him to see Barbara Ellen. The milk house door opened and Elam came hurrying in. As Elam came near the sink, Clayton jumped, being so deep in his thoughts. Clayton moved over a little, thinking Elam wanted to get something in the metal cabinet on the wall next to the sink. But Elam stood with his back against the white cabinet and folded his arms. Facing Clayton, Elam asked innocently but frankly, "I was wondering, would you rather not leave your job here? I mean, I don't want to simply turn you out if this upsets you. I had thought maybe the job was getting boring for you, and when you suggested going to visit your parents in Kentucky, I thought it would be a great idea. But it seems the change of plans is getting you down."

Clayton swallowed a few sobs and without looking up said, "No, the plans of job changing has made my load easier. I don't know where I'd be if I hadn't the change to think about."

Elam stared at him in silence. It was hard to say, but he might as well do it now rather than later. "I'm not going back to Barbara Ellen. I hope you can bear with me." Elam stood silent while Clayton put the pail on the rack. There were tears in Elam's eyes.

At length Elam said, "We will sure bear with you, and I'm glad to hear that our change in work is not affecting you like this."

"If you don't mind, I will go back to Alpheus next week and maybe soon go on to Kentucky."

"However you decide," Elam replied, then left the milk house.

Clayton assumed Elam probably took for granted Barbara Ellen quit him, unless he himself at one time broke up with someone and knows it is still hard, even if you make the decision.

*   *   *   *

Clayton folded another pile of his clothing and arranged them in the suitcase. Now there was still his Sunday clothes to pack. He would put them in a separate box. The two suitcases were full. He had folded the blue shirt and the blue-and-white design shirt, and as he was folding the white shirt he opened it again to take a second look at it. It was starting to show wear as the collar was getting worn at places. It was getting quite thin, almost as threads, and it didn't have such a clean white color anymore. It looked like the shirt would need to be replaced. Who could make one for him? He folded it again and wondered if when he moves home to Alpheus, maybe Ella Mae would make him a shirt or if it was too much to ask. *Maybe Naomi would if I would be there to ask her, but with her two small boys to care for I suppose her hands are full. Well, maybe Seranus's wife would. Her youngest must be about three already.*

As he was packing in the last things, Clayton remembered the few things in the narrow flat drawer in the other bureau. Opening the drawer he saw the card again that had taken him by surprise when it came in the mail the other day.

He had purposely gone to the singing rather late in order that the group would sing without him leading, but the songs weren't going too good and someone informed the ones at the table that he was back in the corner. There was no other way; he had to go up front to the table. He didn't feel as much in a turmoil as he did at the last singings, and he thought if he didn't look he wouldn't know if Barbara Ellen is there or how she is accepting their separation.

It didn't go too badly, but when the whole group in hearty volume and clear voice sang, "When my sad heart aches, till it nearly breaks, is this ought to him, does he care? Oh yes, he cares. I know he cares. His heart is touched with my grief," Clayton had to blink back tears while the others sang on. "When the days are weary the long nights dreary, I know my Savior cares." When the last echo faded, no one stirred or paged through their songbook, but cast quick, expectant glances, so Clayton surmised they must not have sung the last verse. "Does Jesus care when I've said good-bye to the dearest on earth to me?" He couldn't sing anymore, but the voices rang on. It reminded him too much of what Barbara Ellen had said, about leaves and words. He sensed she had said good-bye to what was dear to her.

Number 471 was announced from across the room. Those words weren't as piercing. "Flooding my soul with glory divine. Jesus has said, 'I'll never forsake,'" were some of the words he still remembered. The words seemed like a soothing ointment.

The other day there had been an envelope in the mail addressed to him. He pulled out the card again and read, "To cheer you." There was a picture of a ship out on peaceful water with the riverbank laden with colorful bushes and vines, and the sky a clear blue with fluffy clouds. A lighthouse was on a nearby shore. Inside, the card read, "Warm and friendly wishes. Just to say you're in my thoughts every day." It was signed, "A friend and brother, Landis." Then in his own handwriting Landis had written, "Then nestle your hand in your Father's. And sing if you can as you go; your song may cheer someone behind you whose courage is sinking low. And if your lips do quiver, God will love you the better so."

Clayton hadn't even felt insulted because he knew Landis had walked the road, too, and he felt joy that Landis remembered him and was concerned. Clayton had a feeling it was true that Landis thought of him every day.

Clayton carried the two suitcases out and loaded them on his buggy. When he came in, Elva came in from the washline with some of his clothing and she slipped them in a bag and gave them to him. Then she said, "Did you see the package on the table for you? It just came in the mail today."

"A package for **me**?" Clayton asked surprised, mixed with doubt. Sure enough, it had his name on it. He left it on the table while he went to get the rest of the things upstairs. Now he was trying to arrange everything on the buggy and finally they were on the way. He had left home with Clint and now was going back home with Huckaberry. Home? Where was home? Sometimes he wondered. It was Friday afternoon, and he was heading to Alpheus and Ella Mae's house.

Arriving at Alpheus's, Clayton saw Ella Mae raking the yard. Margaret, the chubby baby, was out with her in the jumper. She jumped faster when Clayton walked up to talk with Ella Mae.

Ella Mae said, "Alpheus is out back plowing. We were looking for you a few days already. I just housecleaned your room, so everything is ready for you." Baby Margaret had been rejoicing, but now she just stared at him. Then she made a fearful sound! Ella Mae said, "I think at first she thought it was Alpheus, but I didn't think you really look so much like him."

When he had everything upstairs, his curiosity got the better of him. Now he must know what this box contained. He ripped it open, and as the last tissue paper fell back, he gasped in astonishment. A white shirt stared back at him! It was so white. He touched the material, almost afraid he would make it dirty. The pure white material prompted a song to come to his mind: "Lord, wash me, and I will be whiter than snow." There was a weave of small diamonds pressed in the pure white material. The shirt was neatly ironed and perfectly folded.

"Who is this from?" he asked out loud to the silent room. "I wonder if it fits." He got hold of the collar and shoulders and let it spread out. In doing so, a paper fell to the floor.

Clayton picked up the paper and read the short message: "Please accept this as a parting gift. I want you to have it; it doesn't fit my brother. I hope you understand. Wish you well. A friend, Barbara Ellen." Clayton suddenly felt weak. Why would she do this? Then it came to him clearly that she had likely made it for his birthday next week and now didn't know what to do with it. And it was true, her brothers were more slender and lightweight. He tried it on and it fit just right. *But how would she know my size?* She had probably noticed his was quite worn.

Slowly Clayton began to unpack his things, still dwelling on the shirt. Then his face lit up, remembering how one evening about two months ago, when they had come home to Barbara Ellen's place, her father had just discovered a broken pipe in the barn. The boys weren't home and there was quite a mess already. Clayton had asked for a change of clothes and had helped clean it up. He remembered again that Barbara Ellen had seemed quite enthused or interested in the shirt he had on, and she had looked at the cuffs that were too tight to close. The shoulders were too narrow, making the buttons tight in the front. At the time he had felt a little ill at ease, and he supposed now that she had been looking how much bigger to make his shirt than her brother's shirts.

Clayton didn't know if it was proper to accept the new shirt, but that was beside the point. He needed it. But could he wear it remembering Barbara Ellen? *I guess as good as she could, keeping it.* He hung it in the closet. Maybe some day he could thank her for it—an excuse to talk with her and let her know that she was no enemy to him.

Putting his other things away, Clayton noticed the birthday card that Jonathan had given him that morning. He opened it to read it again. Then he noticed there was a paper in the envelope. He read the paper. "You're struggling. I see it; I feel it; I hurt for you. But I must tell you, dear friend, I believe you will emerge somehow wiser, stronger, and more aware. Hold onto that thought, tuck it away in a corner of your heart until the hurt melts enough for the learning to have meaning. Elam."

After supper Clayton went over to the shop. Israel was sanding a piece of furniture. Seranus came down to use the phone. Later, Eli Jonas came; after chores, Alpheus came over, too. Still later, Ella Mae brought Margaret in the stroller and Amanda had their baby Cleon along. Amanda had some varnish to do, so she put Cleon in the playpen.

Clayton presumed that this was a usual routine—having a family gathering in the shop in the evening. He was beginning to feel at home. He looked at Israel, who was explaining something to Seranus as he changed the sandpaper in the sander. Then they went over and checked a few boards that were standing there. They were examining the long pieces. Apparently Seranus had an order for something he didn't fully understand. Amanda was varnishing a few small rocking chairs and Ella Mae was visiting with her. Clayton wondered if Israel's friend Emily would actually one day belong to this set-up, too. He still found it hard to grasp, but the young folks had by this time accepted the new relationship as a fact and Israel seemed to think it was worth the waiting.

Clayton enjoyed working and visiting with his brothers, but it was hard to get used to the fact that as he walked up the walk from the shop toward the house, that Ella Mae was in the house instead of Mother. For so many years Mother had kept the house faithfully, but if anyone could take Mother's place, Ella Mae could. But it still seemed Mother should be somewhere in the house.

Chapter Eighteen

Clayton rapped on the door. Mother opened it, wiping her hands on her apron. She looked. The she looked again and said, wistfully, "Have you come, Clayton?" Mother held open the door as Clayton followed her inside. The clocked ticked loudly on the shelf, and the teakettle was singing on the range. Dad's glasses and a few songbooks lay on the stand next to the Bible. The rocking chair was empty. A half-braided rug lay on the regular table. The same dusty blue seat cover was on the double-lidded wood box.

"Have you come all by yourself?" Mother asked while Clayton was noticing the order of the kitchen.

"No, the bus was about full."

"Och, you know what I mean. Where is your suitcase? Did you walk here?"

"I got a taxi to bring me out. I got off at Naaman's and they said I could leave my suitcase there. The children could bring it up on the pull wagon. Where is Dad?" Clayton added, as he washed up to get rid of some of the bus smell.

"He is resting. It seems he needs more rest since his low spell—in November I guess it was." They were discussing Dad's condition further, then Mother said, "If I may ask, is something eating you? Didn't you lose weight?"

"I suppose I did lose some."

Mother asked about the job at Elam's and seemed quite concerned as he explained the change of jobs, and he said it was to his liking. A few moments of silence followed while Mother sat at the table and took the rug in her hands and continued braiding.

Clayton watched her thoughtfully for a few moments, then he blurted out, "How does a person know who's the one God has chosen for them?" She gave him a long look. Clayton further added, "I mean, how did you know that Dad was the right one for you?"

Mother was still looking at him in silent sympathy. "Are you telling me that you are doubtful of Barbara Ellen?" Mother asked in a small voice.

"It's all over," Clayton said simply.

"Was it eating you before or after?" Mother asked, watching him closely.

"I guess before."

"Then you were the one that decided it's best to quit."

"Yes, Mother, but it wasn't easy. She is a nice girl and I didn't want to do it, but—"

"That's better than marrying someone and not having true love."

"But, Mother, sometimes I feel doubtful now. Do you think I was too hasty? Can you tell at four months?"

"I would hope so, and you don't have to know now. When you go back, you'll know if you missed her. By the way, have I asked how long you are staying?"

"I have no definite plans. Maybe a few weeks or so, but, Mother, you didn't answer me."

"Of what?" Mother looked at him blankly.

"How did you know Dad was the one for you?" Clayton reminded her.

"You're the second son that came around asking me this."

"Who else did?" Clayton asked.

"Israel did once a few years back."

"Oh yes, what have you got to say about Israel? Didn't you almost faint when you heard the news?" Clayton laughed.

"The news didn't come to us so suddenly," Mom said thoughtfully in a way that seemed to say there was more to the story than that. Clayton waited, then Mother threw the rug on the floor to see if it had the right shape. She leaned back in her chair.

"It was after Israel broke up with Katie that he asked that question, and he never said anything more. I started asking him about it the third time he had come home with fresh baked doughnuts when he was on an errand for Dad. He said he was so hungry and had stopped at the bakery, but I started getting suspicious. Sometimes the bakery wasn't even on his way home.

"The next time he came home with baked things, I started fishing around. I tried to warn him that I was afraid he was imagining things, as I knew the Rissler girls were quite young and not spoken for yet. Maybe the girl he wanted was one who flirts with all boys and then suddenly falls for someone else. I guess Israel was a little doubtful, too, because he waited until Emily had a chance at others. I was so afraid he would be hurt yet. Besides his age, I thought he was shooting pretty high."

"The Risslers aren't really proud people at all," Clayton added.

"You mean they don't make themselves proud. Other people label them so popular that they seem almost proud."

"I know, but you still didn't answer my question about Dad."

Mother got a faraway look in her eyes and sat back on the rocker. "Well," she began, "where do I start? There were two of the Wenger boys with the young folks—David and Jonathan. Earl was married already. No, first it was only one. When I was nineteen, David started going with the young folks. I was rather impressed. He was everyone's friend and had a voice and will to sing. At times he had a little too much pep, but it was all in fun. The next year Jonathan joined the group, but there was something about David that stood out. By that time I was twenty and he was eighteen. Another boy asked for my company, but I felt I couldn't accept it if I was guilty of being interested in another one. As I was nearing twenty-one, I began to realize that David was watching another girl, which didn't surprise me. At times I asked God to lead David in my life. Other times I asked God to help me give him up. I knew I was losing him.

"The other boy asked me again, but I refused. By now David was more manly. He had joined church and was more serious, but there was another girl in his life. I didn't think very many people knew it, because only if you watched David closely were you aware of it. Sometimes I wasn't sure that girl was aware of David's interest. I often prayed, not my will but Thine be done. This is about as far as my part of the story goes. Maybe since you are the boy you should ask Dad how he knew to ask me for my friendship."

"Mother, you are teasing me. You can't quit there!"

"I'm serious."

"Why don't you just say it?" Clayton begged her.

"I might not get every detail in, and you know Dad likes to talk about it better than I do."

It was no use; Mother wouldn't say any more. Clayton remembered it was always Dad who was giving out hints about some interesting, unusual happenings in their early life.

Soon Dad came out from the bedroom, rubbing his eyes and smoothing his hair.

"Were you talking to me?" he asked.

"No, Dad. We have company."

Father looked at Clayton as his eyes got bigger. "Is it Clayton?"

"Yes, Dad. It's me," Clayton said, getting up and giving him a hearty handshake.

"Are there others along?"

"No, just me."

"Well, we're so glad to see you." Father and son were soon in a good conversation, comparing spring, and how much further the leaves were out here than they were in Pennsylvania, the work at Elam's and quitting, what the boys were doing at the shop, and so it continued. Mother worked on her rug till it was time to make supper.

In another hour Enos came in the door swinging his lunch pail. He stopped in his tracks half way across the kitchen. Clayton said, "Looks as if you do painting."

"Today I did. Wayne wanted me to go along tomorrow again, but I guess Ephraim wants to haul manure." He reached for an apple from the bowl on the counter.

Clayton said, "I came to fetch you since you said you'll be coming back when you are seventeen and I haven't seen you."

Enos looked at Clayton and saw his mischievous look; he blew an apple peel at him. "I haven't had time yet."

126

Mother looked from one to the other and decided they were kidding.

"Stay around a while and you'll find out," Enos said.

When Clayton reminded him again about coming back, Enos said, "Didn't you know a wise man changes his mind?"

This seems so much like home, Clayton thought longingly.

After supper Ephraim's whole family came up. Clayton noticed that Harvey, the oldest, was really stretching himself in size already. No wonder—his mother said he was nine already! Another little girl had been added to their family. Ephraim was the first one of the Wenger brothers to have two daughters, but he had twice as many boys.

Later Naaman himself brought Clayton's suitcase, so it was late till everyone left and they got to bed. It was not until he was in bed that Clayton remembered that he had a question to ask Dad sometime.

*   *   *   *

Naaman's family decided to take the opportunity to have a singing for the young folks on Sunday evening, as was their custom here. Naaman's invited the whole family for dinner on Sunday. Then Clayton, Noah David, and Enos and his girl—Deacon Ian Weaver's Dorcas—all stayed for supper. Clayton got a funny feeling, realizing that Enos had started dating already.

Clayton found it interesting to watch the young folks gather; most were strangers to him. The settlement was a small group, but nice sized. Clayton could tell that they knew each other pretty well. He asked Naaman which was Noah David's girl that they were hearing about.

"Oh, Lucy. She just went into the bedroom with her wraps." Naaman showed him later when she came out with another girl. "Is she older or did she start teaching young if she has been teaching a few years?" Clayton asked.

"Some of each. She only turned nineteen, so she is a year older than Noah David."

Clayton was surprised when the young people started singing. He had forgotten that Mom had written that Noah David had a real interest in singing. He and two other boys took turns leading songs.

As Clayton looked over the group while singing, he found himself more than once taking another look at the girl at the far end of the table. She looked to be an honest and open person, not one pretending to be more than she was. The next time he looked over, she was studying him; they both quickly looked elsewhere. Clayton tried to keep his eyes on his songbook.

Later, the singing died down and everyone was visiting. Clayton was a little disappointed with himself that he had kept looking over her way so often. By now, their eyes had met a few times. He hadn't intended to come to watch girls. It was his last thought. He vowed to himself that he was finished with girls.

Till the evening was over, Clayton had gathered that when people said "Marlene," it meant the girl he had been watching. That's all he knew, and he also noticed she was still there after all the couples had gone. But so were Noah David and Lucy, so he really didn't know anything.

Later, when Clayton came into the living room after most of the people had gone, he found Marlene hunting her songbook. It was hard to remember who smiled first. "They tell me you are a brother to Enos and Noah David," she said.

"That's what I have been hearing," Clayton replied.

"I wonder if they know for sure; I see no resemblance. Maybe you favor Ephraim a little.

"I'm the different one," Clayton said as he brushed his hand over his hair.

"Different from which?" Marlene asked. "Enos doesn't bother much with singing, and Noah David has quite a talent."

"Oh, different from Enos. I—I mean I like to sing." He fumbled for words. *How did that sound, telling this strange girl I have a talent to sing like she said of Noah David?* "But who are you? Marlene—?" he asked, dragging the last syllable.

She finally found her book. "Just another Sensenig, like there are plenty around here," she answered and laughed easily, as she picked up her books and went out the hall door. Clayton entered the kitchen where he told Naaman's good-night, since he was staying for the night.

Clayton tried to tell himself that Marlene was friendly to everyone and that she had been studying him to see if he resembled Enos and Noah David. The way she talked, fitting in proper words at correct places, Clayton assumed that she must be a schoolteacher.

*　*　*　*

On Tuesday Clayton helped Mom make rows in the garden and then he went in the house. Dad was resting on the rocker, so Clayton pulled up a chair in front of him. He had noticed Dad's hearing was a little dull. He asked Dad, "You never did tell me how you knew to ask Mom for her company when you were young. I was wondering how I am to know."

Dad asked, "Did Mom tell me that you broke up with your girl?"

"Yes, I did," Clayton replied. "She wasn't the right one."

"Did Mother tell you how we met?"

"No, she just said that she was desiring you but that you had an eye for another girl. I was supposed to ask you what led you to her."

"God did," Dad said honestly.

"Yes, but tell me about it."

Dad got a far away look, then grinned and had a twinkle in his eye. "Yes, there was a girl I was interested in. I was drawn to her. She was a little young, so I waited. Then one evening there was good sledding. The young folks came together with the horse sleighs and we were sleighing in wide, open fields. Not every boy had a sleigh, so we used to play a game. Some boys and some girls were walking, and if you came up to someone who was walking, you dropped off your passenger and picked up that one. So it continued. When merry bells started ringing loud and clear, it was time for all to head home. You had to take home whomever you had on your sleigh. The ones walking would suddenly find sleighs.

129

"I only had a boy on my sleigh to take home, and we got to talking as we were going home. He begged me to let him ask a girl for me. I said he could if she's the right one; he said he'd ask Jonas's Lydia. I had expected him to say Lydia Horning, but then I realized that her father was Jonas. So I told him he may, and the promise was that since the young folks were invited away for dinner on Sunday, I would pick Lydia up at church if she accepts my company. If not, he would let me know.

"Well, Sunday came and I hadn't heard anything until he told me after church as we walked up to the buggies that 'it went through.' Just as I drove down to the church door, I saw Lydia Horning climb in the buggy ahead of me! I thought he must have meant it fell through. I was just on the verge of telling my horse to go, when out of the corner of my eye I saw a movement. There was a girl climbing into my buggy. It was Lydia Garman!"

"I did some fast thinking. Then I remembered again that they called this Lydia at times 'Jonas's Lydia,' because there used to be another Lydia Garman—Edwin Garman's Lydia—but she was now married. Well, I was still safe. I would take her along to the dinner place. People would think she had no other way to come. And I would explain it to her.

"We really didn't talk much on the way over. She said something about her brother Clarence. I didn't realize at first what she meant. Then I said, 'Oh, yes. I guess that would be your brother that got published today.'

"'You mean you didn't think about it?' she asked surprised.

"'I didn't at the time,' I confessed. To myself I was still trying to remember who I really had in my buggy. Of course, when Clarence was published it hadn't meant anything to me because I wasn't planning to pick up his sister or talk privately with her.

"Then when we were half way over, Lydia started apologizing, asking if it was all right if we go to her home for supper, rather than go to the supper place. Some of her brothers and families from another settlement were coming for supper. They were somewhere in the area for dinner and were planning to come for supper. 'And

130

we are glad, as we don't often get to see them, and Mother was hoping I could come home.'

"I shrugged my shoulders and said, 'I guess we could.' I was thinking that I could drive her home, explain things, and continue on home or to the supper place when Lydia said, 'You don't need to feel out of place. I told my parents, and Dad has a way with people.' I saw that my plan wasn't going to work out. Her parents were looking for me, so I thought I'd go through with it till evening.

"I wasn't going to tell my friend to correct it. He would never forget the joke."

Clayton cleared his throat, "But, ah, if this was Mother, she was always quick to catch on. Didn't she detect that something was amiss?"

Dad smiled, "Yes, she senses things quickly in our family since she knows us all so well. She didn't know me so well then and thought I was quite nervous, because she didn't think I had such a shy nature. But of course she realized I had never had a girl before. She guessed this is how having a girl would affect me.

"Well, then in the afternoon when we started for home amidst the visiting, Lydia suddenly looked at me surprised and wondered if I knew that they didn't live on that farm anymore. Clarence and her sister Ruth lived on the farm where Lydia's family had lived. They had moved to a smaller farm in another direction. I pulled my horse to a halt and confessed, 'I had forgotten. Let's see, was I there at a singing once?'

"'We had a singing since,' she said, then apologized. 'I was going to say something sooner, but I was sure you'd know where we live. But I thought maybe you planned to go up the river road.'

"She ended up telling me which way to go from there. Now of course if I had been dwelling half a week on driving her home, I would have been aware. But it was just like a dream that I couldn't get awake from.

"Anyhow, true to Lydia's word, her dad had a way of entertaining us all, as if we all belonged together. We were at the supper table when one of her uncles looked at me and then at her dad, asking, 'You mean this is Landis?' You know, the brother below Mother.

"Lydia's dad took a drink of water and said, 'No, Landis is on a trip to Indiana. This is a friend who saw that Lydia had a way to get home from the young folks' dinner place' They all knew Harold because he was Ruth's steady for a couple of years already. Her dad soon geared the subject to another direction.

"After the company had left, Clarence and Mabel left, too, and we were sitting there, drawn into the conversation. It was so easy to get involved in her dad's company. Later, as Lydia's dad was talking about something that took place when he was a small boy, he suddenly looked up. Lydia was standing there. Her dad looked at her and then brushed his hands together and asked, 'Am I entertaining your company? Well, I must get off to bed.' It was the first I realized that her dad and I were the only ones left in the room.

"Lydia led the way to a quaint little room where a cozy fire and a glowing little lamp welcomed us. When I asked, she explained what her father had started to say about why his one finger was shorter. I never did get to explain what had really happened—that I didn't belong there. We didn't finish talking that evening and by the next Sunday evening, Clarence's wedding was only four days away and her sister Ruth was published that Sunday.

"It wasn't long until I discovered that Lydia's adorning was not the outward adorning of plaiting hair and wearing gold or putting on of apparel, but the hidden man of the heart. Even the ornament of a meek and quiet spirit which is in the sight of God a great price, as Peter speaks of.'"

"You mean you never remembered the other girl?" Clayton asked, leaning forward in his chair.

Dad got a pleased look on his face. He slowly began, "You're not the first son to ask me that. Now I want to ask you. If you were to seek a five-dollar bill you know is there, and when you came where you thought it was, you found a fifty-dollar bill, would you keep on looking for the other one," he asked, holding the last word, "or would you decide you perhaps had looked wrong the first time?" Clayton sat still, waiting to hear more, when Dad remained silent.

"When did you tell Mother?"

Dad began again, thoughtfully. "Eight months after we were dating I asked my friend who did the first asking, why he suggested to ask Lydia Garman for me. He took a long look at me and said, 'I guess because I noticed she admired you and I thought you needed urging, then you agreed.' That was the first it occurred to me that maybe she wasn't as surprised as I was when being asked for my company.

"My friend wondered why I asked after all this time. I said I thought he had meant Jonas Horning's Lydia, when he said Jonas's Lydia. He had a hearty laugh. I told him not to tell anyone. The other Lydia was at that time dating a guy from another settlement and we heard some questionable things about them.

"Then after ten months of dating, on Sunday evening your mother took me off guard. She had suddenly asked what made me decide to ask for her company. I looked at her, wondering why she asked that. I was afraid word had leaked out. Then she went on, saying, 'I was just thinking it over this past week and remembered that it seemed someone else had caught your attention.'

"I, too, had often wondered why things had worked out like they did, till my friend had told me a few months earlier. I thought I knew the reason, now I was going to prove if it was correct. I looked at her and said, 'Weren't you praying about the matter?'"

Dad smiled and said she blushed and said in a small voice, "Yes."

"Then I reminded her that maybe she should ask God why, or thank him for answering. She never asked me more about it. Then after we were seeing each other about eighteen months, I told her how things really were. After that was discussed, I asked her if she would give her hand in marriage. And we both decided that we could honestly say "yes" at the wedding when the bishop asks if we can promise that we believe that God led us together."

"What did happen to the other girl?"

Dad said, "Aren't you pleased with your mother? We must not lay our hands at the plow and look back."

*   *   *   *

That night Clayton couldn't sleep for a long time. He remembered that before going to his first singing Dad had told him about a guy having the wrong girl in his buggy on his first date, and not knowing where he was going. He also remembered that Mother had blushed when the comment was made.

There was so much to think about, but Clayton just couldn't picture Mother as a young girl. He realized that pictures of Barbara Ellen and Marlene were drifting in and out of his mind as Dad had been talking of his experiences.

*   *   *   *

Working side by side, the two brothers spread plastic on the ground to prepare the patch to plant melons. Clayton was shoveling soil on the edge of the plastic to fasten it, while Naaman was pulling it even on his side. "So you are really starting for Pennsylvania tomorrow?" Naaman asked.

"I guess so," Clayton answered, shoveling more soil.

Naaman said, "I was hoping maybe you'd get a notion to stay awhile, maybe make your home here."

"It's going to be a little hard leaving Mother and Father, but what do I want here?"

"Help raise this produce, and I'm sure the young folks would welcome anyone to make their group a little larger. What's more, if you didn't notice, in the balance of boys and girls, the boys are in want," Naaman said, rising from his knees and looking at him.

Clayton rested on the shovel and said, "I really didn't take notice. Is that why my little brothers are in such demand?" Clayton chuckled.

"Don't you think maybe God is leading you here, too?" Naaman asked.

"I'm not looking for a girl, if that is what you mean. If I would be interested in one, I wouldn't be now. If I'd go get another girl so soon, Barbara Ellen would know I wasn't very sincere."

"Are you planning to go back to Barbara Ellen again?" Naaman asked.

"No, I have no such plans. I really have no plans for anything," Clayton admitted.

"I think maybe you should stay around. You don't give God very much time."

"I thought I told you that I don't want a girl now, and the singing last Sunday wasn't encouraging whatsoever."

"What do you mean?" Naaman asked. "How was it different from the singing we had for you the other Sunday evening?"

"The girl who might be worth learning more about must not attend regularly," Clayton admitted.

"You got me," Naaman said. "I can't remember that there were any other visitors around that time, just the regular group. Tell me more. Describe her."

Clayton wasn't going to tell anyone, but he himself wondered. "You mean what dress she had on?" Clayton teased.

"No, I wouldn't know anyhow, but I suppose you noticed more than her dress," Naaman answered, not to be outdone.

"I don't even know what dress she had on, to be honest. I did gather that she responds to the name of Marlene, and I would think she wouldn't be found any place than a schoolhouse, as handy as she is in selecting the right words at the proper places. She's, well, anything but inferior, but far from bold, and is observant to what's being said."

Naaman cleared his throat. "I didn't know you'd make such a good lawyer or detective. Marlene was a schoolteacher, then she quit when her father became bedfast. After he died, she took care of different shut-ins and now she works for an older couple. Well, not really so old, but they are both rather feeble in mind and the children don't want to put them in a home. The children and the parents are of a higher church and found out about Marlene. She is doing a good job. She talks to them a lot and keeps their minds interested in the present. It's a good therapy. The children and doctors wondered what Marlene was doing, because they noticed a difference in their parents. She has off every other weekend, so maybe you should stay another weekend."

"It sounds like she has a purpose in life already."

"Maybe you could blend in yet with it."

"I guess if that is what God has for me, she'll be around if I come later."

"Boy, you take chances," Naaman replied.

"A few minutes ago you told me I don't give God very much chance," Clayton reminded him. "Now you aren't giving me much chance, and I didn't say I was interested in Marlene."

"Well, I guess I have to believe it that you are going home—and we did get this plastic laid."

Chapter Nineteen

Back in Pennsylvania after his visit to see his parents in Kentucky, Clayton began working for the Singing Pine Brothers woodworking shop. He wiped the sawdust from his face as he went to get another board. He had five more bird feeders to cut yet, but the pile of boards was gone. Israel must have used the last two in his project. So Clayton went over to the other part of the shop and ran another pile of boards through the planer. He hoped this batch was better than the last one.

Clayton looked at his watch and saw that it was past four o'clock already. Another late summer day was so far spent and he hadn't breathed much pure air yet today.

The shop workers were behind in the orders and were trying to get some out of the way. Clayton liked the work pretty well once he got really involved with it, but he missed watching the summer skies and the birds flying about. While at Elam's, he had often taken a moment to pause and watch the sunrises and sunsets when he was working in the fields or repairing the meadow fence.

At times Clayton felt almost like a prisoner in the shop. He hadn't helped Alpheus much with the farm work as Alpheus and Seranus worked together a lot and Ella Mae helped some outside. At times Seranus had been quite busy in his farm shop. Then Clayton had helped Alpheus with the farming and he enjoyed being out in the field and occasionally seeing a thunderstorm approaching in the distance. He would watch the sky change and then feel the changed cool air and the smell of rain and later hear the rain come.

In the shop, at times he thought it was a nice day, then suddenly rain splashed against the shop windows. And Clayton could just try to imagine what all he had missed before it rained.

It would be supper time till he'd get these boards run through the planer both ways. As Clayton ran the boards through the planer, his heart sang,

Dead to the world, would I be, oh Father, dead unto sin, alive unto thee. Crucify all the earthly within me, emptied of sin and self may I be. Open the wells of grace and salvation, pour the rich streams deep into my heart. Cleanse and refine my thought and affection. Seal me and make me pure as thou art.

Clayton found himself hoping that someone would make a singing this week. Lately he enjoyed singing more again; he felt more like putting his whole heart into it. Life wasn't such a burden, and he didn't feel self-conscious about anyone. The hurt had healed pretty well. At first it bothered him a little as throughout the summer he at times could sense that Barbara Ellen was still there and that she was painfully aware of him. He could read the longing.

Clayton had talked with Barbara Ellen once when the young folks were somewhere for dinner and she was a table waiter. He had noticed she was out on the built-in porch filling up dishes and he had slipped out that way instead of going out front with the others. Barbara Ellen had not noticed him till he started talking. He had said, "Thank you, Barbara Ellen. I guess you can see that I needed the shirt."

She had looked up surprised and said, "I thought you did, but I wasn't sure if—" she hesitated.

Clayton finished her sentence. "—I'd appreciate it. I do and I'm glad you count me as a friend."

"You're quite welcome," she quickly said, as a girl was coming in the other door, and he had gone on out.

Ever since then, Clayton felt a little better, but it bothered him that maybe Barbara Ellen had more hope. About two months later, though, she had started dating Warren Brubaker from Cottage Hill, and now it didn't bother Clayton anymore to meet or be around Barbara Ellen.

138

The young folks who started joining the group seemed so young. Three years ago Clayton had been looking forward to autumn to turn into winter and winter passing quickly so spring would bring his seventeenth birthday. Now life seemed to be going fast enough. Would he really be twenty in another half year? Twenty—and his dreams all behind him. The words of a song came to his mind again, "Lord, I am fondly, earnestly longing into thy holy likeness to grow, thirsting for more and deeper communion, yearning thy love more fully to know." He was finding out that there were things in life that had more meaning than youthful dreams.

Clayton carried two pieces of board over to the main part of the shop. A customer had just come in and Israel was talking with him. The supper bell at Alpheus's was ringing.

The meal stretched out well over a half hour, closer to an hour, since Seranus and Muriel and the two boys were also there for supper. Muriel's sister was there, too, since she was helping the women at Seranus's to do a big batch of sweet corn.

Coming out in the shop, Israel asked Clayton to make ten wind chimes. A customer had called and said he would like to have them by morning. The rods and strings and cut-out plastic designs were on the work table. The earlier customer, Ezra Reiff, was still there. The Formica samples were spread out. Reiff must have been ordering or looking for something. Now he was visiting as Israel changed the sandpaper in both sanders and then rubbed an oiled cloth over the varnished boards, making them ready for the last coat.

Israel wasn't talking very much. Clayton guessed he was almost too busy to listen to his customer's visiting. In fact, Israel hardly had a chance to eat supper. Amanda came out and helped with the wind chimes. Eli Jonas was working on a big cupboard project.

The telephone echo bell sounded in the shop. When no one else moved, Amanda went out to answer it. When she returned, she talked with Eli Jonas and they both went to the office.

While working alone on the wind chimes, Clayton was half-heartedly listening to Israel and Ezra Reiff who were talking about

William Nolt, near Cedar Hollow, who was getting discouraged with farming. Israel asked, "Isn't there a son at home yet?"

"Yes, but he just didn't help much, and then when he left the church, William said he had to find another home," the visitor from the east end was saying.

"There are some girls yet, aren't there?" Israel asked.

"Yes, two girls are married, but they each have farms through their husbands. And the single girl, who dates a boy from Ohio, lives out there now. I think she is teaching school. The milking and all is too much. Nolt plans to get rid of his cows first, but with no help and his age, even farming would be too much."

The men switched to another topic and another customer came in the shop. He wanted to see the different knobs for a sink. Ezra Reiff said, "Well, I must be going."

As soon as Ezra was out of the shop, Israel said, "Clayton, will you help the customer? I'm going for supper."

*　　*　　*　　*

Clayton lay in bed trying to unwind from the day. He had pressed to get the wind chimes all together, and it seemed he just couldn't stay at it. He was always running elsewhere—to the phone a few times and to help another customer. As it turned out, Israel never came back in the shop. Ten minutes after Israel left, Emily Rissler had stepped in the side door. All dressed up, she asked if Israel was still there. Clayton had looked out the window to see Israel hurrying from the house all dressed up, his buggy standing in the yard. *They must be going away either for a late supper or else Israel just wasn't getting supper with Ezra keeping him up.*

So Clayton was going in circles in the shop and now as he lay trying to unwind, a conversation came to his mind. A new thought occurred to him. At first it was just a wild idea, a brainstorm. But the longer he thought about it, the more enthused he was getting. Of course, Israel had a lot of work in the shop to do, but, oh well. Clayton reasoned, *I suppose soon he'll be bringing Emily home and training her in the shop unless they make a bakery out of this!* He smiled to himself. Who should he talk to first? He found that thinking of this kind kept him even more awake, and he had been trying to relax.

Two days later Clayton asked Israel for the day off. He wanted to do visiting. He caught the bus in town and got off at Wet Springs and walked to Aunt Sara's place where he got a team and found the Cedar Hollow area.

After asking at two different farmhouses, Clayton located William Nolt's farm. Mrs. Nolt met Clayton at the door when he knocked; he asked if he could talk to William. She invited him in, and he followed her to the kitchen.

"William, there is someone here to see you," she said, rousing her husband from his noon nap on the recliner.

Clayton introduced himself to William. "Oh, yes, I can see that you resemble your grandfather Jonas Garman some."

"That's what I've been told. And more so in the last five years." William invited him to a chair.

Clayton fingered the hat in his hands and asked about dairying. William started explaining the situation and then asked Clayton, "Are you looking for a herd of cows?"

"Not really," Clayton answered, "but I thought you really don't want to quit farming altogether. Wouldn't you want to continue with the farm if you had help?"

The Nolts looked at each other for a moment, then William said. "It's not what we **want** to do. It's what we **have** to do, as help is hard to come by these days. I had been counting on keeping the farm for Martin, but that didn't work out."

Clayton rolled his hat some more and talked about his indoor shop work. He had been wishing to get out in the fields when he heard about this job. "I thought maybe it would be a place where I could get a hired-hand job. You could keep the farm a few more years and see what time brings."

"You mean you would be interested in the job?" William asked. His wife was becoming interested, too. She put in a few words, and William admitted, "The reason that we were pushing off giving up farming is that we really don't know what work we would want to do then." He grinned and added, "I thought you were like the other people. So many people had advice for me to stay on the farm awhile yet, but no one had help. They said I should get someone."

They talked awhile longer and then went out and looked in the barn. A few hours later, William said he and his wife must talk it over again, as they had fully decided to sell the cows and a buyer was interested in some of them. "But we haven't done any business yet. We have to talk it over, and we'll let you know in a few days or so." Before he left, Clayton gave his address and information on how to reach him through the shop phone.

By the time he got back to Aunt Sara's the five o'clock bus had left, so he had to wait for the seven o'clock bus. It was 8:30 till he got back to Alpheus's.

As soon as Israel was in the shop the next morning, Clayton went down and told him the purpose of yesterday's errand. Israel didn't say much. He asked a few questions and said he was surprised Clayton had helped in the shop this long, but he was glad he had helped to finish the fall orders. Israel mumbled something about seeking other pastures, and the folks in Kentucky would like his help, too.

A week later, on a Saturday afternoon, Clayton was washing his buggy when a car drove in. He was rather surprised to see William Nolt climb out of the passenger's side. That explained why no letter had come yet. The men stepped under the barn forebay to get out of the chilly, damp November wind.

Now it was Clayton's turn to think. William told him the buyer would have agreed to give up the deal on the cows, but he sensed it would make the buyer feel better if he kept his word. And some other guy was interested in the rest. William had decided to get rid of this herd and put in another herd for Clayton, and the cows would eventually become Clayton's cows. But the farming he was doing for him. William had said it would be easier for him to give up the milking if it weren't the cows he had milked all these years; otherwise I would be telling you how to do it. Clayton reminded William that he himself would likely at times have to milk, maybe over the weekend or so.

"Yes," William said, "I was hoping you'd give me some chances. I had expected that and that would be easier than stopping

142

all in one day." If Clayton wasn't interested, William would sell the cows and either rent out the land to a few neighbors or sell the farm.

Clayton thought he wanted time to think it over, but he knew that he wouldn't be able to say no to such a challenge. So the plans were made that by the first of the year Clayton would step in. First, he would milk for William until April, when Clayton would turn twenty. Then Clayton would start earning the cows.

After William left, Clayton's mind churned one way then another way until he almost felt lightheaded. There was one thing that Clayton didn't like to think about. That was, he would get separated from the young folks at Stoney Creek because the Nolt farm was twenty miles from here. The farm would be only about eleven or twelve miles from Naomi's home. Cedar Hollow and Elm Grove young folks ran together some, so he did know some of the young folks from being at Naomi's a few weekends.

Eli Jonas came to the barn after Clayton had finished washing his buggy. "Amanda says you shall eat supper with us. Israel will, too. You can get ready to go to the singing first, as supper's not quite ready yet." So Clayton got ready for Saturday evening. He had been afraid Alpheus and Ella Mae would detain him, but Alpheus wasn't in the house and he didn't see Ella Mae, so he wasn't held up. He thought he heard little Margaret in another room. He was off to Eli Jonas's home for supper.

Israel left soon after supper since he had to pick up Emily; her cousin in Cottage Hill was having a singing and they were going there.

Clayton started on his way; at the end of the lane a car was waiting to turn in. A customer at this hour? Well, at least Eli Jonas was there yet.

*   *   *   *

Clayton awoke suddenly, feeling as though he wasn't done sleeping yet. What had awakened him? Then he thought he heard his niece Margaret crying, which was strange as he had never heard her during the night. Maybe she was very sick. He heard Alpheus talking downstairs. He heard it again. No, it was not Margaret.

Then he remembered last evening. Eli Jonas had told him to come for supper, and no one was in the kitchen when he went through to get ready. Then he had heard Margaret in another room. Now he had a good idea of what had happened. That was **not** a shop customer he had met at the end of the lane! Relaxed, Clayton drifted off to another three hours of sleep.

The next morning Alpheus proudly introduced Clayton to baby Lucy. Dad's predictions for his grandchildren were way off. When Clayton was in Kentucky, he had seen Ephraim's little Hannah, and Naaman's had a little girl later in the summer.

Chapter Twenty

As Clayton came in the kitchen and washed up for supper, he saw Alpheus sitting in the rocker entertaining Margaret. Her eyes had a tell-tale sign of tears. Clayton had been afraid the family was waiting on him, as he was a little late. He had finished assembling the marble roller before he came in. Supper was still cooking. Since baby Lucy came on the scene, Ella Mae was a busy mother. The baby wasn't very content and Margaret, too, was unhappy at times.

Clayton sat back on the sofa and decided to read the letter he had stuck in his shirt pocket this afternoon. Alpheus had brought the pile of mail in the shop and sorted it. It was a little unusual that there was a letter for Clayton. He had recognized Naomi's handwriting and stuck it in his pocket till he had more time. Then he had forgotten about it until he saw the envelope in the mirror when he washed up for supper.

He unfolded the paper and read,

Dear Clayton, and all who read this,

We're sending you Christmas greetings to share the blessing we received a little early for Christmas in the form of a little boy yesterday, the twenty-first, with more hair than any of the rest had. More round-faced like his daddy. Clayton, I thought I'll let you know personally this time, so you find out for sure. Ha! We'll still be looking for you, but you don't need to be so surprised like you were with Joel.

John Irvin said we might even see a little more of you, if you are living a little closer. John Irvin said to tell you that we also could use a farm hand, if you had only asked, but guess that wouldn't have helped William Nolt's situation.

Oh, by the way, I was just as happy with another boy baby again, as I remember my happy childhood in our family with all these boys, and it seems just right to me. And when you stop and think, I have nearly as many sisters as brothers. And Mom has quite a row of daughters by now, which seem like sisters to me, so this isn't much difference. I think John Irvin was more disappointed as he was always so close to his sister Julianne, so I let him name the baby to his desire, the name he wanted for the other two boys. You know his dad is named Paul, and John Irvin went to school with a Paul Isaac who always had a special place in his heart, and he always desired to name a boy in his honor. I wasn't so fond of the combination, and thought we could call him Paul David after both fathers, or use Paul or Isaac with John or Irvin, but he says we can use that combination for the next boy! So he is Paul Isaac and by now I'm used to the name, hearing him talk of it so often.

By the way, we plan to have a hired boy this summer, as I see I won't be able to get out of the house, and the men might have to help me. Guess I didn't have enough brothers that we have to get other help. Well, guess we may ask for help, as if we live and stay well, it looks as if we may be able to have help for others. But right now, they are no help.

Just now Emory upset the little rocking chair with Joel on. The crying commotion made the baby cry, so I will help the boys look at a picture book so my maid can do her work.

While they were eating supper, Clayton laid the letter on the table and said, "Naomi has another little boy."

"Another boy?" Alpheus asked.

Ella Mae said wistfully, "I was hoping since we and Seranus and Naaman and Ephraim's all had girls this year, they could have a girl, too."

"The way Naomi wrote, it makes no difference to her. She says she has almost as many sisters as brothers, and Mom almost as many daughters as sons," Clayton said.

Alpheus chuckled, "I guess that's true. She must be hinting that she is waiting for a sister from you yet."

By now Ella Mae was reading the letter.

Clayton said, "I guess David Wenger's family had one too many boys."

Ella Mae said, "No, here Naomi writes she didn't have enough brothers; they must seek hired help elsewhere."

Alpheus took a drink from his glass and thoughtfully set it down. Pushing his chair away from the table and leaning back, he said, "Take courage. God is leading you to another field, remember."

Clayton said, "I hope you know that is the hard part for me, thinking of starting at William's. I would prefer to stay with the group of young folks here if that's what you're referring to."

Clayton saw Alpheus look over at Ella Mae, and Ella Mae looked knowingly at him, with a glow. Clayton had a feeling their eyes had exchanged a few sentences that he hadn't understood.

At length, Alpheus said, "If Ella Mae hadn't come over in another field to care for her uncle, I'd be frying my own eggs."

Ella Mae said, softly, "I'm glad you didn't say washing your own dishes. Since Lucy came, I don't know how my sink would look if you didn't wash them at times."

Alpheus grinned, "My mother used to say, 'Some day your wife will be glad that you learned to wash dishes and put the laundry on the line.'"

"I have been thankful that I have a mother-in-law who raised sons to be considerate of housework."

"Did you tell her already?" Alpheus teased.

"Maybe not in so many words," Ella Mae admitted.

Alpheus looked at the calendar and said, "Christmas would be a good time to do it."

Hearing Alpheus talk raised some dreams of years ago when Clayton had admired Lydia Ann. Clayton used to dream that Lydia Ann would be to him what Ella Mae was to Alpheus, but the dream had long since vanished, healed, and dissolved. Landis and Lydia Ann were married and Clayton was glad for them.

Barbara Ellen's cup of joy was filled and Clayton felt his cup was filled, too, but sometimes Clayton got a longing to share. He wanted to rejoice with someone who cared and understood him. But right now he was aware that he also had to be able to be patient and cheerful and helpful in all situations. *Could I be as thoughtful as Alpheus is when his wife is tired, busy, and late? How different it would be if Alpheus had become impatient and said a hasty word.*

At times Clayton had to marvel that Alpheus and Eli Jonas were really his brothers who had grown up with him. Somehow, it seemed that Ella Mae and Amanda brought the good out in them. He thought of what the Bible said, "Not the outward adorning, but the adorning be the hidden heart of man." It was sort of a mystery to him, he thought, as he went out in the shop later in the evening. He wondered if any good was still hidden in his heart. He doubted that was what the verse meant.

Chapter Twenty-One

It was a hot summer evening and Clayton wiped his brow with his handkerchief. The evening hour hadn't cooled off much, and the air seemed to hang heavy, somewhat hazy, as if a thunderstorm could come over the mountains. As he drove on down the road, Clayton saw quite a few fields where hay was still lying. Not everyone would be ready for rain. Two robins sat on the fence posts and were making melody to the evening hour. He heard a meadow lark calling somewhere overhead, and the song sparrows were chirping on the telephone wires above.

Further down the road, among a freshly mown hay field, a red-winged blackbird was proclaiming summer in a joyous manner. Clayton took more notice to birds since he was living at William's house. William had a few bird feeders around his house and one right outside the window where he could watch them closely. He talked much about birds and knew where a lot of birds were nesting. If a different bird came to the feeder, he checked his array of books to identify it.

Even today, while William was driving the baler and Clayton was stacking bales on the wagon, William had stopped a few minutes and gone over to the fence row to check an old, partly hollow tree where some birds were perched. He thought they might have a nest there, and he had never seen that bird's nest yet. He thought maybe he could find it.

Clayton himself had been eager to get the hay in, but he found that short break had given him a fresh boost. The handling of bales seemed easier again. In the distance, Clayton saw two birds flying high and fast, hurrying along. William saw them, too, and said, "They must have an appointment to meet or are going on a trip."

*   *   *   *

Clayton's misgivings last fall had all been groundless. He had thought that maybe time would get long for him when he left all his brothers and families to work for William Nolt in another settlement. But he found William and Mattie to be like a second set of parents. Quite often while working, like while he was milking cows, William called him Martin, the name of their son. Mattie had, too, at times, but not as often as William did. Once in a while, William called Clayton Walter, the Nolt's oldest daughter's husband. Clayton met the Nolt family and relations in May when their youngest daughter had married.

At times when Clayton worked up a field and asked about picking up stones the next day, William seemed rather amazed and would say, half to himself, "If only Martin would have taken such an interest in the farm." Sometimes Clayton would mention that he had noticed the meadow fence needed to be fixed. It seemed William had been used to telling his son Martin what had to be done next. Thus William had thought that as boys grow up, they don't have foresight.

William told Clayton many things he had been planning to do, and Clayton hadn't minded since he was working for William and expected him to make the plans. Sometimes he felt William and Mattie were staring at him unknowingly, and then William would mutter to himself, "To think that Martin could have done this, too!" Clayton realized that they were grieving over their son. *My presence makes them more aware of Martin. He must have taken no interest in farming.*

Clayton had been considering staying at home tonight after handling hay bales most of the day. He was quite tired by the time he did chores, but William offered to start the milking if Clayton wanted to unload the rest of the hay, and Mattie had fed the calves.

Mattie took such an interest in the calves, even though they weren't their herd anymore. She also took an interest in which cow freshened and how the calf looked. If it was one that didn't want to

150

drink out of a pail, Mattie would soon persuade it to. And William also showed interest in the cows. When the vet was there this morning, he asked if he had looked at No. 16's foot and wondered if it's better. And this evening William wondered if No. 23 was eating better. When he asked about starting to milk, he wondered if Clayton is drying up No. 29 by now. It was handy that the Nolts had such an interest yet, as that way when Clayton asked them to milk, he didn't have to leave many instructions.

William had offered to rinse the milkers for him tonight and finish in the milk house. Clayton said he didn't have to as he planned on staying home tonight. But William would hear nothing of it.

"No, no," he said, "the young folks are looking for you. We don't want this job to separate you from the young folks. Maybe tonight is the time you have been waiting on," he had said with a twinkle in his eyes.

Clayton had to smile at the man's concern and said, "I'm satisfied with Mattie's cooking."

"No, no," William would say, "God said that it is not good for man to be alone. God still has a plan for you."

Clayton smiled again at the frequent times that William would encourage him in that direction. He felt he was far from alone, but William said he and Mattie would not always be here.

Clayton had found the ride over to the singing school tonight very relaxing. After six months, the group seemed like old friends. They had some talented singers. When the singing school teacher had asked the song leaders to take a turn to lead a song or two, Clayton's name was called, too. When the singing was over, Clayton found that in a sense the evening had relaxed him as much as sleep would have.

As for becoming interested in the girls, well, the ones that started joining the young folks seemed so young and vain. Most of the more mature ones were spoken for, but there were some like Sara, Verna, and Anna.

On the way home, Clayton thought how once in a while he had found himself taking a second look at Sara. She was an interesting person and certainly not vain. He had once, a few weeks ago,

151

sort of purposely gotten a chance to pick her up at her home and take her to the supper place and home again. He had enjoyed it.

Clayton, on the sly, had watched Sara closely since, and she didn't show any evidence that she had an interest in him since then, but Clayton knew she wouldn't show it either.

His experience with Barbara Ellen kept Clayton from giving things further thought. He wasn't about to hurt another girl. He prayed that God would lead him to what his will was. It was at the singing before that Sunday, that Aaron Junior was lamenting his troubles about having to pick up Edna and coming down for Sara, then go to Lloyd's for supper that next evening.

Clayton had said, "Well, I can pick up Sara if that helps you any."

Aaron Junior said, "And so it shall be."

But now he had Aaron Junior on his back. He was finding more excuses to have a need for Clayton to go after Sara. But Sara most often had a way with her cousin who lived not too far away. It was just that weekend that he had other plans. To get rid of Aaron Junior when he was begging him to let him ask Sara if Clayton can take her along tomorrow, Clayton said, "Sara can ask if she needs a way to go."

As Clayton got nearer home, he saw the lightning in the distance was moving closer. The whole sky in one split second would light up brighter than day, then become dark again. Then the thunder got louder.

When he reached the Nolt farm and unhitched, he half expected William and Mattie to be out on the porch watching the approaching storms. They always sat on the porch watching a thunderstorm, and Clayton had learned to see the beauty in it. He had never really studied a thunderstorm so much or watched "His power throughout the universe display, but sings my soul my Savior God to thee. How great Thou art, how great Thou art!"

Clayton sat on the porch glider awhile to watch the storm's arrival, but it traveled on around the north. At least the air was a bit cooler now.

Chapter Twenty-Two

Clayton pushed back his chair, still biting his toothpick and digesting his breakfast. William, as usual, had read a chapter from the Bible at the table for all to meditate on God's Word before continuing the day. William now picked up the Bible and was reading to himself.

Clayton was thinking he himself should turn out the cows; the vet was coming for one of the cows. He had to leave her in the barn, and he should move the older calves out of the hutch in the bigger pen so he could put the little ones in the hutch that he just had in the barn alley. There seemed to be an endless amount of things to do.

Clayton asked, "William, do you want me to plow down the oat stubble so we can get it ready to seed, or do you think since it's so nice we should cut the north hay field for a second crop?"

William looked up and considered it in silence, then he laid down the Bible and absentmindedly played with his spoon and fork on his plate and wiped his hand across his face, saying, "I don't know, maybe we should finish the barn chores and go over to Menno's. I know work here is waiting, but we have our health to do it and nothing to keep us up."

Clayton had momentarily forgotten about Menno. He had been over one day to help tear down the rest of the big shed after a twister had torn or wrecked it almost together. William had been over a few times.

"Do they have the lumber to rebuild?" Clayton asked.

"I don't know, but I'm sure they have farm work that has been pushed aside."

Menno had been having pretty much trouble with his back for quite a while, and then the twister had destroyed his shed. Clayton

153

had been so busy with the farming that he hadn't given much thought that they should help at Menno's again. But it was true; Menno had a lot of work.

Clayton and William hurried through the barn chores so they could go help Menno. Clayton had told Mattie what to tell the vet, and he promised that he would change the calves around tonight.

*   *   *   *

There were about a dozen men and boys working on the shed when Clayton got there. He and William had come separately so William could go home at noon for Mattie's dentist appointment. A few teams were pulling in, and later a van also arrived with men climbing out and tying on carpenter aprons. Word had been sent around that they were now ready for workers.

Clayton asked Menno if he wanted everyone working on the shed or if there was something else that should be done. Menno said, "There was some hay raked and a lot more needs to be raked yet. I don't know if the weather will hold if we let it go till tomorrow. Maybe if the people are here, we should get the shed under way."

Clayton said, "Well, with all the people, we'll try to get the hay in, too."

So with Menno's supervision, Clayton got the team of horses harnessed and hitched them to the rake and headed for the hay field. He was out less than half an hour before another team of horses and hay rake joined them. Someone had brought the neighbor's team to rake.

It was a warm day. At times Clayton left the horses rest a little. It wouldn't be long till this hay should be ready to start baling. It was warm, but there wasn't much of a breeze.

Sometime later a man brought the baler and wagon out. Clayton tied his team to a shade tree and helped bale hay while the other team was still raking. Clayton couldn't begin to imagine how it would be to have so much work and not be able to help do it. Menno couldn't help much as his back was giving him a lot of trouble. When the wagons were full, Clayton unhitched his team from the rake, took the wagon to the barn, and helped unload when they got in.

Later, when they had filled it up again and brought the two in, he unloaded the one and drove up further to unload the other one. The team of horses were about up to the yard. He heard water running and looked up as he was unhitching.

There on the other side of the yard fence a young woman stood at the pump filling pails of water. She looked up at the sound of horses snorting. Clayton's face and shirt were wet with sweat and so were the horses. Taking it all in at a glance, the maiden asked, "Do you want a drink?"

"Nothing would taste better than cold well water."

She filled a big tin cup and handed it over the fence to Clayton. As he drank, he felt the water refresh his dry body. "Thank you," he said, giving the cup back

The woman filled Clayton's cup again without asking and handed it back, saying, "I guess we forgot to treat the men in the fields."

Clayton tipped the cup and said, "That's enough. I don't want to spoil my dinner." He reached for the horses as they were pulling away.

Seeing that the horses were leaning toward the water, the young woman asked, "Shall I also pump for your camels?" The horses had stepped over to a little trough that was on the outside of the fence.

Clayton hadn't noticed the trough before. He stood watching the horses as the woman pumped willingly. After the horses had enough to refresh them, Clayton tugged at the harness to lead them away. He looked at the woman who was still pumping and asked, "Are you Rebekah?"

She stopped pumping and looked at him, puzzled. Then her complexion took on more color as she lowered her eyes and said, "No."

As he led the horses away, Clayton said, "Neither am I Abraham's servant." Clayton dared not look back as he turned the horses around to lead them to the trough near the barn. He regretted his comment as soon as he had said it. He likely had humiliated her, but hadn't she called his horses camels? Maybe when they were right in front of her, the horses had looked so big that she thought of camels or because they looked as though they had been working hard.

The woman hadn't said who she was, just that she wasn't Rebekah, Clayton mused as he waited for the horses to finish their drink at the water trough. Then he fed them a little since there was more work to do in the afternoon.

Minutes later Clayton followed the rest of the men and boys through the barnyard past the yard fence and pump, on into the backyard. There the women had set up a table for the men to file by and fill their plates, like a regular barn raising. Clayton saw that no one was at the pump, only a big pail full of washed red beets.

Clayton filled his plate and sat with some men in the yard eating chicken corn soup, red beet eggs, cheese, pretzel sticks, and drinking cold lemonade. He kept glancing to the table where the women and girls were refilling the dishes, but he didn't see who he was watching for. Soon Clarence, a boy from Cedar Hollow, came and sat down beside him and began a conversation.

Later Clayton went back to the table to get his serving of dessert. Mentally he was thinking of what Clarence had told him, of the horse he had bought recently and the time he was having of breaking him to make him road sound. He bought him as broken, ready to drive, but he had given Clarence a few surprises, since he wasn't aware of the horse's sudden spurts of shying. On the way home Sunday evening, Clarence had said the new horse had taken a corner too short and then shied, and in the end, dumped the buggy. Clarence was going to give him a few more chances since he was a nice-sized horse, but he wasn't to be trusted. His main problem was stopping at stop signs. When he was supposed to go again, he horse would start acting up.

Clayton was deep in thought, imagining what he would try to do if it was his horse. He took a piece of cake and set a little dish of dessert on his plate. His sixth sense alerted him, and his eyes lifted without Clayton being aware of it. He looked up and his eyes met a girl coming up the walk with a pitcher of milk. She must have come from the milk house. The moment Clayton looked up, she wasn't looking anymore. Her glance had dropped suddenly and she passed in through the door to the house. Clayton realized then that he must have been watched and that is what made him look up.

Now he remembered—that was the face he had seen by the pump! Something went through him, a feeling he never remembered having before. Walking away from the table, he met Menno, who asked him how the hay was and how far along they are. Menno thanked him for seeing that the hay gets made.

After exchanging the information, Clayton asked Menno who all these people are that are here today. "Oh," Menno said, looking around, "the ones not from this settlement are mostly our relatives, but not all. In a time like this you find out how many friends you have," Menno added with misty eyes. Another man walked up to them and started asking Menno something. The people were slowly thinning out and going back to work.

Clayton went back to the hay field where he found very little time to think of the past happenings. At times he stayed out to bale, and a few times he had come in to help unload.

About mid-afternoon a group of girls came out to the field with a water jug. That's when Clayton remembered the refreshing drink in the forenoon. But this was a group of school-age girls. He wondered who remembered to bring a refreshing drink to the men in the fields; hardly the school-age children.

In the late afternoon as Clayton and Huckaberry traveled back to William's, Clayton left his mind wander. The appearance of the young lady at the pump kept coming to his mind. She had a shining, glowing, radiant face. As he kept replaying the scene in his mind, he was almost startled to realize he was picturing her somewhat like an angel, so to speak. The word beauty came to his mind. Then he tried to think what was so beautiful about her.

He couldn't even remember what color hair she had or how they were combed. He couldn't picture any charming waves or array. What, then, had attracted him? Her dress? He had no idea what color dress she had on. Was it her eyes? Neither could he think what color her eyes were, but then how could he picture her? As a beautiful gleaming face. That's maybe why the word angel came to his mind because he couldn't really picture her in a natural sense.

But if he didn't know how she looked, how did he know that she had been looking at him when he was getting dessert? He couldn't describe it. The word beauty kept coming to his mind; then he remembered what Dad had said about meeting Mother. "By the time the weddings were over, he realized that Lydia had—" What word did he use? Whatever he had said, that was the word Clayton felt about this young woman. But what was the word?

Trying to remember what Dad had said, Clayton thought of the verse; was it I Peter, Chapter two or three, about adorning and plaiting of hair? But this woman didn't adorn herself with plaiting of hair, or hanging on gold, or putting on apparel, or he would have remembered her dress. Or her hair style.

Now he remembered what Dad had said, something about by that time he had realized Lydia's adorning was not of plaiting of hair or wearing of apparel, but the adorning was in the hidden heart of man.

Clayton had seen very little of the young woman and did not know if she was kind, true, or filled with peace and long-suffering, joy, gentleness, meekness, godliness, faith—and all that Galatians says about the fruit of the Spirit. But wouldn't it have shown through in her dress and hair style if she was of outward adorning?

The word beauty came to his mind again. Then something in his mind said, *Beauty is deceitful and oh, something else was vain. Or did it say beauty is vain and, oh*, he couldn't think what it said was deceitful. *Did it say beauty is vain?*

He kept churning it over in his mind, and his heart said further, as his mind listened, *But one that loves the Lord shall be praised.* Now what was that? Did that belong together or was that just another verse that came to his mind? Clayton wondered as he arrived at William's house and unhitched.

William's family was waiting on him for supper, he discovered when he came in the kitchen. William asked if they got the hay in. "Pretty much of it. We only had one breakdown, but even so, I don't think we would have gotten finished."

While visiting at the supper table, Clayton asked who all the people were at Menno's.

"Oh, well, I don't know who you didn't know. There were some of Menno's relatives and maybe some of his wife's. I really didn't take time to think where they all belong."

"I couldn't tell for sure which settlement the van came from," Clayton pressed further.

"From what I heard," William said, "they started off from West View. That's where Menno's brother Stephen is from, and then they met another van at Cloverdale and came with them."

As Clayton went out to the barn, he realized he didn't know more than he had before. He didn't even know if the young woman had come with the van.

That evening, Clayton went up to his room, sat on the chair, and was deep in thought for better than a half hour. Then he reached for his Bible to look up a verse. He checked the concordance to see if "beauty" was there. He didn't know if that was the main word of the verse.

Oh yes, here is "beauty" and it says, "Beauty is vain," Proverbs 31, verse 30. He paged through till he found the right chapter; it was the chapter on the virtuous woman. The second to last verse read, "Favour is deceitful, and beauty is vain; but a woman that feareth the Lord, she shall be praised."

Glancing to the next page, he saw the German version: *"Lieblich und schon sein ist nichts, ein vieb, Dad den herrn furchted soll man loben."* His eye caught the last verse, "Give her of the fruit of her hands; and let her own works praise her in the gates." The young woman at the pump had done good work, worthy of praise. She had refreshed both him and his horses—or camels?—in the gates of the yard fence. If she had not been one whose "work is to be praised," she wouldn't have been willing to pump water for the horses since they could drink it in the barn.

Maybe it was because I was so thirsty and the water so refreshing that I had just imagined all the beauty of her being.

Clayton fell to his knees by the chair and poured his heart out to God, but words didn't come easily. At length, after making different attempts and not being able to express himself, he gave himself up and said, *"Herr Gott, des ist der alles bekannt."* Meaning, "Lord God, this is all known to you. Make of it what you will and lead me so that I choose the way that you prepared for me. And I ask thee, Lord, give me patience to wait on thee. You know what we need before we pray, and I ask that you do not lead me to something just because I desire it, if it leads to my downfall. Rather, help me overcome my desire that I can say 'not my will, but thine be done.' I believe, but God help my unbelief."

As Clayton crawled under the cover, the words were singing in his mind, "To thee I leave the rest."

He didn't have any "puzzle" pieces. Yes, he had one piece, but no border to begin and no other pieces to fit it into.

In the morning when Clayton awoke, his thoughts came rushing back to him and he weighed them again. He was thinking about "Rebekah at the well." Then he got up and found the reference for that in the Bible. It touched him deeply as he read. He sat for a long time. Then a new thought entered his mind. Maybe it was Rachel, but he wasn't Jacob.

He knelt and asked the Lord for strength to meet the needs of the day and guidance for the day, and pleading for a submissive heart, to say "not my will, but thy will be done." Again, he pled "not for things for the pleasure of my desire that would lead to a downfall, but help in overcoming if it is not thy will."

As he went out to the barn that morning, Clayton found himself singing. He listened to the words and was surprised to hear his lips singing, "Have thine own way, Lord. Have thine own way." That was better than what he had been trying to put into words.

Chapter Twenty-Three

The day had come. The entire Wenger clan was invited to the Aaron Rissler home where the whole Rissler family was present. But Dad Wenger had to miss it since he wasn't able to undertake the trip from Kentucky. He had spent a few days in the hospital recently during which there had been some anxious moments. One didn't know if plans of the wedding should continue.

It would be so much more complete if Dad could be here, Clayton thought as he saw the empty place beside Mother, seated in front of the bride and bridegroom. Yes, today the Wengers and Risslers were united, but they would separate again, or would they? *Not all,* Clayton reminded himself as Israel and Emily filed in and took the chairs awaiting them. *Only Israel would now be united with the Rissler family, or would we all?* Clayton was almost surprised at the thought. Emily would now be his sister-in-law.

During the forenoon sermon, Clayton's thoughts were turned to more spiritual values, and the popularity of the Risslers' reputation vanished without his realizing. The sermon brought out that there is no respect of persons, and salvation is open to all. God does not want any man to perish, but he wants all to come to everlasting life. The sermon focused on how we choose our treasures. Do we seek treasures in measures of money? Is our first concern earthly goals? If we want God for our father, we will seek heavenly treasures. For where your treasure is, there is your heart also.

"The five foolish virgins had no oil, so they asked for some oil from the five wise ones, but they had no extra. The foolish had to go buy some. They had too many earthly treasures, or they would have thought to have enough oil. And the five wise didn't have any to spare.

"So it is in our life; we have nothing to spare if we did all that we knew, and still can't stop or boast, or give our faith to someone else. We must still say we are unprofitable servants. We only did what was our calling.

"God said it is not good that man is alone. He made a helpmate. He took a rib from the man's side to build a wife. He didn't take it from the head that he would be a ruler over his wife. Nor from his foot that he would trample her. But from the side, close to the man's heart, that they would work side by side. A helpmate, one for the other, but the man shall be head of the house as Christ is the head of the church.

"There are different examples of seeking a partner, but the most important step is still "in the Lord." The Bible says that it would be better to live in the rafters of the roof than to live with an angry wife, or maybe it says nagging. Lots of nagging is like when a roof leaks. You hear the drops dripping in a pail. It's not a loud noise, but if it continues on and on, it can get rather annoying. It can get the best of you. So it is with a woman. Even if she isn't angry, but just nagging continuously about things, demanding this, nagging about that; it can get weary to the bones. A little appreciation goes a long way in keeping that out of marriage.

"I still feel it is good for the wife to be a homemaker. So many women in today's world take a job outside the home. When they get home, they are tired and there are many things to do since no one was at home keeping house. Soon angry words get exchanged as the helpmate is not there to listen or help. She has no time since she was working away all day. Soon a word is snapped and is followed by other angry words. It is not how God planned it.

"God meant to make a helpmate for a man, to stand by him. The man leaves his father and mother and cleaves to his wife. It does not mean that he shall not have any respect for his parents anymore. The new couple can still take advice from the parents, but the parents can also be a hindrance if they come between man and wife. They can also be a good help in some situations.

"One woman had been married for a while, and by this time some of her husband's shortcomings had come to the surface. Short-

162

comings will show up once people are married; it won't be only the 'Sunday side.' This woman went home to her mother and complained of her husband's shortcomings.

"The mother said, 'You have a good husband.' The daughter complained more, but her mother always said, 'You have a good husband.'

"And so it continued. Now if the mother had sympathized and said, 'Yes, that's how that family is,' or, 'well, you must just make yourself boss,' and taken the daughter's part, more fuel would have been added. It could have been a seed that would have grown a weed and bloomed in a divorce.

"So the advice of parents can still be needed at times.

"We are to seek the good in people, not the evil. Forgive others their trespasses as we forgive those who trespass against us, but I failed to point out the most important thing. How do we find the helpmate that God made for us?

"The first step is in the Sermon on the Mount: 'Ask and it shall be given to you. Seek and ye shall find. Knock and it shall be opened unto you.' Where shall we seek? If we seek where there is much outward adorning or hanging on of gold or outward appearance; if we ask in the world; if we knock on the worldly possibilities, then we shall find the world.

"We need to ask God. We want to seek for inward adorning, the hidden man of the heart which is by God a great price. We want to knock on God's door. We want to find his treasure. A married life can be the most beautiful on earth, but not if love goes out of the hearts and hatred enters in."

Many pleadings, admonishments, and warnings continued to fall on the listening ears. It was stressed further. "It won't affect just the brother and sister who are making their vows today. They will not be starting a home, and if it is according to God's will, their Christian home will affect others. They will be a help to the church, to the community, where the poor will be helped and the hungry filled and the stranger accommodated.

"There is much written in Proverbs on what a virtuous woman is. Her candle does not go out by night. She makes clothes for her

163

family, and thus she is not afraid of snow for her household is clothed. The heart of her husband trusteth her. She stretches her hand to the poor. Proverbs 31 doesn't say that she spends a lot of time making pretty clothes.

"It says strength and honor are her cloth, and her husband is known within the gates. According to that, her husband is ready to help others if he is known to the people. If he would just live for himself and his wife, the other people wouldn't know him. She openeth her mouth with wisdom; that means she knows when to speak and what to speak. A wrong word at the wrong time can stir up much conflict, and a good word at the right time can be a great help.

"Love covers a multitude of sins, but I don't want to take up all the time of reading about the virtuous woman. You can read it yourself, but it says her children shall rise up and call her blessed. That is such a blessing if a mother has the respect of her children. And her husband also, and he praises her. A good marriage goes a long way in having the children respect Mother and Father, and if the father respects the mother and the mother, the father, the children usually have respect, too. I want to read some yet as a text to the wedding ceremony."

More admonishings were brought forth, about the husband being the head of the house, but how divorce can come forth if the man is too hardnecked and unforgiving. As the bishop went on explaining, Clayton's mind was still dwelling on the words which the bishop had said about a virtuous woman, what all she does, and how the man is known in the gates, because he helps others. And thus he will be known and how the couple can be a help to the neighborhood, the church, etc.

Clayton found that instead of picturing Barbara Ellen or Lydia or any such girl, he had been picturing William and Mattie Nolt, who made themselves helpful to the neighborhood. Many times Clayton thought they had a lot of work planned for the day, then William thought of someone who needed help. This and other examples had taught Clayton, and he respected William highly.

Now as Clayton listened to the bishop's words, a new thought occurred to him. Is Mattie, a virtuous wife, the one who brings out

164

the good in William? Well, he didn't know if she gets the credit, but on the other hand, if Mattie was a demanding wife and said, "No, today I want so-and-so done; you have helped them enough already," then, of course, William couldn't be such a blessing to the neighborhood.

Clayton woke from his thoughts as Bishop Paul asked the bridegroom and the bride to come forward. Clayton caught himself thinking that Emily perhaps should have brought a little foot bench along. Israel stood at least a head taller, but the bishop had no trouble tying the knot.

It wasn't until the family was seated around the dinner table that Clayton realized the truth: he was the only person without a partner. As he looked around the table, he was aware that all of his brothers had their companions along. Yes, Enos and Noah David had Dorcas and Lucy along. In fact, Enos and Dorcas sat by Israel and Emily's side in the forenoon as witnesses.

Clayton thought he must surely look odd with the family— no friend, eating with his left hand, and his hair combed to the opposite side as that of his brothers. But he remembered that at his age Israel hadn't had Emily either. His train of thought was soon derailed. Naomi and John Irvin, across the table from him, had started visiting, and Seranus and Muriel also joined in, so at heart Clayton still felt he was one of the family even if he appeared different.

Chapter Twenty-Four

The woods seemed silent, deep, and dark on this late December day. Only a few birds sang hurried songs, and a squirrel ran through the dead leaves and scampered up a tree as Clayton entered the bush area between William's northeast fields and the west fields of neighbor Lloyd. The wide fence rows had lots of stones gathered off the fields over the years.

For a moment, Clayton stood looking at the big tree that lay sprawled on the ground. A few branches of other trees had broken off when the tree fell against some smaller trees. Clayton looked at the space where the tree had stood and noticed another maple tree, standing straight and tall, stood there right next to it. By the length of the one that lay on the ground, Clayton thought the trees must have been about the same size. He wondered if perhaps they had grown side by side for many years. Maybe they had been planted together and had weathered many storms together.

In early fall when Clayton came back here for a stroll, he hadn't noticed any dead trees. The big tree must have brought forth leaves this summer, but now that it lay broken off at the trunk, he could see that some of it had been losing life on the inside for a while.

As he started sawing the tree, Clayton's thoughts went back to when he was sixteen years old and was cutting a tree with his Doddy Wenger. He had compared the life of a tree to the life of a man. Today, as Clayton worked and saw the remaining maple tree stand, his thoughts went to a few months ago when Emily and Israel had married. They were planted together side by side as these two trees probably were, to stand by, shelter, and protect each other in storms of life until death doth part.

He wondered if he was to live as a tree standing alone, taking the full force of the storms. No side tree to shelter the storms or help weep in damp autumn when the leaves came sweeping down. No side tree to stand by in the spring when the birds gather on the branches and sing spring melodies from the treetops, and the frolicking spring winds sing merrily through the leaves.

A few times he had thought a tree was planted by his side, but they had not grown. Lydia Ann and Barbara Ellen were not meant to grow by his side. They were planted in other ground where they would grow.

Clayton's thoughts went back to September when he had gone to Menno's and met the young woman at the pump. It had left quite an impression on him. William was constantly reminding him about his concern of Clayton's seeking a helpmate, since he and Mattie were getting older and might soon not be able to help as much. So there was a need to seek a companion so that there would be more help. "A man alone on a farm isn't worth much," William would say.

Now and then William would try to open the subject to Clayton, but Clayton didn't give satisfactory answers. Some weeks ago while they had been cleaning manure out of the heifer pen, William asked Clayton if he had been around unhappy marriages, since he doesn't seek a companion. "Do you have a fear of something that maybe you should discuss with someone? Clayton had smiled at his concern and had told William that up to this time, things had not worked out, and he is praying for God's will to be done, but he wasn't always patient.

A few weeks after the gathering at Menno's, Clayton had spent one weekend visiting Cloverdale and one weekend at West View settlements. He realized that even though he prayed, he couldn't just sit on the nest. Even if God promised to care for the birds, they still had to go out and hunt food. So he thought if it was God's will, he might be able to meet the woman he had seen at Menno's. But both times he came home disappointed.

He had enjoyed the gathering and had made new friends, but his plans had not been fulfilled. In fact, he had gone to West View twice. He wasn't even sure if he would recognize the woman, but the memory of the day he had met her had since failed to give him any interest in other girls.

As the days wore on, Clayton found himself thinking of the incident at Menno's more as a dream; it was becoming dim in his memory. He began to wonder if it had really been so, or if was his imagination. Would he lose the value of his dream? If someone had told him at age sixteen how it would be at age twenty, going on twenty-one, he wouldn't have believed it. Dreams vanished about as fast as the years did.

Clayton's spirit lifted as a sparrow perched high on a treetop nearby sang an assuring, trusting song, even though it was alone among dead trees. Well, these trees weren't dead, but they appeared so since they were barren of leaves, and a dreary, chilly air surrounded the bush. Clayton's courage was lifted by the faithful bird, and he started swinging the ax faster and was soon singing. "Have thine own way, Lord, have thine own way. Thou art the potter, I am the clay. Mold me and make me after thy will—"

There was a rustling through the undergrowth in the bush. When it continued, Clayton looked around. Maybe a deer was coming. Surely no bear. As he looked around, his mouth fell open in disbelief. His brother Israel was walking toward him! Clayton was stunned and couldn't utter a word.

Israel walked up nearer before talking, as if he was weighing a message and wanted to say it right. When Israel looked at him, Clayton knew there was something wrong.

"It's Dad," Israel said.

Clayton suddenly felt weak and asked, "I thought he was better again."

"Yes," Israel said. "After our wedding he was better and was wishing he had come. He was helping a little more with small things at Ephraim's. In fact, the other day he had a good day and even hitched up the horse and went to town alone. But this morning he fell on slippery snow and no one was with him, and he overdid himself trying to get up. Mother found him and went to Ephraim's for help. His heart pill didn't help anymore, and he refused to go to the hospital. He only lived for one hour."

"Israel," Clayton gasped, "you don't mean it's over?!"

Israel wiped his nose with a handkerchief and said, "Dad said he was so tired and said, 'Please don't put me in the hospital. I want to sleep. Please let me sleep.' He died before the doctor came."

Clayton was frozen to the ground with grips of shock.

"They are having the funeral out there and bringing the body to Pennsylvania for a funeral and burial here. Dad said he wanted to be buried in Pennsylvania because probably Mother will want to move to Pennsylvania again. The funeral is on Tuesday at Alpheus's and then at church. Further plans at this time are unsure."

Clayton didn't remember all that Israel had said. He left as suddenly as he had come. Clayton hadn't even asked how he was traveling. After Israel left, the tears came. It just couldn't be! Dad had been low now and then, but he had always pulled through. To Clayton it seemed part of himself had died. After all, he was flesh and blood of Dad. The advice and admonishing Dad had given him were always based on Scripture. How could he go on without that source?

Clayton tried to pray, but only tears came. Dabbing the tears with his handkerchief and blowing his nose, Clayton saw the fallen tree before him. So like Dad—he had sheltered many a storm and wind but had crumbled from a weak body. Then he noticed the other maple tree standing true and faithful. Yes, Mother would have to stand and continue on after the many years that they had stood together.

Words of a song went through Clayton's mind. "Does Jesus care when I've said good-bye to the dearest on earth to me?" Who was nearer to him on earth than Dad? Clayton had also talked things over with Mother, but for a serious matter Mother would send him to Dad for a heart-to-heart talk. Fresh tears came again as a longing engulfed him. *Couldn't it have been me instead, for Dad could have done much good yet in helping to raise the family? And what has earth to bind me here?* He knew he must not let such thoughts come. Satan would try to get him discouraged. For many times the ministers said that we all have a purpose in being here. If we had no purpose, we wouldn't be here anymore. If God's purpose is fulfilled, he calls us home to rest.

Clayton started walking back to the buildings. He couldn't stay here; he was too alone. He wanted to go where he could talk with William or Mattie. William probably was waiting on him since Israel surely had told him the news.

How grateful Clayton was for William's support. William could give Clayton sympathy without feeling his self pity.

When Mother came to Pennsylvania, Clayton soon realized that they had to be strong for her sake. When he realized Mother's sorrow, he began doubting the urge he had at times to have a life companion to love and confide in and stand by and be understood. Clayton realized that Mother and Dad had been one, and now half of Mother had died. He thought maybe it would be better to go alone through life than to one day endure such grief.

Time had no meaning for a few days. On the day of the funeral, so much comfort and sympathy came forth that Clayton thought he could see his way to continue on and trust, but he found that as the days passed, his heart was hurting and hungry again. He needed strength to continue. If only life would not have to go on. But William was wise and told Clayton to come back to work two days after the funeral. William knew that Clayton would need to keep occupied.

There seemed to be one bright spot in the whole matter of changed plans. Mother was nearer home again. Many plans had been discussed, changed, rebuilt, cast aside, and reconsidered, and most of January had passed until Alpheus and his family moved on a farm nearer to Ella Mae's parents. Yes, almost to the Ohio line, and Eli Jonas and Amanda moved in the farmhouse, and Israel and Emily in the main part of his new house. Mother was now living in the basement kitchen with a bedroom and living room as hers.

Enos and Noah David returned to Kentucky. Noah David was working for the same people, and Enos was hired out to someone out there. Naaman's and Ephraim's had sent up Mother's belongings. Nothing much was said of the house Mother and Father had left empty. Clayton supposed Enos might be needing it soon. First Eli Jonas and Amanda had planned to move out there, but Israel said he had to have Eli Jonas in the shop, so he would do the farming with Seranus's help and work in the shop when he could. Likely Mother would help in the shop once she learned a little bit about it.

As Clayton opened the kitchen door to go to the barn, the damp February air sent a blast of sleet in his face as a morning welcome. His depression deepened. Life seemed cruel. He had forced himself out of bed this morning. The winter seemed unending.

When Clayton got to the barn, the cows all knowingly looked at him and begged for their morning meal. Stanchion No. 25 was empty. Clayton opened the door leading to the other part of the barn that had box stalls. There lay cow No. 25, looking sicker than she had last evening. He would have to treat her again for milk fever. Clayton wanted to do nothing more than crawl back in bed and let the February wind howl and moan, but, no, that wouldn't do. He would only sleep a few hours, then he would lie awake and think too much. He treated the cow and fed the other cows, then started milking.

Mattie came out to feed the calves using pails. She said William still had some backache. William hadn't helped with the chores for two days, and Clayton had missed him. The workload loomed before him. But today was Sunday and there were only the regular chores. When Mattie brought the calf pails back, she said, "Sandy doesn't want to drink." The calf had had fever for a few days already, so Clayton went to check her.

By the time Clayton went to the house, he didn't know if he was beginning to get sick, or if discouragement was overwhelming him. The bacon and egg smell didn't make his mouth water like it usually did. He played around with the egg and bread, trying to get it down. He didn't know one could cut bread into so many pieces.

Although William had backache, he still was cheerful at heart and carried on a conversation. William gave him a few long looks when Clayton's answers came in a few short words. Clayton felt as if a load was pressing down upon him. He had looked forward to having his sorrow lighten as days changed into weeks, and weeks into months. But it seemed the pressure was increasing by the day.

171

Clayton considered going back to bed, but William advised him to do otherwise. He wondered if he had any plans with the young folks. If not, maybe he could take them to church, as he didn't feel like taking the team alone with his aching back. So as a favor to William, Clayton hitched up and took the family to church when otherwise he would have stayed home. The ride to church had lifted his spirits some already, as he had no time to dwell on discouragement.

In the morning as the congregation sang, Clayton's heart was touched as they sang,

Ach, Gott! Erhor mein seufzen und verklagen, lasz mich in meiner nobt nicht gar ferzagen, Du veiszt mein schmerz, Erkennst mein herz, Hast du mirs auferlegt so hilf mirs tragen.

Tears of pity dampened his eyes. Clayton didn't want to be reminded. "Let me in my need not faint altogether," but the last two lines were a new thought to him, as if he was talking to God, saying, "If you laid it on me, then help me carry it."

The next verse said,

Du kanst ferfluchen und auch veider segnen, Ich bin dein kind und habs ferdeint, Gieb vormen sonnerschein noch truben regen.

He found himself praying the words with the writer, "You can condemn, but bless again, I am your child, I earned it, give warm sunshine after the dreary rain." The words tasted better than the bacon and eggs did at the table.

The third verse continued,

Planz nur geduld durch dein geist, in mein herze, und hilf dasz ich es aucht fur keine scherze.

That's what Clayton needed, patience or submission.

The admonishing continued,

*Ich veisz, du hast nochmeinern nich fergessen, Dasz
ich fer leid sallt mein herz abfressen.*

It was hard to believe or agree when it said, "I know you have not forgotten me."

The next verse was the most encouraging yet, saying,

*Es hat kein unglicht mie so long gevahret, Es hat doch
endlict viede auf geharet. Beut mir die hand, und
mochs ein end.*

Clayton read it again. No ill luck has yet so long continued, but it always comes to an end, so hold my hand, and make it an end.

Later when the minister was speaking, he explained the verse, *"Es hat kein unglicht mie so long gevachet, es hat doch endlich vieder augehoret."* Then he went on to explain that the king was assigned to write a sentence to encourage the depressed and bring down the exalted, that they wouldn't be so proud. The same sentence was to be an admonishment for the two opposites. He had three days' time to write it or he would lose his office. He worked hard. The days passed, and on the third day he came up with a sentence and it passed trial. His message was, "This too shall pass away," so when we are feeling low in sorrow and heavy burdens, we must remember that this too shall pass away. If we feel lighthearted or good after receiving praise, we must remember that this too shall pass away. Like a song writer wrote, "No ill luck has so long continued, but it always comes to an end."

After his heart was softened, more words of encouragement and admonishment were received. In singing the last song, it seemed whoever had chosen the song must have known the submission that had taken place in his heart the past few hours.

*Ein herz, sez zurfrieden, betriebe nicht. Gedenk dosz
zum bestern dir alles geschichkt vann dir vas begegnet*

als ungluck regnet, Bald kommt die sonne mit
frohlichem schein, mein sez nur zufrieden dein trauen
ein stell ein.

"Oh heart, be content, trouble ye not, think you receive the best, if get this. If it rains ill luck so soon, the warm sun shines again. Then mine, be satisfied put on your trust."

The next verse revealed the same comfort,

Ver recht fergneset, dem gar nichts gelricht, ver sich
laszt fergnusen, un Galtes ferfugen Der behet
gluckselig ouf errdischer velt, Veil er ist zufrieden, vie
Gott es gefallt.

"Who truly is content and holds nothing back, he who lets be led under God's leading, he lives good happily on this earth, as he is satisfied how God makes it." Further in the song he noticed a line saying, "content of heart is more worth than gold.

The last verse sounded as if the writer had won the whole victory.

So then, I will be satisfied with my God, He sends me
joy, He sends me pain, so shall I in all His will fall,
For He knows what is best and good for me, So I am
satisfied, it stays with me.

Clayton himself had not won all victory, but on the way home from church he was looking through eyes different than when he had gone to church.

Throughout the day and following weeks when discouragement tried to crowd in, Clayton would convince his heart of the submissive words and repeat them over and over till discontentment had to leave.

Chapter Twenty-Five

Clayton stood for a moment at the barn doors, after turning the cows out for a little exercise. He watched them wandering down the cow lane as they headed toward the meadow. Gazing over the countryside, he noticed the meadow and fields were getting a little green with life. It must have been after the warm rain last week. Was spring really on its way? Yes, the trees showed signs of buds. Another season was approaching.

Clayton marveled at the thought that all that had seemed dead over the winter was now showing signs of life, even if there really wasn't that much warm weather yet. Still, the earth must have felt the awakening. He himself hadn't given much thought of spring yet, but the Bible said summer, winter, heat, and frost would continue as long as the earth stands.

It was true that time didn't stand still. Clayton was very much aware of it this week when he saw what time did to the Nolts. Over the years, William and Mattie had also made some gradual changes. Quite often William had backache and didn't feel up to helping with the chores, and during the summer it was more than Clayton could handle alone. So that's why the neighbor boy Edward had started to come and help with the feeding and milking on mornings and evenings and at times with haying, etc. It had worked out good since Edward's parents had wanted work for him since younger brothers were doing the chores he had been doing at home.

The changes had come gradually. Just like the grass. It was showing a hint of green, and one day it would be green and the air warmer and it will be another spring, and no one will know just exactly when spring began.

The seasons turned into years. Each year brought little changes easy to adjust to, but as the years continued almost unaware, the changes did show up if you took them all together. Like he saw on Friday when his whole family was together, except Ephraim's. He realized that even though not many changes had come into his life the last years, the results still showed up.

As Clayton closed the barn doors and went out to the heifer shed to turn off the water, he was trying to think how many years it was since Dad died. Enos and Noah David hadn't been married yet at that time, but how long had they been married? He couldn't think of a reminder when Dad died. Oh yes, now he remembered again. It was in the winter he had turned twenty-one in spring. Now he was about to turn—would the next month make him twenty-six years old? Then it must have been five years since Dad died—a little over five years. Had all those changes come in that time?

Noah David and Lucy had come to Pennsylvania for Lucy's aunt's funeral and Naaman's had come along. Enos and Dorcas had invited Mom's whole family on Friday before they left, and it seemed the years had brought changes to all the family except Clayton.

After Noah David and Lucy married, Enos and Dorcas had bought a house and a few acres only one and a half miles from the Singing Pine Brothers Shop. They moved there to help Israel in the shop, and Noah David and Lucy moved to the house where Mom and Dad used to live in Kentucky, and where Enos and Dorcas later lived.

As Clayton came into the house, he noticed the kitchen was empty. William and Mattie were getting ready to go to church. Their carriage stood in the barnyard, so William was going to drive. Clayton had started to look forward to the times William asked him to take them along, as somehow he started feeling sort of out of place driving his buggy up to where the young boys tied their buggies at church. The sixteen- and seventeen-year-old ones seemed so young. He felt sort of self-conscious. He guessed they probably called him a bachelor. Maybe he was.

Going upstairs, his thoughts went back to Friday again. He stood staring out the window as he thought of when they were at Enos's sitting in the room visiting and Lucy had come and handed

176

one-year-old Louise to Noah David, asking, "Could you care for her? I want to feed Murray."

Noah David had put the little girl on his lap and smiled at the baby, talked a little to her, and she leaned against him as Noah David continued visiting. It seemed very usual. He was used to seeing Enos with a child or two on his lap. But Noah David, his youngest brother, a father of children? Clayton could hardly grasp it. Of course he knew it, but seeing it was something different.

Sometime during the day he had gone to the porch. A boy was sitting on the bench and a girl, a few years older, was pulling on his boots and another was blowing up a balloon for the boy. The older of the girls looked up and smiled at him. He recognized her as Alpheus's Margaret, helping her brother with his boots, and Lucy was blowing up the balloon. Time sure had a way of changing things. It seemed only a little while ago when Margaret and Lucy kept Ella Mae so busy that Alpheus had to do the dishes. Now they were helping Ella Mae with the younger children.

It seemed the tradition of boys went with the home place as Eli Jonas and Israel both lived at home and had all boys. People often mistook Israel and Emily's two boys for twins, and if they heard their names, they thought so even more. If people called them by their first names, Reuben and Ralph, they sounded like twins. And if they used only the second names, James and Jacob, it still did. Emily dressed them like little gentlemen with suit coats and ties—just like the Aaron Rissler family, sort of old-fashioned in a fantastic way.

Clayton's thoughts ran on, and when he got aware of time again, he thought, *Why go to church? I could sleep this forenoon.* But William stressed that you go to church if possible, so with a rather late start he got ready.

As he was arriving at church, Clayton saw to his dismay that the boys were walking to the church house already. He sort of felt out of place with the boys, but still didn't like to walk in all alone. They probably didn't even notice that he wasn't with them. As the wheels of the buggy crunched on the stones, a few of the boys looked back to see who was coming and walked on. But strangely, Henry Martin swung around and walked away from the others. He walked up to Clayton, who was getting out of the buggy.

While Clayton tied his horse, Henry waited and said that he doesn't like to go alone. Henry was maybe about eighteen years old, and Clayton really didn't know him that well. They visited a little as they waited to blanket the horse, and then they walked into church together.

Clayton suddenly felt glad that he had come to church. Maybe the younger boys respected him more than he thought. And to think that he had never gone out of his way to be kind to Henry. Maybe Henry felt self-conscious at times and Clayton never took time to notice and assure him. They hadn't talked much, but it was the deed and thought that warmed Clayton's heart. He was sure Henry would never know how much he did for him.

That evening, as Clayton was doing the milking, his mind felt troubled again. He couldn't explain himself. He had no desire to go where the young folks were invited for supper. He thought it would relax him to come home to the cows who were expecting him. Edward fed the cows and hurriedly left since they were getting company for supper. William and Mattie had walked over to the neighbors for the evening.

Clayton had a lonesome feeling that almost hurt, but if Edward would have stayed, he hardly would have talked with him. Edward didn't talk much when he came and when William was out in the barn before they left, they hadn't visited much. Clayton had a hard time understanding his own feelings. It seemed almost as if the approaching spring was a dread to him. What season could be more joyful than spring time with sunny skies, nature blooming and budding, and birds singing? He couldn't explain it; it just depressed him. It seemed he was not ready for spring.

That evening Clayton went for a walk and then went up to his room. He leafed through his songbook, but couldn't honestly get himself interested. He felt like a two-year-old child who doesn't know what he wants himself. For a while he sat staring in the dark windows. His thoughts drifted to his mother. He wondered if she was often lonely too. Israel and Eli Jonas were there, but she probably at times felt not included.

Clayton remembered a Sunday a few months after Dad had died, and he had gone home to Mother. After visiting awhile Mother had fallen asleep, and for something to do, Clayton had picked up the box that held her sympathy cards. He was looking through them and he was reading some of the letters when he came upon a poem. After he read it, he read it again. He felt a strength go through him, like a refreshing drink after being thirsty.

He found a tablet and copied the poem to take along. He used to read it once in a while, but he had forgotten about it since. Now he wondered where it was. He looked through his drawer a few times then leafed through his Bible. Yes, here was the folded sheet in the back cover of his Bible. He sat near the lamp and read it.

Don't despair, when heart is aching
And there is hardly strength for prayer,
When you're lonely, feel forsaken,
And no friend your burden share
Faith in Jesus almost ceasing
You can scarcely stand the strain
Don't despair with loads increasing
Though the efforts seem in vain.

Don't despair, Christ too was lonely
And he understands your heart
Burdens are for this life only
Left on earth when we depart
There will be joy beyond all measure
If you sit at Jesus' feet
He gives peace instead of pleasure
Life in Jesus is complete.

When your life on earth is finished,
May you hear the Lord's "Well done."
Leave your work and come up hither
Where I have prepared your home."
All the burdens and the heartaches

*Will seem naught when day is over
And you go to dwell with Jesus,
Sing his praises evermore.*

Clayton read the song again and put it back in his Bible. Maybe he didn't sing enough praises. Maybe he dwelled too much on troubled thoughts and wasn't grateful enough for his blessing.

As the weeks passed, Clayton's intentions failed. He felt himself dip into depression. At times he had a hard time falling asleep, and then he would worry that maybe something was wrong that he couldn't sleep. In the morning he awoke too early and the thoughts instantly settled on his mind so that he stayed awake and thus wasn't getting his rest. So his body energy lacked and with energy lacking, his appetite decreased. He was dragging himself around until the weekend came and he had a bad cold and stayed at home to try and rest it out.

On Tuesday right after dinner, William came out of his bedroom with an envelope. He handed it to Clayton and said, "There isn't so much to do today. You may take this to the doctor in town and pay for Mother's last appointment. I had forgotten my pocketbook that time. See if he has something to help you get your strength back." Clayton obeyed.

He had to wait until two other patients were finished. When he was called in, Clayton said he wanted to pay Mattie Nolt's office bill and he would like to talk with the doctor.

The doctor asked Clayton to step on the scales. He shifted the weights and moved the spacer. "It shows 176. Is that what you usually weigh?" the doctor asked. In a relaxed manner he looked over the form Clayton had filled in while waiting.

Clayton looked at him, thinking he was joking. When the doctor looked at him innocently, Clayton looked at the scale and said, "At home I usually weigh 198. Maybe it didn't show right."

The doctor looked back at the form and asked, "When did you last weigh yourself?"

Clayton couldn't remember. "Maybe half a year ago."

The doctor looked at him silently, then said, "If you have a few minutes, come and sit down." He gave the nurse instructions about taking Mrs. Heffner in to take her blood pressure. The doctor closed the door and sat down. "Have you been eating as usual?"

"No," Clayton replied, "I haven't been sleeping too well and then work doesn't go so well, and then I guess I don't get so hungry since I don't work so much. Then last week I got a bad cold and everything tasted alike."

The doctor asked about his job and wondered if he liked working at William's, were they easy to work for, and a lot of other questions.

"Yes," Clayton truthfully said, "I like my boss and my job if I feel like working. But just now it's a drag since I don't have my strength."

"What keeps you from sleeping?"

"I don't know. I guess I'm not working hard enough now to get really tired."

The doctor smiled, "Now wait once. You're going in circles. You can't sleep, then you can't work, then you don't get tired enough to sleep. We'll talk about other things while that goes on the merry-go-round."

The doctor asked about Clayton's family and how much he sees of them and how close their relationship is. After an endless row of questions surrounding the family, the doctor said, "I gather that all your brothers are married. Have you any prospects?"

"No," Clayton answered.

The doctor waited. When Clayton said no more, he asked a lot of questions in that direction. Did he ever date a girl and why did they break up? Before he was aware of it, Clayton had told the doctor all about his experiences of younger years. Now and then the doctor asked a question and thus the story lengthened. He had to answer a lot of questions until the doctor was convinced that Clayton wasn't still grieving over Lydia Ann and hating himself for Barbara Ellen.

"What then has kept you from dating another girl?"

"Well, I wasn't really interested in any others particularly."

They discussed it back and forth till the doctor summed it up. "But you were slow to ask another girl because you were afraid you would hurt someone like you did on your second friendship?"

"Well, yes, I suppose I would have fallen for someone else if I hadn't that fear."

"But now—there is no girl you cherish?"

"No, not at all."

The doctor had been watching Clayton closely and sensed that it took a few seconds till he said no, as if he almost hesitated. "If there is no one, why do you feel discouraged? Is there something about your work or life that stirs up the depressed feelings? I mean, when do you most feel depressed?"

Clayton admitted that the awakening of spring, the signs of life coming back, the greening of spring and warmth of the sun left him with a depressed feeling. "I just don't feel prepared for spring. I don't want the spring to rejoice when I can't help. Oh—" Clayton ran out of words.

"You mean the earth is rejoicing in new strength and has been alluring in its beauty? The sun shines, the birds sing, the air whispers, and it makes you depressed to realize the season is going on and you would want to stop?"

Clayton nodded.

"And why can't you rejoice? Is there maybe an ache in your heart? A longing that thirsts more as spring beckons with its gay spirit?"

"Well, yes, maybe you could call it an ache. If it were a tooth, I would get it pulled."

The doctor was persistent and asked Clayton that if everything in God's power was opened to him, what would he do first? What important thing would he attempt if he suddenly had all of God's knowledge to use?

"Maybe nothing now," Clayton simply said.

"Why not now?" the doctor urged.

Clayton ended up telling the doctor about the experience years ago that at one time was too sacred to speak about. The girl at the pump. He admitted that at one time it bothered him a lot, but it had dimmed in his mind. "And cured me of all girls."

The doctor asked every question surrounding it. He was in deep thought awhile then asked, "I take it you are a praying man?"

Clayton explained how much he had prayed about the matter and had after a while resigned himself to the silence.

The doctor moved his chair closer to Clayton as he rubbed his hand over his near-bald head. A look of eagerness shown on his face as he began talking. "I remember a reader we had in school many years ago. It was about a little girl who got a pair of red rubbers for a birthday present from her parents and she was very delighted with them. She looked forward to being able to use them, but the weather stayed nice. She often looked at her beautiful rubbers and kept waiting, thinking, *Sometime I can use them.* The nice weather continued and she cherished her rubbers.

"Then one day she remembered to pray for rain. She prayed for rain every day, but every morning the sun rose again. As the days wore on, she got a bit upset at the sight of the sun, and the sight of the sun made her sad. If it weren't for the rubbers, she wouldn't have minded the sun. She became a disturbed little girl.

"Soon she wasn't very pleasant to her parents, since it was her parents who had given her the rubbers she couldn't use. The parents disapproved of their daughter's disposition, not knowing why she was so hard to get along with.

"One morning the girl got up without being called and greeted her mother with a 'Good morning,' something she hadn't said for a while. She asked if it was time to eat.

"'Yes, it is,' her mother said. 'What do you want?' She asked for a piece of toast and an egg, which surprised the mother because her daughter had recently been drinking only orange juice and eating sugared cereals. She gladly made an egg and toast for her daughter.

"After breakfast, the little girl put on her sunbonnet and said she was going out to play. She put on her rubbers when her mother couldn't see her, and she went out and smiled back at the sun. She wasn't upset. She had plans of her own. She took her little pail and filled it at the springhouse and carried it up to the field lane that went past the pumphouse.

"There was a thick layer of dust. She would pour water there and make a mud puddle and use her rubbers. She had to fetch water at the springhouse because the pump handle was too high and heavy for her to pump.

"As she came around the pumphouse and was about to lift her little pail and dump the water on the dust, she was amazed to see a big puddle of water and mud! The ground around it was dry and the sun shone bright. While she stood there confused, the girl saw her brother come. He explained that Dad had filled the tank on the wagon with a hose, set up with suction from the supply tank next to the pumphouse, and he had left the tank run over."

The doctor paused. Clayton aroused, almost forgetting where he was, and said, "I guess that's what you call faith?"

The doctor nodded. "Faith with works and willing to do what she could with what she had. She went in faith."

Clayton got up. The doctor handed him a small envelope and said, "Here are some pills to hasten your cold away, and if it's no better by next week, I want to see you again."

Clayton left in a much different spirit than when he arrived.

All through the evening two thoughts seemed to rise above the others. The prayers of the girl in the doctor's story were not answered until she had changed her gloomy spirit and was willing to do what she could with what she had.

The milking turned out to be a more pleasant chore. Clayton and Edward talked more than they had for a while, and William and Mattie were so pleasant that evening. As he went to bed, Clayton realized he felt emptied out. The talk with the doctor had cleared him of things that he had been bottling up. He actually felt tired in the evening.

When he awoke the next morning, Clayton was surprised when he looked at the clock and it was almost time to go out in the barn. He felt so tired yet. He had slept better, but it seemed it would take time to catch up with the sleep his body had lost. The more he slept, it seemed the more sleep he needed.

*   *   *   *

On Saturday morning William, Mattie, and Clayton lingered around the breakfast table. Clayton looked out the windows and saw light rain. He thought to himself, *Now the girl could use her rubbers.* He pushed back his chair, William sat back in the rocker, and Mattie started gathering up the dishes.

Clayton then sat on the sofa and picked up a book, but he soon stacked the pillows on each other, stretched out, and laid down his book. He yawned and decided to catch a nap in this rainy weather. The words, "Here am I and ready at thy bidding, Lord. Send me," were going through his mind as he rested and then fell asleep.

Clayton sat up with a start and tried to open his eyes. Why was Mattie in the middle of the church house looking concerned and coming his way? He opened his eyes further, blinking, trying to get awake.

Mattie asked him if he was okay. A sizzling sound sputtered and a cloud of smoke rose up by the range. Clayton jumped up and leaped toward the stove, grabbing a kettle of milk that was boiling over. Then he realized that he had burned his hand.

Mattie quickly brought the honey jar and poured honey on the burn, which made it feel better. "Now put on some more when that melts off," she said. Then she asked, "Are you sure you are all right?"

Clayton nodded his head and wondered why.

"You made such a scary, fearful moan right before you awoke. I thought something had come over you. Then I forgot that I had milk heating on the range to make cracker pudding," Mattie said as she used sandpaper on the range top.

Clayton went for his raps and chuckled, "I thought I was in church and strange things had happened." He looked at the clock and saw he had taken a good, long nap. William likely was out doing the rest of the barn work.

On Sunday morning as the congregation was singing and the ministers were walking in, Clayton suddenly remembered something and almost felt lightheaded when he saw Bishop Paul from the home district among the ministers. No wonder he felt lightheaded, as fast as his heart was thumping.

After the rude awakening and uncalled for excitement yesterday when he had awakened from his nap, he hadn't given his dream much thought. But now, seeing Bishop Paul, the whole dream rushed back at him. How real it had seemed!

He had dreamed he was in the home church and Dad was still living. Before dismissing the church, Bishop Paul had said, "It is yet to be announced that a couple is minded to step into matrimony, and if you are still minded, please come forward. This is Clayton Wenger and Kathleen Musser." In the dream, Clayton had tried to speak but couldn't. He tried so hard to talk that he must have made a loud sound. That's when he had awakened and Mattie said he had moaned.

Today when church was over, the deacon did publish a couple's name to be married, but not Clayton's. After church Clayton kept his eye on Paul and lingered around. Maybe he shouldn't. Paul was a good sober bishop, but if you knew Paul well, he had a good sense of humor.

When Paul was walking away from a group of men, coming towards the church, Clayton greeted him. Paul shook Clayton's hand heartily. "That's right, I guess this is where you are at home."

Conversation was exchanged and Clayton asked him where they were going for dinner. After Paul answered, Clayton dragged his shoes over the crushed stones and felt his blood rise to his head as he asked, "Who is this Kathleen Musser that you published me to?"

Clayton saw his bewildered face, and Paul said, "I didn't publish anyone."

Clayton chuckled, saying, "I know. Just when I saw you here this morning I thought of what I had dreamed yesterday about you. I was in church and you published me with a Kathleen Musser, or something like that. And I thought I'd have to kid you about it."

Paul looked at Clayton with an expression he couldn't determine. He asked huskily, "Shall I?"

"Not without me knowing anything about it," Clayton said, "but I have no fear. I don't know of someone as such. I just wanted to tease you a little."

Paul didn't even smile. Clayton regretted that he had said it, but seeing Paul had brought the dream so fresh in his memory.

When Paul did talk, he said, "Maybe you aren't keeping yourself busy enough that you dream about such things." Then they talked about his work at William's.

As Clayton was about to walk away, Paul asked, "But you didn't tell me yet, who really is your girl? I can't remember the couples I meet at weddings."

When Clayton stammered and words failed him, Paul asked, "Aren't you seeing anyone?"

"No."

Just then someone else walked by and shook hands with Paul, and Clayton slipped away. Clayton felt quite humiliated. He wished now that he hadn't even talked with Paul. Anyhow, not on that subject. He had thought Paul would take a joke. Clayton reminded himself that marriage was a serious matter, not to be taken so lighthearted.

A few Sundays later Clayton had been home to Mother on Sunday and found himself avoiding Paul at church. He felt sort of shy or guilty. Paul didn't search him out, and he didn't hear anyone say anything about it, so it dimmed from his memory. Bishop Paul must have kept Clayton's dream to himself.

The second to last week in May, the annual equipment sale was five miles from William's, and Clayton always liked to go there. If for no equipment business, there were always a lot of people to meet from surrounding areas. Clayton was looking at some stock tanks that would be handy to have in the heifer shed when he heard his name. As he turned around, he saw Bishop Paul was walking up to him. He gave him a handshake and asked how everything was with him today.

"I guess you'd say pretty good. Maybe I should be home farming."

"Is your corn all planted?" Paul asked.

"No, we still have a little over a field to do, but if the weather holds, it shouldn't take long anymore." Sometime in the course of the conversation Paul invited Clayton to go along to visit some shut-ins and sick ones. Others were going, but they still had room.

"I thought likely you aren't going with the young folks regular, and maybe you'd enjoy such a day for something different. It does us good to see how others have it."

"I'm not good at such a sort of thing," Clayton humbly admitted.

Paul said, "I suppose if you were sick for a while, you'd be glad for everyone who came, not only for smooth talkers and gifted speakers, but just to show that the people thought of you."

"Maybe," Clayton thought out loud. "Are there more young folks going or will you be singing maybe?"

"Yes, usually someone asks us to sing for them," Paul said, his face lighting up as if he had a wonderful thought.

"Do you mean visiting back home in my area?" Clayton asked.

"No, no," Paul said, "we're going up country in the area of Dry Hill or Cloverdale, somewhere around there. Some are going to visit relatives and they are trying to fill a van."

"When is this? Will I need to go home to get picked up?"

"It's two weeks from Tuesday, June eighth. Only a few are coming from our way. We'll get the rest on from this area and more on the way up. And I'm counting on you."

"Guess it won't hurt to take the day off."

"It usually pays, and we'll be there before eight."

Chapter Twenty-Six

As Clayton was pulling on his shoes to go to the barn, he looked at the calendar, wondering if this was the day that the vet was coming for the herd health check on the heifers. But no, that was not for another week. Why did he have June 8 in his mind?

Suddenly, he remembered—he had promised to go away today. He'd better move fast if he wanted to be ready before eight o'clock. Edward would have to finish up after breakfast. *But what about the hay*, Clayton wondered as he went out the door. A dreary, misty day greeted him, and what to do about the hay was immediately settled.

When Clayton came in from the barn, he asked Mattie to make an egg sandwich for him. "I was asked to go along to visit some sick folks up country." He wasn't more than upstairs to put on better clothing when the van drove in. He hurriedly finished dressing, came downstairs, and hastily took a drink of milk. He grabbed his sandwich, eating on the way out.

Mattie called after him, "Was I supposed to pack lunch?"

"I don't know. I have money along." He never thought of songbooks.

Observing Clayton putting on his jacket and eating a sandwich on the run with his hat set halfway on disheveled hair, Paul asked good naturedly, "You about made it, eh?"

"This morning a little after five I first remembered I'm going."

Paul smiled, amused. Clayton pulled out his comb and used the driver's mirror to get his hair in place. There was an assortment of people in the van by the time the driver had gathered everyone along the way. Now and then they dropped a few people off, who were visiting relatives. Paul was up front telling the driver where to go; the others were informing him of their plans.

They pulled in a short lane leading to a green and white house. A smaller barn and a few green houses were also on the place. Paul said, "Here's where Clayton and I are getting off."

Clayton got out and stretched his legs, taking in the surroundings while Paul talked with the driver some more. When the van turned around, Clayton looked at Paul and asked if they were the only ones getting off here.

"Yes, we won't all travel together. Big groups aren't ideal for visiting shut-ins. This is where my daughter and family lives. We'll get a team here to go on farther.

Just then a man came out of the barn, leading a horse all harnessed up. Paul grabbed the shafts and helped hitch the horse. Paul's daughter came out of the house with her sweater hung over her shoulders to shield the drizzle and visited a bit.

"Well," Paul said, "I'll see you later today. We really have to be going."

As the forenoon wore on, Clayton had automatically started counting his blessings. Bishop Paul usually informed him about the people he expected to meet in the house. They ranged anywhere from a couple caring for a retarded, difficult daughter to a thirty-three-year-old man who had both legs broken to a two-year-old who was burned badly but had started to get better to, oh yes, that old couple.

As they went along a little country road, Paul read, "Country Food Salvage Market. Sound like a good place to get dinner?"

"Sounds all right. I didn't bring any dinner, and my breakfast has been digested awhile already," Clayton laughed, remembering his lone sandwich and drink of milk.

Clayton stood for a moment looking across the countryside and the scattered buildings. As he was ready to go into the store, Paul came hurrying out with a pack of cheese and a box of crackers in his hand. He stopped and said, "Now just take your time to eat. I have another call to make up the way here while you eat, so take your time till I come back. You can look around and eat a big dinner." Clayton didn't ask any questions. He guessed the bishop wanted to make this call alone.

Just as Clayton came in the door, one of the employees came out the door as if she was looking for something. Clayton walked on back and looked through the aisles to get an idea what was available to eat since it appeared as though he would have some time on his hands. It seemed the cashier who had come back in the store was now looking for something in the store. Or was she watching him? The employee came around the corner and looked sort of puzzled and asked him if he needed help in finding something.

Clayton said, "I'm just looking for something to eat."

Taking a quick look at him, she asked, "You aren't with Paul, are you?"

"I came with Bishop Paul. While he is on an errand, I will get something."

She gasped, cutting off his words, "That's not how we treat our travelers, eating out of the store. In just a few minutes dinner will be ready. You can eat with us."

"I suppose Paul will soon be back," Clayton replied, moving further up the aisle.

"Hardly! His son-in-law lives a piece up the road here. He probably won't be back for a while, so we'll have dinner. Didn't you come a distance already this morning?"

Clayton nodded and more words failed him. When he looked at her, he saw her gentle, serene face, something like an innocent child who was eagerly trying to do something that took all her ability. She was saying, ". . . in fact, Paul said he has a visitor here and wondered if I could get him dinner and see after him till he returns. I was trying to find someone. I thought he meant one of his grandchildren from up the road."

"You wouldn't have needed to bother," Clayton said.

"It's no bother. I'm making dinner anyhow. I'll go check that customer out there and then we will have dinner."

Clayton walked on through the store, but he wasn't really looking. He wondered why Paul would have said such a thing. A young, tall boy came in the door, and the woman was giving him instructions.

"Now it's dinner time," said the woman as she came back through the store. She led the way through the side door into a warehouse, and on through a built-in porch, where a door opened into a cozy kitchen. It somewhat resembled a "grandmother" kitchen—tidy, inviting, and humble. She motioned him to a chair. In a few quick motions she had slapped cheese sandwiches together in a pan and poured a little water in a kettle and moved it further front on the stove. While she set the table, she asked if any more people had come along with them.

Almost before he had finished answering, the woman said, "I must go fetch Delores." She disappeared in the direction of the built-in porch and out through another door. A corner outside the kitchen window hid his view.

Seeming only a few minutes later, she was back with a little girl. When her cap was removed, her light curls fell everywhere. The sunny little girl smiled at Clayton as she set her on the high chair. The woman got a pack of crackers from the warming closet in the range, set the soup kettle on the table, and said, "Now we're ready to eat."

It was then that Clayton saw there were only two plates on the table. He had expected her husband to come in the door any minute. *Maybe he works away through the day.* While they were eating the simple but delicious cheese sandwiches and chicken corn soup, she asked where they had been visiting in the forenoon.

"I don't know if I still remember names. We were at a place where a man in this thirties was laid up with both legs broken from a runaway team."

"Oh yes, I guess John Reiff is home from the hospital now. He was in the hospital quite awhile. And then there was a place we stopped for a few minutes with a couple that had a severely retarded boy."

"Yes, that was nice of Paul. I'm sure Sam and Ella were glad for company as they can't go away much."

192

"We stayed longer than Paul figured. And then there was a two-year-old that had been burned and was healing again."

She nodded. "He is recovering better than we thought he would for a time." Delores was crying and in doing so she rubbed her hair in her face. The woman lifted her on her lap gently stroking her curls out of her eyes saying, "Kathleen didn't comb you, did she? But I think Delores is tired now."

Clayton continued relating how the group had also stopped at a place where there was an older couple. The man was in a wheelchair but seemed the better of the two.

"That must have been at Phares's. His legs are worn out but not his voice or sense of humor."

"After a day like this, you begin to realize your blessings," Clayton said as he cleaned up the last of his dessert.

"Then we should go visiting more?" she asked knowingly. The eyes under the curls of blonde hair had fallen asleep.

"Did you say Paul's son lives somewhere near here?" Clayton asked as she started clearing off the table after laying the girl in a crib.

"Yes, up the road and around a few turns. Didn't Paul say?" Clayton shook his head. She continued, "It seems they have their share of problems." Clayton looked at her blankly. "He has struggles to keep up his spirits. I am sure they were glad to see Paul."

While eating dinner and talking more with this woman, Clayton began thinking maybe he should know her. He seemed to recognize her but couldn't come to any conclusion.

As the visiting continued, Clayton asked, "On the way over, I was wondering if there is a livestock auction somewhere near here."

"Yes, Four Acres is about four miles across the fields to the north."

"I thought it looked a little familiar in this area."

"Have you been there already?" she asked.

"Yes, some months ago when my calves were picked up. The driver was talking about another auction and I wondered where it was. He said he'd take me there sometime. I went with him one time and spent the evening there; I thought it might have been somewhere in this area."

A bell rang out on the porch and the woman said she must go see what was needed in the store. While she was gone, Clayton looked over the kitchen area and noticed more signs of children. The wraps on the wall looked like boys' clothing as did a pair of shoes by the stove. Looking at the wall of wraps, a strange feeling came over him. There were no signs of any men's wraps, shoes, or anything.

He picked up a magazine and started reading it and was soon lost in the story. As he turned the cover to read the last part of the story, he sat up with a start when his eyes caught the address on the magazine. Kathleen Musser! He felt struck. His face felt warm. Surely not. He suddenly felt weak. He had heard the name Kathleen mentioned earlier when she talked to Delores about her uncombed hair. He had assumed she was referring to someone where the girl had been in the forenoon. Just then the woman came back in. Clayton couldn't look up. He pretended to be reading.

She apologized for running off. He said he didn't want to keep her from her work while he waited on Paul. "If you are interested, you could come along over in the warehouse. There are some shipments to unpack and things to take care of." He had thought the warehouse looked rather interesting, so he went along.

To himself, Clayton was pondering, *Does she know? Did Paul tell her?* Then he remembered that she had been looking for Paul's grandchild to give dinner to and watch over until he came back. She went over to a stack of boxes and opened the top one.

Completely unaware of his thoughts, Kathleen said, "These boxes have anything in from pineapples to dog food. Whatever goes in a tin can." She threw some empty boxes over. "They have to be sorted. Over there are some more empty boxes if you need more. I'll check over this order." She walked to another stack of boxes on a pallet where some cases were open.

"Do you operate this salvage store?" Clayton asked as he started sorting tin cans.

"Others help. I couldn't do it alone." She went on explaining about the store as she filled boxes and lifted them around. Clayton kept stealing a glance her way. He didn't know any Kathleen Musser. *When have I seen her before or who does she remind me of?* Occasionally she went in the kitchen to listen if Delores was awake; the last time she brought her along out to the warehouse.

194

Clayton mused, *Paul set a trap, and I walked right in.* Once, when he looked up to ask her something, he found her watching him. She smiled a quick smile. "Is there anything else you want done?" Clayton asked.

"Well, if you don't mind, this stack of peanut butter cases here will need to be gone through. I think there are broken jars in some of them."

The warehouse doors from the store opened and a voice exclaimed, "Kathleen, I'm home." She looked around and gasped in happy surprise, "John Mark, it isn't that time yet, is it?" A boy came slightly limping across the warehouse. "Were you hunting for me?" she asked apologizing.

"I looked in the kitchen and then in the store. They told me you were here." John mark smiled at Clayton, then suddenly almost frowned.

Kathleen was watching and said, "Did you think it was Albert? This is company. While he is waiting for his driver to pick him up, he is helping us. If I'm right, it's Clayton," she said looking over at Clayton in a way that made him want to learn to know her more.

He nodded his head and wondered some more. She continued saying, "He is visiting around here and came to the store for dinner. Now we make him work." The look in the boy's eyes turned from fear to that of friendliness. It seemed that Kathleen was putting on extra friendliness on his behalf. Clayton noticed that the children didn't call her "Mother."

John Mark said, "I'm going in the meadow to pull grass and things for the rabbits. It's not raining anymore. The sun came out a few times."

"Put on your everyday clothes first."

When John Mark left, Clayton asked, "Are you baby-sitting that they call you by name?"

She gave him a puzzled look and bent over a box as she answered. "I am their legal guardian. After Jonathan died, I worked in a hospital and got acquainted with children. Through that, I got in touch with the homes of the children who came to the hospital. I didn't leave them all there," she chuckled.

"Jonathan?" Clayton repeated looking her way.

Without looking up, she said, "Jonathan Leid, a boy who died from pneumonia a few weeks before his planned wedding when he was painting his house." Clayton stood thinking. He had heard that before.

His silence caused Kathleen to look up. "Did you know him?"

"No," Clayton said coming back to life. "I was just trying to think what I know about that." He was remembering aloud, "Eli Jonas had gone to fetch Amanda."

Kathleen raised her head, "Yes, I know Amanda. She came for the funeral."

"I'm trying to think why I remember that. Oh yes, that's how it was. I went to my first singing that weekend because none of my brothers were at home, and Mother promised someone transportation."

After a few minutes' silence, they both said together, "That's over ten years ago." They looked up at each other, amused at how they both had the same thought.

It was something about her shy smile that made him look again. Clayton asked, "Is the UPS truck here? I heard a horn."

"We have to go to the kitchen. We can't see from here." Crossing the porch she looked back and said, "Maybe it's someone for you."

"For me?" Clayton asked.

"I thought maybe to pick you up," Kathleen said.

"I came with Paul in a carriage."

"Maybe he took the horse home and came with the driver," she said looking at the van.

"Well, it does look like the van we came with," Clayton said slipping on his wraps. He thanked her for the meal and the company.

"You're quite welcome anytime," she replied.

"When is a good time for you?" he asked resting his hand on the door knob. Her brown eyes shifted as she stroked her hand over her already smoothed down hair. "The store closes all weekdays at five and Saturday at three." At the toot of the horn, Clayton hurried out. As he climbed in the van, he saw only Paul and the driver. Paul was occupied in telling the driver where to go next. Clayton had been dreading to face Paul, but Paul seemed not aware that he was on the van as he continued relating a story to the driver that they must have been talking about before he came out.

Chapter Twenty-Seven

Reaching the little knoll on the road, Clayton saw part of the brick house with its shed and porch attached. It made his heart beat faster and his footsteps slower. He was looking forward to it, but now he almost quivered with nervousness. It was two weeks since Paul had led him here. Clayton had not had the opportunity until this week. He now hitched a ride with Bob, who was taking some cattle to Four Acres to sell for other people and then to haul some beef back. Clayton had told Bob to drop him off at the corner and to pick him up at the third house on the left if he was not at the auction. He explained that when his visiting was done, he would walk to the auction.

As he reached the yard, Clayton started cutting across the yard around the house and suddenly heard voices nearby. There in a circle were some assorted lawn chairs occupied by the little family with some pails around them. Just as he was ready to speak, he sensed silence. They were looking his way. "Looks like you could use some help."

"We have one more pail to do," Kathleen said as she put more hull peas in her lap. "But you don't look as if you came to help work," she added taking another glance at him.

John Mark also had a little bowl on his lap and a pail beside for the empty shells, but he momentarily forgot about peas. Kathleen picked up a bowl that was standing on a lawn chair next to John Mark and nodded to Clayton to have a seat. Delores and John Mark were on either side of Kathleen, so now they formed a circle. Clayton took some newspaper that was lying there and put it on his lap for the pea pods and a bowl for the shelled peas.

"And how are you traveling?" Kathleen asked. "Or where did you come from?"

"I came from William's with Bob, the livestock hauler. He goes to Four Acres pretty regular; so I hitched a ride. I hope it is all right. You said anytime, didn't you?"

She chuckled, "It's fine if you don't mind our—" She laughed, glancing down over her everyday dress and apron and bare feet, embarrassed. Her bare feet and work clothes did not change her appearance. There was a tenderness and friendliness that seemed to glow from somewhere deep within.

Clayton replied, "If I would have minded, I wouldn't have come this way." As the visiting continued, Clayton at times asked John Mark if he should open some pea pods for him when he had trouble. John Mark looked over at Kathleen, who smiled and nodded to him. He would put some into Clayton's lap and looked at him gratefully, as Clayton opened them easily. Although darkness was settling about them bit by bit, Clayton had recognized an appearance of sacredness that he hadn't caught two weeks ago on their short visit.

Delores had fallen asleep; the last peas were out of the pail. Kathleen said she would put Delores to bed and light the lamps before they finished. Clayton's lap was about empty too, so he took some peas from John Mark.

As they came in the kitchen door, Kathleen came in the door from the hallway after putting Delores to bed. She had changed into a clean dress and apron and put on shoes. Her hair was obediently brushed under a covering though a few strands had strayed out from the wear of the day.

Kathleen got a container from the freezer. "Now we'll have a little treat after our day's work."

John Mark rejoiced, "Ice cream." The visiting continued while they had the cool refreshment. Clayton saw that John Mark watched him as he was eating. He reasoned that John Mark likely had not often seen someone eat with his left hand. He stared a little but didn't ask any questions.

After the treat, Kathleen looked at the clock and reminded John Mark that it was bedtime. Somewhat quietly he asked, "No story?"

Kathleen said, "Well, maybe no story tonight. Delores is asleep."

He looked disappointed and asked, "Then maybe we could sing?"

Clayton looked at John Mark's eager face and suggested, "Why don't we? Do you like to sing, John Mark?" John Mark nodded his head eagerly.

Kathleen did not oppose, so John Mark bounded over to a little narrow cabinet, opened the drawer above the doors, and came back with a small, thin blue book. Paging through it, he opened it wider and held it for Clayton to see, pointing to No. 571.

Clayton asked, "Do you know that song? He nodded his head happily.

Clayton started singing,

> *I have decided to follow Jesus.*
> *I have decided to follow Jesus.*
> *I have decided to follow Jesus,*
> *No turning back, no turning back.*

When Kathleen joined the singing, John Mark started singing too.

> *Though none go with me, yet still I'll follow.*
> *Though none go with me, yet still I'll follow.*
> *Though none go with me, yet still I'll follow,*
> *No turning back, no turning back.*

Clayton paused. John Mark looked at him and Clayton continued.

> *The world behind me, the cross before me.*
> *The world behind me, the hope before me.*
> *The world behind me, the Heav'n before me.*
> *No turning back, no turning back.*

When the song ended and John Mark started paging through the book, a paper fell on the floor. John Mark picked it up and looked at it.

Kathleen asked, "What's that? Is that the new song you learned at school?" He nodded. Looking at Clayton, Kathleen said to John Mark, "Maybe he could sing it for you?" To Clayton she explained, "They learned that song in the last month of school, and he wanted me to sing it at home. But I don't know the song and couldn't quite learn it from him without hearing someone else sing it."

Clayton took the paper and smoothed it out. As Clayton read the words John Mark asked, "Do you know the song?"

Clayton nodded his head. They waited, and he started singing.

> *Have thine own way, Lord! Have thine own way!*
> *Thou art the potter, I am the clay.*

John Mark got a smile on his face and nodded his head in earnest and sang along in his boyish ability.

> *Mold me and make me after they will,*
> *While I am waiting, yielded and still.*
>
> *Have thine own way, Lord! Have thine own way!*
> *Search me and try me, Master, today!*
> *Whiter than snow, Lord, wash me just now,*
> *As in thy presence humbly I bow.*
>
> *Have thine own way, Lord! Have thine own Way!*
> *Wounded and weary, help me, I pray!*
> *Power—all power—surely is thine!*
> *Touch me and heal me, Savior divine!*
>
> *Have thine own way, Lord! Have thine own way!*
> *Hold o'er my being absolute sway!*
> *Fill with thy spirit, till all shall see*
> *Christ only, always, living in me!*

Halfway through the song Kathleen joined the singing, too, after getting the idea of the tune by then.

Kathleen looked at the clock, saying to John Mark, "It's bedtime."

He looked suddenly unhappy and asked with a fearful look, "Are you going somewhere?"

"No, no. I will just be down here visiting until Clayton's driver comes back from the auction." The she added, "Maybe some other day he will help us sing." John Mark looked at Clayton and gave him an assuring smile. Then he was off to bed.

Left alone in the kitchen, Clayton and Kathleen continued visiting. At a lull in the conversation, she said, "Maybe I shouldn't ask you, but I was still wondering from the other time. I take it that tonight you had plans of coming here, but it sort of seemed to me two weeks ago you hadn't known you'd be visiting here."

Clayton chuckled, "That's right. Two weeks ago I had as little warning that I was coming here as you had warning that I was coming. Or maybe you had more if Paul told you to make dinner and that I would be here all afternoon."

"I didn't know who it was, but I did wonder why he had that mischievous look hidden in his sober expression. What possessed Paul? After I think of the expression he had when he told me that he had company along for me and that I was to give him dinner and entertain the company, I felt he wasn't as innocent as the rest of us were. I haven't come to any conclusion."

Clayton studied the floor a bit and answered without looking up. He wiped his hand over the arm of the rocking chair and said, "Well, sometime ago I talked with Paul about something I didn't fully understand. In fact, I thought it was a joke and I told Paul about it in that manner. I thought Paul rebuked me for it. I left it at that, but Paul didn't. He told me nothing about his thoughts leading it to this."

A whole row of question marks lined across Kathleen's brow, but silence remained. Clayton scratched his head then straightened his hair again as he took courage and said, "But I am wondering, too, just since I arrived here tonight a thought entered my mind that leaves me wondering."

At length Kathleen asked, "Is it something I can help you with?"

"Maybe. That's why I wonder . . . . Oh—, . . . until two weeks ago I didn't know you. I almost thought maybe I should recognize you, but I didn't. I learned your name by the address I saw on the mail when I was here before. But after this evening I was wondering if I had met you before or did I talk with you before? You knew my name without me telling it."

"I knew your family faintly through Amanda being married to Eli Jonas. But I really didn't know one from another by that."

Clayton realized that she was only answering part of the question. He then finished the answer for her. "Then later we did meet and you learned which one I was?" Clayton asked, guessing what she hadn't said and looked her way.

"It helped a lot," she said, her face getting more color.

"When I asked if you were Rebekah?"

She blushed and kept her eyes cast down as she said, "You didn't ask who I was, so I didn't know you wondered, but I tried finding out more about who you were." He wondered some more things, but felt the subject had gone far enough in that direction. He asked about John Mark and Delores. Kathleen relaxed to a more usual topic.

Clayton listened in earnest as the clock unnoticeably made a few more rounds, faithfully catching the minutes and turning them into hours. Kathleen explained that she worked in the hospital, first doing cleaning and often in the children's ward. That's how she got acquainted with the children. "At times I did more than cleaning. When John Mark was in the hospital for his polio, I learned that he came from a children's home. I felt rather sorry for him. He received few visitors. I found that when I showed interest in him, his often sullen appearance and signs of fear melted away. He was in and out of the hospital frequently for a few years. I made some visits to the home or I would meet him in the hospital. Until another year I found myself working in the home and while there, I learned that at times John Mark went to foster homes only to return with all the confidence and sunny disposition I had worked to build up ruined. I asked about the possibility of giving him a home. It wasn't all that easy, but after having him for a few months at a time, the people at the home started seeing that the results were good for his welfare.

"My mother was still living at that time. She really wasn't in favor of it, but she really got attached to him and gave me permission to adopt him before she died. It has been two years since I adopted him; four years since he came regularly."

"And that makes him how old?" Clayton asked.

"Eight. He had polio at two and a half. I never met his parents. His mother died when he was a year old. His father remarried and his next wife didn't accept him. He lived in different homes before he came to the home and eventually to the hospital with polio. He has had many unpleasant experiences and he still has a fear. As a rule, he doesn't have much confidence or respect in men, and he has reasons for it."

Clayton remembered the sullen fearful look that had come to his face when John Mark first noticed there was a stranger in the warehouse two weeks ago. Clayton had thought John Mark was the neighbor boy who helped in the store at times.

Kathleen said, "I never knew him to accept a stranger as quickly as he did you this evening. We didn't talk much about you these two weeks. He didn't ask much, but your being willing to sing to him and knowing the song he was learning was a highlight in his world. I have rarely seen the eagerness in his face as I have seen tonight. He still has a fear that I will leave him. His father never came back to see him since I have him. I don't know where he and his wife live.

"Then there's Delores. She has seen a lot less and has a more happy, trusting state of mind. Next week she has to go to the hospital again for a few days. Perhaps you noticed that she has a hare lip. She was born to a single girl who disowned her at birth because of it. Her mother simply abandoned her in the hospital and either changed her own name or fled. The authorities haven't been able to contact her, so the home was notified. They weren't eager for such a small baby, and since some more hospital stays were before her with her handicap, foster homes weren't interested either.

"Someone remembered me, however. It was a trying time for me as I as good as promised Mother I wouldn't adopt any more children. But Mother wasn't living anymore, and I decided to bring Delores home with me. I had started the salvage store already and was able to be at home. I started keeping her after her hospital stays, which proved to be a tonic to John Mark. That was a little over two years ago. The home would like if I'd adopt her, rather than their paying me to care for her. I just haven't yet, but we have an agreement that she is not available to go to foster homes. I'd try to adopt her before I would give her up. They allowed me to make the agreement since I paid the costs of her last two operations.

"She was bald the first seven months of her life. I don't believe those curls." The clock ticked on.

Till the evening was over and the cattle truck at the side of the road gave a short toot, Clayton and Kathleen had an agreement of meeting in two weeks again in the same manner. They had exchanged addresses if there was need to contact each other.

*   *   *   *

As the summer wore on into autumn, visiting every two weeks soon turned into weekly visits. Each Thursday evening Clayton came along when Bob went to the livestock auction. At first William Nolt wondered why Clayton didn't attend his own area livestock auction more often if he had such an interest in these auctions.

When William expressed concern that he might be in bad company, Clayton told him, "I didn't say I go to the livestock auction. I said I go with Bob when he goes to the auction. I go to a place you'd approve of." After that William asked no more questions about that subject. Occasionally Clayton got himself in a tight spot by mentioning something that he and Kathleen had talked about, but he was able to just pass it off rather than finishing his line of thought.

Paul once asked him if he would go along to visit shut-ins, but Clayton simply replied, "I guess not this time."

Paul added, "Or do you know your own way by now?"

Clayton could truthfully say, "I haven't gone visiting shut-ins since." But Clayton felt Paul look at him deep enough to see right through him. He felt like a guilty child, whose face betrayed him. Paul said no more, but there was a twinkle in his otherwise sober face.

Clayton realized that he wasn't being good company to William and Mattie as his mind was often preoccupied.

Chapter Twenty-Eight

During the last several months, Clayton had learned from his visits with Kathleen that the place where she lived was willed to her from her mother for as long as she needed it. The property included two fields and a pasture besides the buildings. Since Kathleen's neighbor was farming the fields, she almost forgot they belonged to her. Other boys had offered friendship toward Kathleen, but the scars of Jonathan Leid had been too deep. Although most of the scars had healed, she had a fear of going through it again. She hadn't even known that Jonathan was sick when the fatal message was suddenly delivered to her. She developed a panic toward messages. She had even fainted a few times after that when she thought someone was delivering bad news. She tried to overcome her fear, but panic still gripped her at times.

Lately their visits had begun to center on the future. Clayton had talked about the opportunity at William's and about people needing time to make a change. He gathered that Kathleen was torn between two: the sake of him, and the sake of John Mark who was now used to a regular home and friends at school that knew and understood his life situation. They had come to no decision.

The following week Clayton brought up the subject of their meeting at the pump. They saw it as God's will and made a promise to walk life's way together. Clayton recalled how Dad asked Mother, "Haven't you been praying about it?" He asked Kathleen, "Were you maybe praying about it since we met there?" She admitted that she was. She also confessed to being a little hasty in making efforts to attend some singings in his area soon after that.

When he asked where he was, she replied, "At the singings but not watching girls."

It was then that Clayton told Kathleen of the dream he had as well as what he had told Bishop Paul. It did not matter to him if he was not able to continue at William Nolt's. He also considered John Mark's life. How would more changes in his life affect him? This was not Clayton's home district, nor was William's his home district. It didn't matter to Clayton one way or another, but soon William must be informed that there will be changes.

Instead of coming to a decision on their future during their next visit, Clayton found Kathleen's mind quite preoccupied. He had expected her to say what was on her mind, but she hadn't. He found himself jittery, fearing he would receive a letter through the week, a letter he didn't want to receive. He was almost holding his breath.

Thursday evening had come and so did Bob, his driver. Clayton found himself sweating as he walked up to Kathleen's door, but his fears vanished as soon as she opened the door. He saw that their friendship was still in bloom and that he was quite welcome. By now John Mark and Delores were precious to him. He enjoyed visiting and playing and singing with them for an hour or more till they went to bed. But he enjoyed even more when he and Kathleen could visit alone.

It was a hard week for him. He hadn't meant to, but when he said, "Kathleen, I'm not going home till you tell me what's on your mind," he broke out in tears.

"I know I should have told you, but I almost didn't know how. I thought maybe it would take care of itself and I won't have to trouble you, but I didn't realize you were aware that my mind was weighed down."

She sat down beside him and said, "Someone from the hospital came out the other week to see me and give me some information. She said I was to come in and talk with them. Then last Tuesday I was at the hospital as well as three different days this week."

"I'm listening," Clayton reminded her.

"It's a baby girl," she started fresh. "A baby girl was brought to the hospital some weeks ago. There was an accident where a young couple got killed. The baby was quite injured. She is out of intensive care and the hospital is concerned that she needs someone to care for

206

her, to love her and give her something to live for. The nurses don't have time.

"It sounds as thought the couple had recently moved to the area from Louisiana. The hospital officials had difficulty contacting any family members, so the couple was buried in the area. But no one is concerned about the baby. The hospital had hoped to get more direction. They are still waiting, but they want someone to love the baby now. And I didn't know if I want to get involved."

Clayton remained silent for a while. Then he said, "What would you do if you wouldn't know me?"

Kathleen answered, "That would make it harder yet. The baby has a gash in her head, but the most serious condition is her internal injuries."

"You have become attached to her already, haven't you?" Clayton asked.

"Yes, I have, and she seems to respond to me already. I wasn't prepared for how the doctors and nurses automatically rolled the care and concern on me—as if I was the mother."

"The couple's car was searched, but no name could be found for the baby. Since they knew the couple was from Louisiana, someone called the baby "Annie" and it stuck. So far, she is Annie and we believe her to be about five months old."

Most of the time was used in discussing Annie. Kathleen looked at the clock in alarm and said, "You have to tell me what to do before you leave!"

"All I can say is, 'Do unto others as you would have them do unto you.' Let's love her if she needs love, if you are willing. We have enough strength today, and if the need continues, we will get new strength tomorrow."

Before Clayton left, he advised since the neighbor family with growing children had taken such an interest in the salvage store, they should discuss moving the store over there by January. If Annie would be joining the family, Kathleen wouldn't have much time to help in the store, and Clayton was beginning to see some opportunities for the buildings.

*   *   *   *

William Nolt was quite disappointed when Clayton told him that he would be quitting in February. But William was overjoyed to hear that Clayton was taking a wife and thought it would just suit fine for them to continue farming at Nolts. He and Mattie would find a house to move into till they get one built. Edward and his father and brothers were ready to farm the extra acres and instead of hiring Edward out and have the next son helping at William's as they had earlier planned, they would take over the dairy and keep their sons at home.

It worked out well. Clayton had been home on the Sunday before Christmas and told Mother all that was taking place. He told her that the Sunday after New Year's, when Eli Jonas with Mom's help had invited all the family for dinner, he was planning to tell all his brothers and Naomi that he and Kathleen plan to be published in two weeks from then. He would like to bring Kathleen there that day to meet everyone.

*　　*　　*　　*

A cold, clear breeze was sweeping through the countryside, but the sun moderated the temperatures to a friendly winter day. Snow was sprinkled over the fields and the yards, but the roads were bare again.

The house on the Wenger home farm was filled with activity. The table had been stretched and a few settings were filled, till all the group had eaten.

While the women cleared the dinner away and washed the dishes, there was much visiting. Many little children were playing underfoot, from one room to another. And Grandmother, as everyone called her now, was always holding a child or two on her lap, while the dishes were being washed by younger hands.

In the sitting room a more lively conversation was in session where the sons and son-in-law were visiting. It was days like this that Dad's death still was felt as there was so much missing.

School-age girls were playing games in another room. School-age boys had been out in the fresh air, resulting in rosy cheeks. But after the cold started getting through, the boys sought the hay loft and were building tunnels in the straw.

When the excess volume of visiting was exchanged, most of the men moved out into the kitchen and blended their voices in singing.

While they were singing, a team came in the lane. It turned around and left off a few passengers who walked toward the house. Amanda recognized Kathleen right away and said as she went to the door, "Oh, that's right. I saw Kathleen was in church. She's one of my friends from Cloverdale. I didn't even get to talk to her since we left right after church." She opened the door and welcomed Kathleen, explaining that she had Eli Jonas's family here and that's why they rushed off after church and didn't get to meet her.

Quite a few of the men looked around to see who was coming. Clayton didn't need to. Amanda, out of habit, took the baby off her arms while Kathleen was taking their wraps off. Then Amanda looked at Kathleen and asked, "Who is this? It can't be Delores, since I think she's standing behind you."

As Kathleen took the wraps off Annie, she told Amanda how Annie came in her home. Naomi had gotten up and greeted Kathleen and was listening to the conversation.

John Mark paid full attention to the singing for a while until Nevin and Paul Isaac brought the tinker toys out of the drawer and started building things. Then John Mark moved their way and was soon building things and they started visiting together. Clayton looked up from his songbook long enough to notice, and it was a joy to see John Mark mingle so soon.

Sometime later Amanda and a few of the other women put drink and cookies on the table. They were filling the cups for the children who were gathering from every direction. The songbooks were set aside and visiting came into motion again.

Clayton was sitting on the bench against the wall and Naomi was visiting with him. He felt a tug at his clothing and, looking up, he saw Delores standing in front of him. She smiled when he looked up. She was stretching, expecting to be picked up. Clayton lowered his glass of grape drink, "Do you want a drink?" She nodded her head. The little curls that had worked out of her braids decorated her forehead.

Naomi smiled, amused at the incident, and continued visiting. Clayton matter-of-factly said, "I'm quitting at William's."

She raised her eyebrows, "Are you really?"

Clayton nodded.

"And what are you going to do now? Help us?"

"I'm getting married!"

"Clayton!" she exclaimed fearfully. The men around the table looked over. At Israel's questioning look, Naomi said, "He said he is quitting at William's and I asked what he will do and he said he is getting married!" Seranus chuckled and Israel had a good laugh. The others had grins.

Israel said, "You are about old enough."

"I took you as an example," Clayton said looking at Israel.

Israel chuckled and wiped his fingers across his eyes as if getting the tears out from laughing. With a mischievous look, he asked, "Oh, yes, didn't you say she was only about eleven or twelve at the time you were eighteen?"

Naomi quickly remembered the brothers' kidding about that some years ago. Laughing, she looked from Clayton to Israel and back at Clayton.

Clayton cleared his throat and smoothed his hair slowly, saying, "No, I think she was twenty-four or twenty-five then and was wondering where I was."

Israel chuckled over the memory.

Naomi told the listening brothers what Clayton had said when Israel and Emily started dating. Having a longing for some good old-fashioned fun with her brother, Naomi urged him on, "And when will this be?" she asked, trying to sound serious. By now it was the main topic in the kitchen.

"We're getting published in two weeks," Clayton replied. He heard a few gasps.

Naomi was stunned. She wasn't going to believe him yet. She said, "I dare you."

From the other side of the table near the stove, Emily jumped up from her chair, clapping her hands, and springing to life, saying, "It's Kathleen! Why else would she blush so?"

Now it was Clayton's turn to blush as the family looked from one to the other. Naomi sat down on a nearby chair. The brothers' grins widened.

Amanda was the first to speak. "Kathleen!" she gasped. "I can't believe this!" Delores crawled up on the bench and was watching the grown-ups' excitement. Clayton looked at her and she slid into his arms.

Naomi looked at her mother and asked, "Did you know?"

She nodded her head and said, "Not for long yet." And soon the whole kitchen was humming. Many questions had to be answered.

Clayton and Kathleen had planned to marry in church before the services and have the family and some relatives for dinner at Kathleen's home. Till the afternoon was over, the family had not changed the wedding date of February 3rd, but they had changed the location. Mother, Amanda, and Naomi thought Kathleen shouldn't have to prepare everything herself, with the small children and Annie still a bit frail. Since there weren't many close relatives on Kathleen's side; the Wenger family would provide the wedding.

Clayton and Kathleen planned that if it suits the church that day, they would marry before services in Clayton's home church. The wedding meal would be at Eli Jonas and Amanda's home. Naomi and Muriel also offered to do it, but since Amanda and Kathleen were long-time friends, Amanda insisted. They could spend some days together bringing back friendship memories since Kathleen said she would help Amanda a few days or so.

Chapter Twenty-Nine

Clayton mixed the milk replacer and poured the solution into three different pails, all ready for John Mark, who was nearly finished feeding the calves in the other pen. For a moment Clayton stepped back and studied the lower part of the shed. He hadn't fully decided how he wanted to finish out that lower pen. Maybe he would put another hay manger in a little lower. If he puts some smaller calves in there at times—

"Daddy, are there only three pails?" Clayton looked up to see John Mark picking up a pail of milk replacer. It still seemed rather strange to hear someone call him Daddy, but John Mark nearly always remembered. It was a joy for him to do so since having a father made him feel more like the other boys.

"Yes, only three tonight. Remember, Bronco doesn't get any tonight; he gets some only once a day now."

John Mark picked up two pails and went over to the next pen. He had seen that all the calves had names. Clayton had brought quite a few of these calves along from William's farm.

John Mark had more trouble remembering to call Kathleen "Mother" since he had called her "Kathleen" for so long. Even though John Mark had been adopted earlier, Kathleen hadn't urged him to call her "Mother."

He and Clayton had spent a lot of time in the calf shed already. Before the wedding when Kathleen went to Eli Jonas's to help prepare for the wedding, Clayton had come to stay with John Mark so he could continue going to school. Then Clayton had time to start remodeling the shed. He had made a good start at it.

The neighbors had moved the salvage store over to their basement and had used a shed for temporary storage, and now they had built an addition to the basement.

John Mark brought back the pails and Clayton said, "That's all for tonight. I'll feed the two that are learning to drink from the pail."

Clayton washed the pails in a corner near where he had fixed a drain and sink for that purpose. He took down the lantern near the calf pens and hung it up near the area that he was remodeling. He would work at that trough yet tonight.

As he tied the carpenter's apron around him, Clayton saw that John Mark had vanished into the feed room which was the part of the warehouse that connected to the porch. He had made that into a feed room and the rest of the warehouse and store he had been remodeling as pens for calves. They also had had a raising to build an addition to the building.

As Clayton was driving nails in boards to build a trough, he thought that it's been a little over a month since he and Kathleen were married. He smiled to himself as he thought of the time he had gone to Bishop Paul and said he could publish them now.

Paul had said, "I was beginning to get worried. I expected to hear from you sooner and wondered so much how things worked out." But Paul admitted that he had suspected things were working when he had talked with Clayton one time about going to visit shut-ins again.

*   *   *   *

One spring night Clayton was roused from a deep sleep. Kathleen was shaking and calling him, saying, "There's something wrong with Annie! I can't quiet her. She usually sleeps all night." Minutes later Clayton was going down the road a short distance to a neighborhood telephone booth to call the ambulance.

It seemed like a few hours till the ambulance arrived. Clayton wanted to go along to the hospital when Kathleen did, but one of them had to stay with the other children. Kathleen felt responsible to go in as likely a lot of questions would be asked that Clayton wouldn't have answers for.

Clayton tried to go back to sleep, but there was no sleep. After a while, he got up and tried reading but ended up thinking.

Two months of wedded life had gone by so softly and sweetly. It should if "there's love at home." His thoughts went back to the wedding day when he had heard in the sermon that life cannot be all sunshine or we would wither. There have to be rainy days, although the need may not seem so at the time. It refreshes us like a warm rain does the growing things. All sun would scorch our life; we would lose the need of God.

Clayton had planned to buy a cow for the family's milk supply rather than fetching milk like Kathleen had, but then the doctor recommended giving goat's milk to Annie, so they had gotten two milk goats and they all learned to use goat's milk. That was a delight to John Mark because one of his school friends had goats and John Mark had longed for some. So the goats were serving a few purposes.

Clayton was doing chores in the barn when Kathleen returned from the hospital. He and Kathleen had time and again rejoiced with each other, but with one look at Kathleen, Clayton knew what had happened. They wept together.

After Kathleen had released some of her sorrow through tears, she said, "Annie lived only about two hours. They had done an emergency operation in the area where her internal injuries had been when she was in the accident. We hadn't known she had injured her liver, but there was a scar right there and it had grown as the liver grew. Then it ruptured and she hemorrhaged, which caused her death."

Annie's death was hard to accept since lately she had been growing more plump and was not so frail anymore.

John Mark shed some tears when he was told, but after a few hours he said, "I'm glad though that we could love her this long, and we still have Daddy." A child shall lead them!

Kathleen told Clayton as the days continued that it was the comfort of John Mark's words and the truth of those words that carried her over the waves of sorrow. Annie had been loved and not just left in a home unloved, unclaimed. Clayton could not sing, but the words of a song comforted his soul.

> *Death shall not destroy my comfort. Christ shall guide*
> *me through the gloom.*
> *Down we'll send some angel convoy, to convey my spirit*
> *home.*

214

Two months before Annie's death, Clayton's family had gathered with him to rejoice as lives were added to his. Now two months later, the family and many friends gathered to weep and sympathize with him when a life was taken from him. The Lord giveth and the Lord taketh. Blessed be the name of the Lord.

Annie had never been legally adopted into the Wenger family. The law in this case had required them to wait two years to see if any relative would seek to claim her.

Realizing the declining of Kathleen's good spirits and her lack of interest in regular tasks, Clayton felt the depression that was taking hold. It was destroying her comfort and she was faltering in the gloom.

Only a baby's grave, a foot or two at the most, of tears and dewed sod, but a loving God knows what the little grave cost!

Clayton's heart also mourned, but sensing Kathleen's sorrow, he felt a need to rise above the gloom. They could not wait until sorrow passed. They had to rise as the writer wrote in the book of words of comfort and cheer, "He does not send the rainbow before the cloud, but when the cloud appears, the rainbow is seen in it." But Clayton realized the sun must reflect in the cloud to cause a rainbow.

Clayton made himself quite busy with the remodeling and building and with the strawberry plants that had arrived during the warm weather. He planned to plant a large strawberry patch. Time and again he asked Kathleen to help John Mark with the calf feeding. At times he felt rather cruel putting so much of the chores on her knowing she wasn't quite up to par. But her arms were so empty. Clayton knew Kathleen needed to be more occupied rather than waiting for sorrow to pass.

As Kathleen continued to manage the calves with John Mark's help and help with the garden and berry patch, Clayton slowly saw some enthusiasm coming back in her life. Tending the calves and learning when they were ready to wean made Kathleen feel needed. Kathleen tenderly cared for the young ones and patiently taught them to drink out of a pail. Sometimes Clayton was almost caught up with odd jobs and almost didn't have excuses not to be helping with the chores.

As Kathleen's spirits lifted and she rose above the gloom, she found more to occupy her time—things that she had been neglecting. Slowly Clayton took on more of the chores again.

After Annie's death, Clayton and Kathleen had received many sympathy cards, and Clayton had continued singing a tune from a verse that was on a letter. Sometimes Kathleen and John Mark helped him sing and sometimes he heard them singing it themselves. Yes, Kathleen was singing again.

> *Pure as a lily, spotless as snow,*
> *Baby was the first of our family to go.*
> *Singing with the angels, dwelling on high.*
> *We hope to meet her in the sweet bye and bye.*

Other times Clayton found himself singing, "nearer my God to thee, nearer to thee. E'en though it be a cross that raises me."

*　　*　　*　　*

The following January the earth was clothed in white; a few inches of snow lay over the countryside. The branches silently held their snow, and bushes everywhere calmly let the new-fallen cover rest on them.

Clayton was now resting. He had slept very little during the night. He thought of the words in the German songbook, *"Veinen, Das vor mein erst stimm, mit vein'n var ich geborn, mit vein'n tragt man mich vieder hin."*

Crying was baby Josiah's first voice during the night. And even now there would be tears if his life should come to an end, and even if baby Josiah gets to grow up, Clayton was thinking, like Dad. Even though Dad had been in his fifties already, there had been many tears. Baby Annie had been only about nine months old and still there were many tears as she was carried out.

The birth of a baby is a happy occasion and reason for real joy. Clayton, now a father, realized more the truth that first come the tears and the baby's first voice is crying, and when the baby dies there are more tears.

But two hours later as John Mark and Delores gathered in the bedroom to meet their baby brother, there was great rejoicing. The joy that showed on Kathleen's face as she rejoiced with the children put a new joy in Clayton's heart. Later as he was out choring, still filled with awe and wonder of the birth, Clayton thought of a verse in the Bible, but he couldn't remember the reference.

Later that day Clayton sat in the bedroom where everyone was and decided to check his concordance for the verse he wanted. Just as he was about to give up, he found it by paging through the first four books of the New Testament. It was in John 16, verse 21. The words were so true; he read over the last part of the verse again: "She remembereth no more the anguish, for joy that a man is born into the world."

Josiah was now that joy. How could a baby of 81/2 pounds bring so much anxiety and now enough joy to forget the anguish? Clayton and Kathleen had wanted to call the baby Rebekah if it was a girl, for the sake of the memories of their meeting, but he was Josiah.

Although Clayton was filled with a new joy, his mind at times dwelled on Annie, remembering her sunshine and happiness and how soon Clayton's joy turned to sorrow. Should he hold himself from exercising his heart to lust in this joy? Is a sorrow foreboding? He tried to shrug the troubled thoughts off his shoulders, but it wasn't so easily shrugged off. Clayton's faith strengthened when he saw Kathleen trusting, never fearing.

Last fall Clayton had been quite concerned about Kathleen because she had fainted a few times. When he wasn't at home and someone had come on an errand, Kathleen panicked in fear of a tragic message. She admitted she had to fight her fear that her present joy would suddenly turn to sorrow as it had when her friend Jonathan had died.

But now she was at ease again. Clayton prayed much on Kathleen's behalf that she would gain victory over her struggle. She needed faith to stand and trust whatever it may be, even if an unpleasant message came. Clayton himself had never been on the scene when she passed out. He hoped he never would have to be, unless he could somehow strengthen her power at that time to lessen her fear. Clayton still wondered if such a great joy as Josiah would be given without any sorrow in the cup.

Chapter Thirty

On a March day as John Mark came bounding home from school, Clayton was in the house repairing something at the cupboard. The one drawer slide had failed to work. After having the drawer set on the floor beside the cupboard for a while, Clayton was finally making other slides.

John Mark was telling Kathleen about some event at school and then he had come over and watched Daddy awhile. In a few minutes he was off upstairs to change into his everyday clothing and then came down and talked to baby Josiah who was cooing for attention. "May I pick him up, Mother?" he asked.

"Yes, will you?" she answered from the sewing machine. "I am almost done with this mending then I can take him, if he's not satisfied."

Clayton had meant to be a little observant, but John Mark had been so friendly that he had relaxed and got involved in his repair work.

Kathleen had told him that of late John Mark was sort of moody and at times would sit in silence, his eyes staring and his face wearing a troubled look. At times John Mark gave some ill-tempered answers, like the John Mark Kathleen had known at the home years ago, when she first had him.

Clayton and Kathleen had discussed that maybe John Mark's behavior was about the baby, but he seemed to like Josiah as much as anyone. They had talked with his teacher and she said he was his usual self and talks happily about the baby. When doing chores with Clayton he was friendly as usual, but Clayton had also noticed that at times he was a little sullen when they were all in the kitchen.

Later Kathleen brushed past Clayton as she was starting supper and gave him a knowing look. Clayton caught the message and looked around. Delores was playing on the floor with blocks. Baby Josiah was lying on the sofa next to where John Mark sat. John Mark was looking out over the baby, not seeing. He had a very dejected look on his face that made Clayton think of rebellion.

Clayton gathered up his tool and said, "Well, now this drawer is fixed." John Mark stared on. Clayton reached for his clothing and said, "John Mark, do you want to go with me to get straw down from the barn to take up to the calf shed yet before supper?"

John Mark came back to life and suddenly changed his expression to a willingness as he slipped on his wraps and helped Clayton take his tools out. When they had a few wheelbarrow loads of straw hauled over to the calf shed, it was time for supper. Clayton hadn't mentioned anything; he had no clue. Supper was a pleasant time as usual.

The Wenger family lingered around the table as usual. Clayton was telling about some calves he was getting from a neighbor and that he was hoping the guy who was getting those five started ones would soon come for them. He would soon be getting more little ones.

Clayton wasn't aware of anything until Kathleen said, quite urgently, "John Mark, why are you up on the counter top? Watch that mirror!" A hand-held mirror was dangerously near his foot, ready to be swept off the counter. "And what are you doing with the mirror?" Kathleen asked sort of jokingly.

Clayton expected John Mark to smile mischievously, but he didn't smile at all. He almost pouted. Kathleen started to tell him to put the mirror away, but Clayton looked at her with an unspoken command, "Don't say anything more now."

John Mark took the mirror in the bedroom. When he came out, he was holding back tears. Kathleen looked bewildered. Clayton looked at the clock. He stood and picked up a magazine and sat on the sofa next to John Mark. Clayton showed his son a few things in the farm magazine until he was a little friendlier. Clayton then asked him what they had played at school and then asked him if his loose tooth bothered him lately.

"No, I mostly chew on the other side," John Mark said.

Clayton asked to look at the tooth. After he had taken a look at the tooth, he casually asked, "Maybe you had the mirror to look at this tooth?"

John Mark shook his head.

Clayton asked, "What were you looking at then? I will look at what you wanted to see if you tell me what."

John Mark looked at him longingly, tears were bidding.

Clayton looked at him, urging him on, and John Mark said, "I don't look like you."

"I didn't look like my father either," Clayton said, trying to collect his thoughts. "Why does it trouble you?"

"When our company came to look at our baby, they all said he would look like you or Mother and—" he got more tears and left the last words unsaid.

"Even if you don't look like me, you still belong to me and Mother."

"But I was looking if I, in some ways, looked like you or Mother."

Clayton sat deep in thought then said, "Maybe I'm the one that doesn't belong here. You and Delores and Mother all have brown eyes. Even Josiah's eyes look rather dark, and mine are blue. And you all eat with your right hand, and I eat with my left hand, and—"

John Mark cut him off as he flew at him and said, "I don't care if you have blue eyes. I want you for my Daddy."

Clayton hugged him and let him loose and asked, "Then you still like me even if I look different?"

"Yes, Daddy. It doesn't matter."

"Then neither does it matter if you don't look very much like us."

"But Josiah?" John Mark asked.

"Well, his looks will change. Some will say he looks like me, then some will say like Mother, and some will not know which of us he looks like. I didn't look like my brothers either. Only one of them had blue eyes, but he was taller than me and not so heavy. In fact, I am broader than any of my brothers. And none of them combed their hair over on this side, so maybe it's good we came together if neither of us looks like anybody."

"Daddy, we look like someone, but not like each other. And not like Mother," John Mark said, reprovingly in fun but still meaning it.

Clayton smiled, "Maybe Mother should have married someone with light curly hair, so he'd look like Delores."

John Mark shook his head in disagreement, "No, we wouldn't want any other Daddy."

Kathleen was sitting on the rocker tending the baby, the dishes still on the table. She had wanted to hear the conversation. "Well, we have to do chores now," Clayton said. "If we have time, I want to tell you something tonight. If not tonight, some other time. Something you will have to remember."

Hours later as Clayton came in from chores and washed up and dried his face on the towel, he walked over to the shelf and picked up the Bible and sat on the rocker.

John Mark was soon at his side asking, "Daddy, didn't you say you were going to tell me something?"

"That's right. I have a story to tell you." He paged to Romans 8, verse 18. "Here it says, 'For I reckon, that the sufferings of this present time are not worthy to be compared with the glory which shall be revealed in us.'

"That means that the things we suffer here, the bad of it, cannot even be compared to the good that will be given us. Maybe that means the good that awaits us in heaven, or maybe it means the good we learn from our burdens, is a lot more valuable to us than the sufferings were. But to make it a little easier for you, I will compare it to things of now, of your life.

"Suppose Mother hadn't loved you so much, and she had left you at the children's home. You and I don't know where you would be. Maybe you would have been taken into homes where you couldn't have been happy at all. Maybe you would still be at the home, which wouldn't be pleasant.

"Now most people know your life, why you are a little lame and why you don't look very much like us and that we have you because we love you. But you will at times meet people who do not know and maybe at times someone who doesn't know will innocently say, 'Well, he sure doesn't look like his brother or his father, and maybe at times someone will make an unkind remark and won't think how it would sound to you.

"However it is, you must then remember this verse, thinking that not looking like your family is not nearly as hard to have to hear at times. Then the happiness is great that you may live with us and not have to stay at the home all this time. Always when something happens like that, something being said that makes you feel sad, before you get upset you have to stop and think. This remark or fact cannot even be compared to how it would be if you couldn't be here with the family and would have to always live in the home. Wouldn't you rather have this trouble of Josiah looking more like me than having the burden of always staying at the home or go into foster homes?"

"Yes, and even if my other father had taken me long ago, the other woman may not have liked me, so I'd much rather be here."

"So the home was better than the places where you weren't treated nice. And this is better than the home, and I think you have even less troubles this way."

"Dad, can we mark that verse so I can find it sometimes?"

"Yes, sure, we'll mark it and try hard to remember that the troubles can't be compared with the joy because the joy is so much greater. Always say that to yourself when you are ready to become upset, and if that doesn't help, talk to us. We all need each other."

*   *   *   *

Clayton was sobbing into his pillow. Kathleen stirred a few times and then she got up and walked to the door, then came back and checked the crib and was ready to crawl back in bed when she asked, "Clayton, is it you? I thought I heard one of the children. Aren't you feeling well? Can't you tell me what's wrong?" she asked, concerned when only sobs came as an answer. He blew his nose and tried to explain.

Kathleen said, "I don't understand why you feel upset. John Mark was so happy the last three days since you had that talk with him. I think it really means something to him."

"But he's only nine years old. How big will his battles get yet? I just feel too weak. The load looks too heavy."

Kathleen came to Clayton's side of the bed and fell to her knees and prayed, "Satan, get thee behind us, you don't want what is godly." She prayed that three times.

Clayton knelt beside her, and Kathleen led in prayer which was unusual, as usually she wanted him to lead. She only led in prayer with the children or when she was alone. She pleaded for strength for the day. "Help us not to take thought for the morrow. For the morrow shall take thought of the things itself. Sufficient unto the day is the evil thereof. Help us to seek first after your kingdom and righteousness, and then these things shall be added unto us," Kathleen paused.

Clayton prayed, "I believe, but help my unbelief; the spirit is willing but the flesh is weak. I thank you, God, for leading me to a virtuous woman. The heart of her husband doth safely trust in her, so that he shall have no need of spoil. A woman that feareth the Lord shall be praised, and we say not our will, but Thine be done."

As they went back to bed, Kathleen reminded Clayton that if he ever gets so depressed again, he should awaken her. They talked for a while and Kathleen asked, "Did you see that John Mark started combing his hair to the other side?"

"No, did he really?"

"Yes, I noticed it this morning. When I said something to him tonight if he is going to comb his hair like Daddy, he said, 'Yes. I asked the teacher and she said she doesn't care if my parents don't.' I almost laughed in his face, but I quickly turned around, pretending I was getting something from the cupboard. It struck me funny that he asked the teacher."

As Clayton was drifting back to sleep, he realized the truth in the words of I Peter 3:3: Let the adorning be not of "plaiting the hair . . . or of putting on of apparel; but let it be the hidden man of the heart, in that which is not corruptible, even the ornament of a meek and quiet spirit, which is in the sight of God of great price."

Chapter Thirty-One

The Wengers were traveling toward home on a warm August Sunday after being away for dinner. The children were in the back seat since John Mark wanted to hold Josiah. He was becoming attached to the baby since Josiah was seven months old—old enough to enjoy entertainment.

Clayton was lost in his own thoughts until Kathleen gasped. He guided the horse further to the side, thinking that maybe she had seen a car coming too close. Kathleen slumped forward and John Mark cried out, "Daddy, she's fainting!"

Clayton stopped the horse. "Put her head down between her knees," John Mark said, putting the baby on the seat and trying to get over the seat. Delores and Josiah were now crying. If it wouldn't have been for John Mark, Clayton would have stopped the first car for help. At first, when Kathleen started responding she was very tired.

When they were ready to start driving again and the two children had quieted, Clayton asked, "Is something bothering you?"

"Yes, I could see home."

Clayton quickly looked in that direction, expecting to see a building on fire, but in the distance he could see a team standing there. "Maybe they are bringing us company."

"Not hardly. It looks like two men. They would tell the neighbors to tell us if it was an ordinary message, or leave a note."

Clayton was curious but not alarmed. As they rode in the drive near the driving shed, they recognized the men as Minister Wayne from Dry Hill, and the other one was a neighbor to Wayne.

The men greeted Kathleen and Clayton and after a few words,

they said they had come to inform them that Clayton was in the lot at Dry Hill to ordain a deacon. Clayton and Kathleen were both speechless!

When he could, Clayton spoke, "I don't understand. We're not of that district."

"We didn't come to collect excuses," Wayne said. "The candidates are scheduled to meet at church on Monday afternoon and the ordination is on Tuesday."

Clayton was stunned. As the men were leaving, Kathleen said, "Remember, we were over in Dry Hill Church some weeks ago when they had council about ordaining another deacon since Franklin is getting rather sickly."

"No, they only announced council that Sunday."

Later in the evening, Kathleen told Clayton he didn't seem very disturbed. "Maybe I would be more, but since that experience on the way home, nothing else matters much. For a few seconds there, I had thought I would be left alone. And, you know, you **would** make a good deacon's wife!" Clayton added.

Kathleen was stunned and gasped, "I thought they're making a **deacon!**"

Clayton chuckled at her accent on the last word. "But if you weren't my wife, I wouldn't be in the class."

"Is something wrong with you?" Kathleen asked in alarm.

"No. But seriously, it's true. Because then I wouldn't be living in this area," Clayton reminded her.

"I think we better go to bed and sleep before you think of more strange things."

Clayton realized that they had about the same distance to Dry Hill as to Cloverdale, but they most always went to Cloverdale and took communion there.

When the candidates met for observation on Monday, Clayton's load seemed lighter. Six others were helping him carry the burden. With seven men carrying the load, it wasn't so heavy. One was younger than he.

But by Tuesday the strain seemed heavy again. He felt almost stricken when they arrived at church; he noticed quite a few of his brothers were there, and he glimpsed William Nolt in the crowd. What were they all doing here? The thought of letting his family know never occurred to him; someone had, though. Seeing his family there put an alarming fear in him.

The forenoon was a blur to Clayton. When he heard the words, *In die schwagen bin ich machtig*, it seemed a heaviness was pressing on his chest so that he could hardly breathe anymore. The tears came freely after he had risen to get his book with the others and had it lying on his lap. The load on his chest was weighing him down and the book was so heavy. He started praying for deliverance.

A mighty load was lifted when the bishop picked up the book from Clayton's lap. When the bishop paused and started speaking, the burden fell on his shoulders. As the bishop asked him to rise, Clayton felt the weakest of them all, but he was grateful for the deliverance of the weight which now rested on his shoulders rather than on his chest and lap. He could go on; he wasn't alone. Kathleen would help him in his new responsibilities.

In the evening, after the children were in bed, Clayton and Kathleen talked for a few hours before retiring for the night. Kathleen trusted that God would be with her husband in the difficult times of his deacon work, like he had given him words when John Mark needed them. She wanted to be willing to share her husband in that way and maybe others could be helped.

Clayton trusted that since God had through Kathleen carried him through the dark night in spring when he was at the weakest when he saw no other way, so he wanted to share his wife. Maybe a sick one or troubled one would be helped. An hour later as they were in bed, a song was going through Clayton's mind.

> *Let none be your idle saying, there is nothing I can do,*
> *Gladly take the task he gives you, let his work your*
>   *pleasure be.*
> *Answer quickly when he calleth,*
> *Here am I, oh Lord, send me.*

Clayton asked, "Are you sleeping?"

"No, why?" Kathleen asked, wide awake.

"It just came to me now that I had been praying for this."

"Why do you say so?"

"I was praying so much for a way that you could be helped of your weakness of fainting at messages, and now I feel that with people coming on church errands and tasks, you will get used to having people coming and not knowing what they want. You won't need to panic, for over the years there will surely be unexpected callers on errands and messages. I didn't realize what I was praying for."

"Maybe," she admitted.

Clayton said, "I think of that poem that says something about,

I asked for strength that I might achieve;
He made me weak that I might obey.
I asked for health that I might do greater things;
I was given grace that I might do better things.
I asked for riches that I might be happy;
I was given poverty that I might be wise. "

"There's more, something about I was given weakness that I might feel the need of men after asking for power. And then after the last lines it says, 'I received nothing that I asked for, but all that I hoped for.'"

"My prayer was answered."

Later as he heard Kathleen breathing in peaceful sleep, Clayton thought of the words, "He giveth more grace when the burdens grow greater. He sendeth more strength when the labors increase."

His thoughts ran on to what he had read in the *Streams of the Desert* book, a book Kathleen had been given when Jonathan had died.

"We pray for patience and our Father sends those who tax us to the utmost, for tribulation worketh patience. We pray for submission and God sends suffering for we learn obedience by the things we suffer. We pray for unselfishness and God gives us opportunities to sacrifice ourselves by thinking on the things of others and by laying down our lives for the brethren. We pray for gentleness and there comes a perfect storm of temptation."

Now Clayton's mind went to the things Proverbs says about a virtuous woman in Chapter 31. "Her husband is known in the gates, when he sitteth among the elders in church and the heart of her husband doth safely trust in her, so that he shall have no need of spoil."

How would life be if he had sought for a woman who adorned herself in plaiting of hair and putting on of apparel and gold? Peter was wise when he counseled that the adorning of the woman"let it be the hidden man of the heart, in that which is not corruptible, even the ornament of a meek and quiet spirit, which is in the sight of God of great price. . . . Likewise, ye husbands, dwell with them according to knowledge, giving honour unto the wife, as unto the weaker vessel, and as being heirs together of the grace of life; that your prayers be not hindered."

Clayton's soul sang, "After this life with all its strife, Heaven will surely be worth it all." As he was drifting to sleep, more words rang in his mind, "Let but my fainting heart be blest with thy sweet spirit for its guest to thee of God I leave the rest. Thy will be done."

— The End —